Steadying the Ark

Steadying the Ark from Rebecca K. Jones is an impressive debut novel. Mack is a very engaging protagonist with her heart and head in the right place while working on her trial. She is written as singularly focused and driven while building the case which rings very true to me.

I must mention the book cover art is what drew me to this novel. It is stunning. As well the title, once it is explained deep into the story, is a thought-provoking religious conundrum of faith. And it is the perfect fit for the novel. I wholeheartedly recommend this new author be added to your to be read lists.

-Della B., NetGalley

I'm impressed. I thought this courtroom drama was riveting and great. It touched on so many topics such as sexual abuse, rape and religion. I thought the book was beautifully written. Well Done!! I recommend.

-Bonnie A., NetGalley

Hard to believe this story came from someone who has never had a book published, it's that good. If this is a sample of Ms. Jones skills as an author, I look forward to reading her next book because I'm sure there will be others. Very enjoyable read.

-Bonnie S., NetGalley

After reading *Steadying the Ark* by Rebecca K. Jones, I must tell you how impressed I am with this book and the author. This is the debut novel for Ms. Jones, and honestly, I'm having a really hard time finding anything to criticize. The story is practically flawless and very entertaining. I can't wait to read more from this author. If you love a courtroom drama filled with excitement, suspense, and thrills, then this is the book for you.

-Betty H., NetGalley

Steadying the Ark is a fantastic debut—I cannot wait to read more from Rebecca K. Jones in the future.

-Natalie T., NetGalley

STEMMING
THE TIDE

REBECCA K. JONES

Other Bella Books by Rebecca K. Jones

Steadying the Ark

About the Author

A proud graduate of Choate Rosemary Hall, Middlebury College, and the University of Arizona James E. Rogers College of Law, Rebecca K. Jones now lives in the Phoenix, Arizona area, where she has been fighting crime since 2012. This is her second novel.

STEMMING THE TIDE

REBECCA K. JONES

BELLA BOOKS

2023

Bella Books, Inc.
P.O. Box 10543
Tallahassee, FL 32302

Printed in the United States of America on acid-free paper.

First Edition - 2023

Editor: Heather Flournoy
Cover Designer: Kayla Mancuso

ISBN: 978-1-64247-488-6

PUBLISHER'S NOTE

To my parents. You make this book,
and everything else, possible.

PROLOGUE

Just another Tuesday evening behind the bar, waiting for karaoke to start at nine. It's quiet, a few regulars scattered around the dim room, lit only by the Christmas lights that stay up year-round. We're off the main drag—don't get many customers who just stumble in. It's easy to get to know people, get them talking. We learn their usual drinks, don't make them waste time ordering. For some of them, the ones who come on a schedule, I even have their drinks waiting when they come in. They eat that up, feel like big shots.

It's unseasonably hot out, and I've got the AC on full blast, overcompensating. It's not as bad as it was back in the depths of summer, but it's still bad enough that I send Willow to bus the tables on the patio rather than risk sweat stains. Appearances matter in this job. No one wants to get their drinks from an ugly bartender, and I live on tips. I buy a stack of new shirts three times a year, when the old batch is bleached to the point of no return. It pays to look sharp.

I find myself watching a couple so *clearly* on a first date it makes my teeth hurt. They're out of place, too young for this bar, and one of them can't keep their hands off their phone. They can't pay attention to the other one for more than a couple seconds at a shot. Either the date is going really poorly, or they've got some ADHD they need to address. Or both, I guess. I wonder if they're even old enough to drink and remember that I don't care. I've had this place a couple years, and in all that time the cops have never pulled an ID check. Never seen anything like it any place else.

As the door swings open, I glance up, hoping it's her before I see her. It is. A slow smile spreads across my face. She's a regular, yeah, but she doesn't keep to a schedule. I've known her ten years, since she was just a kid. The days of her crashing in my office are long past, but we still keep in touch. I'll text her, call her, but she's bad about responding. Usually, I just have to wait until she comes in. Like tonight. Sometimes, she'll come in a couple nights a week for three or four weeks in a row, then disappear for two or six or long enough that I've almost forgotten her by the time she pops back in. But I'm always glad to see her. Watching her walk in is almost as nice as watching her walk away. I wonder who's going to join her tonight. It's too much to hope that she's here for me. Her friends are pretty, nice, and they make for a laugh, but they're a distraction.

She smiles back, and I fill a pint glass with Angry Orchard and slide it to her with a wink. She blushes. Not to brag, but I know the effect I have on women, and this one is no exception. The scar on her cheek is new, red and angry against her skin. It doesn't look like a casual injury. It looks like someone hurt her. I feel a surge of anger, a swell of rage that I breathe through. I don't let her see my reaction.

"Long time, Pumpkin," I say, my voice friendly.

She raises her glass and salutes me. "Too long. I missed you, and this place." She takes a deep pull on the drink and sweeps her long blond hair over one shoulder. She's gotten a tan since I last saw her. Taking advantage of the nice weather while it lasts. The silver chain around her neck reflects the overhead light. I can't quite get a look at the charm. It's tucked under her black Henley shirt, unbuttoned just enough to give me a peek at cleavage. Teasing.

"Been busy?"

She nods. "Same peanuts, brand-new circus. You?"

Some jerk down the bar gestures to get my attention and I grimace, performing for her. Just a little. Just enough to keep her interested. I've known her so long—I know what works. She winks as I head that way.

I'm interrupted by more patrons, clamoring for beer and our two-for-one well drink specials. Animals, all of them. I don't drink, myself. Never developed a taste for the stuff. By the time I get back to pour *her* next drink, it's crowded and loud. The heat rolls off people, and I'm sweaty despite my best efforts. A trio of frat bros commandeered the stage half an hour ago wailing country music released long before they were born. I grin and bear it, although I'm surprised this DJ even *has* these songs in her catalog. More people means more drinks, and the sweatier they get the more refills they order. I never fudge the receipts or their change. It'd be stupid to get caught making trouble for such a small payoff. I just keep making eye contact, smiling, and watching the singles roll in.

The next time I swing by, Pumpkin's not alone. A young—very young—redhead who I've never seen before is leaning into her, and I can't tell if they're pressed together so they don't have to shout, or for some other, less innocent, reason. The redhead's got a black tank top on under an open leather jacket, and it's way too revealing. She has her chest right up against the other woman's arm. If Pumpkin looked down, she might see a nipple. The redhead is talking directly into her ear. Pumpkin seems uncomfortable, and my backup bartender must see a chance to play the hero.

"Get you another?" he says, pointing at her empty glass.

"Make it two," the redhead says, throwing a twenty on the bar. She means to be cool, but her execution is flawed. It looks like she's never tried that trick before, and I bet she won't try it again any time soon. The bill lands in a puddle of some asshole's spilled G and T. He frowns and picks it up between finger and thumb, showing her—showing both of them—his disdain. He wipes the bill on a bar towel.

"Can I see some ID?" he says.

She throws an ID—it can't be hers, she's too young, but who can really care—into the same puddle. He glances quickly at the card and silently fills two pint glasses.

I get called away before he's formulated his retort, and the next time I look over, Pumpkin has slipped something into the redhead's hand. She looks stern. Still hot, but mad, almost, and the kid looks disappointed, like she was expecting something more. She polishes off her drink and disappears into the crowd. Pumpkin follows her, and I lose sight of them as I rush to satisfy the vultures, already rowdy even though it's not nine thirty yet.

Pumpkin comes back, upset. Her face is red, and it looks like maybe she's been crying. Her mascara is smudged. Still the prettiest girl in the place, though.

"She a friend of yours?" I say when I get back to my favorite spot at the bar, right in front of her.

She shrugs and starts to speak, and then someone says "Mack!" and she spins at the same time I glance up toward the voice we've both heard.

It's Anna. Haven't seen her here in a long time. Thought she must not like me, or maybe she just hates the bar. Haven't exactly been mourning her absence—I've been getting Mack all to myself when she deigns to come in at all.

"Hey, Doc," Mack says with the biggest smile I've seen from her in a long, long time. She runs her hand up the sleeve of the brunette's leather jacket and pulls her closer by the back of the neck. There's an easy familiarity born of habit, but—last I heard—they'd been broken up for years.

"Can I get some help here?" one of the wannabe cowboy karaoke stars shouts from the other end of the bar. I've never been less interested in doing my job but move reluctantly down the rail.

When I look back, they're still kissing. The next time I look, they're gone.

CHAPTER ONE

Mackenzie Wilson groaned as she faced the stack of boxes in front of her. No matter how many the tall blonde unpacked, their number didn't seem to decrease.

"You have too many books," Dr. Anna Lapin said, removing her Astros cap and wiping the sweat off her face with the hem of her Michigan State T-shirt. "When you said, 'Come help me organize the office,' I pictured some light unpacking of files, not building your own legal library."

Mack was distracted by the sight of the psychologist's tanned stomach and set the books she was holding on the ground. "Way too many." She looked at the shelves that lined her new home office, already half-full, and gathered her long blond hair in her fist. "I maybe should have listened to you when you said to donate some before the move. I guess it's too late now—they're already here! Want to take a break?"

Anna grunted and reached for another box. Like the others they had unpacked that morning, this one was labeled *BOOKS*, but it was lighter than a box of books should have been.

"What's in here?" she asked, pulling the lid off.

Mack peered over her shoulder and shrugged, then pulled a brown expando-file out of the otherwise empty box. She opened it.

"Oh, shit," she said. "I know what this is. It's the case file on the girl from the desert. I was wondering where this got to."

"What girl from the desert?" Anna asked.

"I might not have told you about this one," Mack said. "I think you were out of town when they found her, and the case never went much of anywhere, but I was *obsessed* with it when it happened." She looked around the room. The desk chair and futon were still covered with boxes, and the ceiling fan wasn't cutting the heat in the south-facing room. "Let's take a break. Do you want a beer?"

Anna looked at her watch. "Isn't it a little early to start drinking?"

"Suit yourself," Mack said. "But it's a long story."

Once they were settled on Mack's new living room couch with bottles of Kilt Lifter and the case file between them, Mack pulled a school photo out of the file. The girl was pretty, in a bland sort of way—light brown hair curled for the photo, freckles across her upturned nose, a winning smile.

"This is Sabrina Fisher. She was sixteen when this photo was taken. A year before her murder."

Mack pulled six more photos out of the file and spread them on the coffee table. She tapped on one, showing a skinny young white man in a blue tank top pointing away from the camera into the desert. The picture was blurry. It had been taken at night with the camera's built-in flash.

"Back in 2011, this guy and his girlfriend were riding ATVs in the desert, out by Rita Ranch one night. You know, like people do. The girlfriend saw what looked like a bonfire, so they rode up to it, just curious, but when they got close they saw that a human body was burning. They called it in, thankfully. By the time police got out there, they'd put the fire out by shoveling dirt on the body, which—"

"Which eliminated any trace evidence," Anna finished.

"Nailed it."

"What was the cause of death?"

Mack took a long swallow of her beer. "Inconclusive," she said. "The medical examiner thought maybe strangulation, because the hyoid bone was damaged, but he couldn't rule out drugs or just about anything else, because of the state of the body."

"How did you get involved?" Anna was fanning herself with a travel magazine that had been sitting on the coffee table, her olive skin flushed from the heat of the office. Mack watched a bead of sweat roll down her forehead and lost her train of thought. Anna nudged her. "Easy, there. Focus. How did this turn into your case?"

Mack shook her head. "Just luck of the draw. I was the on-call attorney that night, and they wanted a prosecutor to come see the scene, get a sense of where it happened. I know prosecutors hate going to scenes, and I'll deny it if you repeat this, but it was actually super helpful. It's really desolate out there, and it's a miracle those kids saw the fire. If they hadn't, the body might never have been found. But then I went to the autopsy, watched them interview the people who found her, and got hooked. Something about her just spoke to me."

Anna paged through the reports in the file. "Anything interesting from the autopsy?"

"Lots," Mack said. "This killer was careful. He'd cut off her fingertips and smashed her face up pretty bad."

"No prints and no dental records," Anna said.

"Exactly."

Anna tilted her head, thinking. "This wasn't his first crime. It was too clean for a newbie." Mack loved talking cases with Anna. It was so nice to be able to talk about anything, no matter how gruesome, without worrying that she was going to offend the other woman. Most people didn't want to listen, but Anna usually would. Anna's career as a forensic psychologist, dealing with the full spectrum of human monsters, made her comfortable brainstorming cases, unlike a civilian, who could be forgiven for shying away from talking about murders on a Saturday morning.

"That's what we thought, too. But the medical examiner still did a rape kit, despite the condition of the body, and actually got lucky. One sperm in the vaginal vault."

"Whoa! Very lucky! Not to interrupt your story, but I've told you about the defense attorney who asked me in an interview if it was true that vaginas were fireproof?"

Mack laughed, sputtering through her mouthful of beer. "You have," she said, "but it makes me laugh every time. And, hey, this time he was almost right! Just the one sperm, but, luckily, enough to get a profile."

"Any matches?"

"Not in CODIS," Mack said, referring to the national database of DNA from convicted felons and unsolved cases. "They wanted to run the guy who found her, just as a rule-out, but they wound up not being able to find him again by the time they wanted his info."

"Did he give fake contact info to police?" Anna asked. "I mean, it is pretty weird that he found the body and then disappeared. Did they ever find him?"

Mack shrugged. "No idea if he lied, or just moved and didn't keep in touch. I mean, people move. But they never found him, and it seemed like maybe he had something to hide, right? They looked for him and the girlfriend, and never found anything on either of them. But, like, maybe patrol wrote their info down wrong, or maybe they lied for some totally innocent reason like they were drug users, who can know?"

They sat quietly, drinking their beers. Mack remembered this case so clearly. It was the first time she'd ever seen a dead body outside of the morgue. She hadn't even wanted to go, had been woken up by the phone call and "asked" to drive thirty minutes out into the desert. The scene was bad—the stink of the burning body, the crunch of soil beneath her shoes as she walked from the air-conditioned SUV into the blazing desert, the knowledge that no one in fifty miles could have seen what had happened there. Even on scene, she knew it would wind up being a cold case. There was no way they'd be able to pin it on anyone, even if they could find a legitimate suspect. After the autopsy, Mack went home and spent an hour in the shower, trying to get the sickly stench of death off her skin and especially her hair.

Anna pointed at Sabrina's school photo. "So how does she come in to it?"

"Right. So we needed to ID the girl. There was a little, like, not a purse, but almost a pouch that had been burned with her. There was a school ID card that was partially burned, but we could tell it was from Sahuaro High. We went to the school, cross-referenced attendance records with missing person's reports. Hit on Sabrina. The medical examiner found traces of an accelerant on the body, but we were still able to get DNA, and Sabrina's mom Susan gave us Sabrina's toothbrush."

Mack cleared her throat.

"That meeting with Susan was one of the worst things I've ever had to do. Sabrina had fallen in with some stoners, was starting to act out. She ran away three days before they found her body, and Susan blamed herself. Said if she hadn't been so hard on Sabrina for missing curfew, she never would have been killed. It was the first time Sabrina had ever been late, but Susan thought she needed to take a hard line, keep her from going down the wrong path. Nothing I said eased her guilt. I'd never understood the term 'wracked with grief' until that afternoon."

Anna scooted closer to Mack on the couch and put an arm around her shoulder, pulling the blonde tight against her side. Mack relaxed against her.

"So it's still unsolved?"

"Uh-huh," Mack said. "We never got any leads. We talked to Susan, talked to Sabrina's friends at school. No one came up as a possible."

Anna pursed her lips and rubbed the back of her neck with her free hand. "The attempts to disfigure the corpse suggest that the killer didn't know the victim. Disfiguring isn't a thing people typically do to a loved one or intimate partner. But I'm sure you talked to the boyfriend?"

"None to talk to," she said. "Sabrina was gay. Newly out. Single, as far as anyone knew."

"A woman didn't commit this crime."

"Yeah. That's what we think, too."

"This is a terrible case, Mack, but why did it hit you so personally?"

"I'm not sure. It was the first homicide scene I ever went to. I think you always remember your first. She was so young, and gay, so I guess I identified with her. She had so much potential, and it was just crushed for no good reason. I hate that I never got a resolution for her." Mack reached for the file and pulled out a stack of greeting cards. "Every year, Susan sends me two cards—one for Christmas and one for Sabrina's birthday. She says she knows I still care about her daughter and if—you know and I know that prosecutors don't solve cases—but Susan says if anyone is going to solve it, it'll be me."

Mack couldn't begin to explain how many hours she'd spent with these detectives, trying to help them develop this investigation.

How many late nights she'd spent with the autopsy photos just trying to find some new detail. Eventually, though, other cases claimed her attention. Other victims cried out for justice, and she took the path of least resistance, devoting her time to the cases she knew she could win. It must have been two years since she'd last looked in this file, other than to add Susan's new cards to the others.

She rubbed Anna's knee and leaned against her shoulder. She closed her eyes. Her girlfriend smelled like laundry detergent and perfume and something else that was just Anna. "We should get back to it, I guess."

Anna smiled and stood, pulling Mack with her. "Susan definitely got one thing right!" She kissed Mack firmly before walking toward the office. "If anyone can solve this, it's you. She's lucky to have you on her side."

Mack reassembled the case file and placed it in a desk drawer, pausing one last time over Sabrina's school photo.

"Hey, maybe that's an upside of this new job," she said. "Maybe I'll finally have time to figure this out. Give Susan some peace."

Give myself some peace, she thought, but did not say.

CHAPTER TWO

The October sun was low in the sky that Sunday evening as Mack lazed in the hammock Anna had put up for her in her new backyard. It was still hot, but she could tell a change in the weather was coming. It was starting to smell like fall. She inhaled deeply and took stock.

The next day, she would return to the Tucson District Attorney's Office after almost three months away—first on vacation and then, when she still couldn't face going back without vivid flashbacks of Benjamin Allen's attack on her—extended medical leave. It was probably time. She had been cleared by the doctor to return to all regular activity weeks before and had been going to the gym ever since, gradually building back her strength and stamina. She wanted to be certain her body was in top form in case another violent perp decided to take revenge and invade her home as Allen had done. Though the scars had faded, her wrists sometimes ached from where he had bound her to the chair in her living room. The nightmares still came, but only occasionally. Not every night, as they had in the weeks just following the attack, even after he had been killed in jail. At first, the dreams pulled her out of bed, and she spent the rest of the night on her feet—first in Anna's guest room and then in her new house—with a drink in hand. She slept best when the sun was up, when she could see into the corners of the room and check under the bed. Now, though, she usually stayed in bed and breathed through the dizzying rush of panic that woke her and left her gasping for air.

That morning, she'd gone for a long walk and paused on her doorstep before letting herself back into her house. That moment of putting the key into the lock had been hard since the attack, but time had transformed it from an insurmountable challenge to a brief hesitation. She'd tried to talk to Anna about it as they cuddled on Mack's couch, but Anna just held up a hand.

"Have you heard about the brain surgeon who was obsessed with his job?" she asked.

"I don't think so."

"He came home from work and said 'Honey, take off your hat!'"

Mack didn't get it.

Anna rubbed her eyes. "I'm glad you're starting to think about getting some help, but I can't be your therapist. I'd love to refer you to someone, if you want."

Mack let it go.

Her ribs still ached if she moved the wrong way, and the doctor warned that might never get better. The scar on her cheek would also never go away, but she'd decided to embrace it. She'd always known she was pretty, but now her face had character.

Michael Brown, the district attorney's executive assistant, had called her Wednesday evening with the news that she was being reassigned from Sex Crimes to a newly created public relations position. The position would operate on a one-year rotation, with Mack as the guinea pig. Despite being technically a promotion—complete with a four percent raise—the job was simple; Mack could do it in her sleep. The problem was equally simple: Mack had no interest in being Peter Campbell's PR flack. She was a born and bred trial prosecutor. Sitting behind a desk for a year wasn't her idea of putting her time or skills to good use. She had tried to refuse, to say that she appreciated Mr. Campbell's confidence but she would prefer to stay in Sex Crimes, thankyouverymuch, but her objection was shot down. Despite Michael's emphasis on this as a good thing—a résumé booster, a chance to get some executive experience, a negotiating tool for when she would rotate off the desk in a year—Mack couldn't help but feel like she was being punished. Campbell hadn't reacted well to the fact that Allen's attack had disrupted the Andersen trial. Not that she was responsible for the attack, of course. And not that the Andersen trial had gone badly. Jess Lafayette, Mack's second chair, had saved the day with her closing and the pair had sewn up an appeals-proof guilty verdict for the prominent community figure who used his power and position to manipulate church doctrine to serve his pedophilic tendencies. Even Jeannie Bea, the courtroom commentator who had taken up residence in Tucson for the six-month trial, hadn't found much to ding them on. But still. This promotion would keep Mack in the background, when she should be riding the publicity generated by the Andersen case all the way to a judgeship, or a book deal, or even just the next high-profile case.

Mack had sold her condo—she hadn't even gone inside it after surviving her encounter with Allen—and bought a house in a nice neighborhood on the east side of town. Her mom had flown out for a few days to help her get moved in, and Mack had spent her time off work getting situated. She liked the new place. It was bigger than the condo, only ten minutes from Anna's, and less than twenty from work. She thought maybe it would start to feel like home if she painted a few of the walls.

Who was she kidding? If *Anna* painted a few of the walls.

In September, she and Anna had decided, after much discussion, to start dating again. It was Mack's idea—she was the one who first broached the subject of missing Anna as more than a friend. They were taking it slow, and on a day-to-day level, not much had changed. They still saw each other multiple times a week, as their schedules permitted, and Anna understood better than anyone why the assault had left Mack skittish when it came to sex. Mack felt safe in Anna's arms, and she knew the sex would follow. That had never been their problem.

Jess had seemed shocked when Mack had taken her out to lunch and confessed that her relationship with Anna had taken a turn back toward the romantic. The older woman looked at Mack searchingly across their salads. Mack had dreaded this conversation for a week, knowing how Jess felt about Anna. Her friend had surprised her, however, taking a deep breath and saying only, "If you're good, I'm good" before changing the subject. Mack found herself grateful for Jess' protective streak, and equally grateful that she knew when to let things go.

Mack's mother, on the other hand, had been ecstatic, immediately planning a trip for Mack and Anna to visit her in Cleveland. She had grown close to Anna the first time they'd dated, and her time at Anna's house after the attack had solidified their bond. She respected the psychologist's cool, analytic manner and thought she tempered Mack's impulsiveness.

Three days in Cleveland wasn't exactly Anna's idea of a vacation, but she'd gone willingly enough. They'd checked out the zoo and a baseball game, eaten at all of Mack's favorite restaurants, and endured an afternoon of Mack's mom's friends filing in and out, like a funeral visitation. They'd come home five pounds heavier.

Mack was looking at the empty bottle of pumpkin porter next to her, considering grabbing another from the cooler, when her phone rang.

A photo of Jess in an old Halloween costume—Morticia Addams, her hair coated with black hairspray, her face painted deathly white—flashed on the screen.

"Well, well," Mack said. "This is a surprise. Shouldn't you be doing trial things?"

Jess groaned. "Don't say that word." Jess had been ensconced in a messy trial for the better part of a month. The defendant was a college athlete, and Jess worried that the jury was falling for his "aw, shucks" routine, when she and her case agent knew he had strangled a young woman to death, angry that he couldn't sustain an erection during their first sexual encounter after a date. "If I never hear the word 'stiffy' again, it will be too soon."

"Gross." Mack laughed. "What's up, friend?"

"I'm calling to see how you're feeling about tomorrow."

Mack considered the question, swinging back and forth in her hammock, the purple bougainvillea that took up half her yard coming and going from her line of sight.

"Did you know a million people live in this city?"

"Excuse me? What does that have to do with your new job that starts tomorrow?"

"No, really. A *million* people." This was the first time in Mack's life that she'd ever had a yard of her own, and she was enjoying the process of learning how to take care of the desert xeriscaping.

"I mean, maybe when school's in session."

"Nope, all the time." Mack idly pushed her hand against the pavers, causing the hammock to swing gently. "That's bigger than forty-nine state capitals! The only state with a bigger capital is our state. A million people's worth of crime. Murders, rapes, even drug sales. Organized retail theft! And starting tomorrow, what am *I* going to be doing? Sitting on my ass in an office with a view of Fox Theatre. Coming up with talking points for the district attorney. Giving community safety lectures to the snowbirds."

"Ah," Jess said. "I see the connection now. Took me a minute, but I got there. What are you doing right now?"

Mack stood, shakily, not sure if the motion or the alcohol or the existential crisis was the problem. "Nothing, navel-gazing, why?"

"Put the lint down. Let's go out."

"Say what? It's"—Mack checked her watch—"after eight. On a Sunday. And you're in trial tomorrow. And I have a meeting with Campbell bright and early."

"So what?" Jess asked. "Let's go out! We can even go to Paradise, if you want. You can't say no to Paradise!"

Mack considered. Paradise *was* her favorite bar. And Jess rarely suggested they go there, claiming it was too far from her house. Anna was spending the night at her own place and wasn't expecting to hear from Mack, and it wasn't like Mack had any work to do.

"Okay," Mack said. "I'll go to Paradise. But you're buying, right?"

Jess laughed and hung up without answering.

As Mack walked in, she saw Jess sitting at the bar, chatting with the bartender. Her friend's long brown hair was down and hung over her bare shoulders in loose waves, and she wore a black blouse that was surprisingly low-cut for a casual Sunday night, especially compared to Mack's own tattered jeans and old Ani DiFranco concert tee. Jess laughed at something the bartender said and flirtatiously touched his forearm.

"So much for this place being farther for you," Mack said as she pulled up a stool. "You don't get to pull that card anymore, not if you can beat me to the bar."

The bartender's face lit up. "Mack!"

"Hey there, can I get a—"

"Angry Orchard?"

She smiled and nodded.

The bartender moved down the bar and she turned to Jess.

"He's *so* cute," Jess said.

"You say that every time we come here." Mack looked at the bartender again, straining to see him through Jess' eyes. "I mean, I guess so. If you like that muscle-y, rugged, unkempt thing."

"Yes. Yes, I do."

"Is that why you suggested we come here?" Mack asked.

Jess coughed. "No. No, of course not. I suggested we come here because it's clear that you need cheering up."

Mack rolled her eyes. "Uh-huh."

"Well," Jess said, drawing out the word and looking over Mack's shoulder. "That, and him—and I also need a favor."

The bartender set Mack's drink in front of her and winked before heading to another patron.

"That makes more sense." Mack took a long sip of her cider.

"To be fair," Jess said, "I wanted to ask you before you got this new PR gig. In fact, I'm not sure I *can* ask you, now that you're not on a trial assignment."

"Go on."

"I have this trial coming up. It's messy. Hard facts, mostly circumstantial, high stakes, opportunity for media attention. Right up your alley."

"And you want me to second chair it? Can I think about it? Get my feet under me in the executive suite?"

Jess frowned. "You can," she said slowly. "But not for long. We start witness interviews in two weeks, and trial starts in January."

Mack stared at her best friend, momentarily speechless. She'd need to be up to speed on the witnesses she would be handling before the interviews began, which could entail reading thousands of pages of reports, not to mention listening to untold hours of recorded police interviews. She sucked down the rest of her drink and gestured to the bartender for another. "Two weeks? Of course we do. Okay. I'm in. Lord knows, I owe you for Andersen. Whatever you need. I'm here for you."

Three drinks and a bowl of popcorn later, Mack was feeling optimistic about the whole trial.

"You know," she said. "I'm almost sort of looking forward to this."

Jess laughed. "That's the cider talking."

Mack giggled. "Probably," she admitted. "But we do make a good team. The Andersen trial notwithstanding, we've had some good times in a courtroom, you and me. You'll send me the case file in the morning?"

"Sure," Jess said. "We can discuss after I get my verdict. Probably Wednesday." Her eyes remained on the bartender.

Mack noticed and waved for his attention.

"Hey!" she said. "Garçon!"

He walked toward them, slinging a towel over his right shoulder. The motion caused his white button-down shirt to tighten around his biceps. The towel was the perfect shade to bring out his eyes, and the shirt was unbuttoned just enough to show a curl of chest hair. Mack had to agree with Jess: he was a good-looking man.

"I'm sorry," Mack said. "That was terribly rude, but I don't think I actually know your name."

"Adam. Adam Bennett."

"Adam! That's a good name."

Adam smiled, showing a slight gap between his front teeth. Jess blushed, and Mack could feel her elbow digging into her side.

"Adam, what are you doing working in a lesbian bar?"

He laughed. "Lesbians are great tippers," he said. "Plus, not every woman here is gay. Less competition for me on the straight ones."

Mack and Jess laughed, too.

"Adam, my friend here"—Mack gestured to Jess, who shrank on her stool and almost fell—"thinks you're cute."

Adam studied Jess across the bar. He had a nice smile, Mack thought. The stubble really emphasized his sharp jawbone, and his eyes were a lovely color. He was tall, too. At least six four. Jess loved tall guys.

"Jess," Mack said. "My friend's name is Jess Lafayette."

Adam reached out to shake Jess' hand. "Hi, Jess Lafayette," he said. "Any chance I could get your number?"

Mack giggled all the way to her Uber.

CHAPTER THREE

The first day of Mack's new job went smoothly. The slight hangover when she woke up was easily overcome by a long, hot shower and a stop at Starbucks for egg bites and a skinny vanilla latte. Mack arrived at her office, now in the executive suite, right next door to the district attorney's chief assistant Michael Brown and only three doors down from the big man, Peter Campbell, himself. The Facilities team had relocated the contents of her old office—the stuff in the desk drawers, the Ruth Bader Ginsburg bobblehead, and everything in between. Nine file boxes were neatly stacked next to her new bookshelf. She slipped the lid off the top box, found that it contained the contents of her "just in case" drawer, and cringed. Mack would have preferred doing the packing on her own. She wasn't thrilled that men had been responsible for moving her stash of tampons and extra deodorant, especially men she didn't know, but it was too late now.

She took in the view of downtown Tucson from her new window. The city was beautiful, even in the half-light of an early October morning. Her old office had looked out over an alley where people often camped. This didn't seem like as much of an upgrade as it should have—all Mack wanted was to be back in her Sex Crimes office, trying not to get caught staring at the occupants of the encampment.

Mack made it through unpacking three boxes before the executive suite started filling with attorneys and staff members, all popping in to welcome her. She'd been fortunate throughout her career to avoid much contact with the administration, so it wasn't that people were renewing previous relationships. She wondered just how much was curiosity based on the circumstances of her transfer. Finally, the influx of people overwhelmed her, and she let the remaining six boxes sit, unopened, where Facilities had left them.

She met with Campbell at nine, which she suspected was early for the elected official, and heard all about his grand plans for Mack's new position. He was up for reelection in two years, and he envisioned his community liaison acting as a free one-woman publicity campaign. Mack would hold the job for one year, as a "reward" for her hard work in the Andersen trial, and then some other deserving attorney would rotate in. Mack could have her pick—within reason—of trial units to return to, but Campbell hoped she might choose to stretch her wings a bit and not return to Sex Crimes.

She went into the meeting prepared to ask for permission to try Jess' homicide case with her in January and was surprised by the resistance she faced. The office, Campbell said, felt that two senior attorneys should not be paired together, and, instead, they should each be focused on mentoring newer prosecutors.

That was news to Mack, who reminded Campbell he had personally approved of Jess trying Andersen with her, given the high-profile nature of that case. He'd thought they *needed* two senior attorneys to ensure that justice was done. Surely, she pointed out, he wasn't suggesting that only victims whose cases were subject to media scrutiny deserved such justice.

Campbell, abashed, responded that if Jess' homicide warranted a second senior attorney and it didn't conflict with the requirements of her new position, she could participate. Mack smiled, pleased with her win. That sounded like permission to her, and she would run with it. She then smiled wider to cover her disdain for how easily manipulated Campbell had been.

The job itself had two component elements: interacting with the general public through educational presentations, media appearances, and tabling at events; and training law enforcement to follow the DA's office policies and procedures.

The media hadn't been friendly to Campbell's administration. The office had been plagued by delays in charging cases, perceived failures to take police brutality seriously, and allegations of racial disparity in drug cases since Campbell's election. No matter what changes he'd made, public opinion of him remained low. In addition to not improving his polling, the changes had actually damaged Campbell's popularity with law enforcement. The DA had won his first term with his tough-on-crime and pro-police stance, but local police departments saw the office's new policies as betrayals and held them against his employees, too.

Mack fought to avoid rolling her eyes. She couldn't imagine any job in the office she was less suited for. The foundation of her relationship with law enforcement was that she didn't tell them what to do. That wasn't her place as a trial attorney, and it would mean a significant shift in her perspective. For a prosecutor to direct an investigation would put their qualified immunity at risk. They could be sued for any harm suffered by a civilian.

Mack usually enjoyed interacting with law enforcement. She had generally had good relationships with the detectives and officers she'd known over the years. So long as everyone kept their roles in the system in mind, conflicts were few and far between. Interacting with the unwashed masses, however, sounded like a nightmare. Each week, she'd be expected to give at least four community presentations—to churches, schools, Rotary Club meetings, whoever she could get to invite her. The presentations could be on anything the organization wanted, but she would be provided with PowerPoints on internet safety, child safety, and pool safety, and encouraged to stick with those when possible.

Once a month, Mack would be expected to meet with Campbell, Brown, and a few other high-ranking people in the office for a "status exchange." Mack would report on what trainings she had done and for whom, while the other "members of the team" gave her new material to push for the month ahead. It all sounded very corporate and political, much to Mack's chagrin. She'd set out in her career to avoid both of those worlds, but now—for the next year, at least—she would have no other option but to immerse herself in them.

Her first week went smoothly, to Mack's surprise, and so did the second. Before she knew it, Mack found herself gliding into her third month in the frictionless position. She didn't care about the mission, wasn't interested in acting as Campbell's PR flunky, and did the bare minimum to satisfy the participants at the monthly meetings. Otherwise, her time was her own. There was no one checking where she was at any particular time, and she took full advantage.

"Honey," Mack called to Anna's dark foyer. "I'm home!" She'd stopped to pick up salads from the sandwich shop down the street. Anna had been working extra hours the past several weeks, covering two therapy groups for a colleague who was out on maternity leave. That gave her an extra twenty patients, and Anna was being stretched thin. Mack was doing what she could to pick up the slack, from meals to household chores.

"In the dining room!"

Mack set her keys on the console table near the front door and made her way through the house. "Dark in here," she said. She set the bag on the table and gave Anna a quick kiss before continuing into the kitchen for plates and drinks. She found an open bottle of Riesling on the counter, poured herself a glass, and carried the bottle with her to the table.

Anna stood, stretching her back and shoulders. "Yeah, I've been sitting still for a while," she said. She still had her work clothes on—black wool slacks and silk blouse, topped by a black cardigan. Her dark hair was neatly contained in a very short ponytail. Mack looked at her feet, surprised to see she hadn't even changed into house slippers. "Trying to catch up on probation reports on Michelle's guys. How was your day?"

Mack paused from unpacking the salads. "Umm, it was fine," she said. "I had lunch with James Harris"—the supervisor of the Sex Crimes unit and Mack's former boss—"and then ran a few errands this afternoon. Did a little shopping. Talked to Jess. She's been on like four dates with that bartender already. She likes him a lot. Then, let's see. Worked on house stuff. You?"

"Busy," Anna said. "Very busy. I had a group session, four individual patients, and I'm writing up two evals." She eyed the salad she was handed skeptically. "Is this the chicken apple?"

"Oops," Mack said, swapping the two. "Yours is the Thai chicken, mine is the chicken apple. Better?"

Anna started eating. The meal passed in silence, and Mack couldn't tell if Anna was tense or just tired. A thank-you would have been nice, she thought. It's not that she wanted effusive praise for picking up takeout—which they both knew was the extent of her kitchen abilities—but she didn't think basic politeness was too much to ask for.

"What do you want to do tonight?" Mack asked once the salads were cleared.

Anna opened her eyes and sat upright. "I have a couple more hours of work."

"Oh," Mack said, feeling hurt. "I thought maybe we'd get to spend the evening together." She scratched the back of her neck, aware she was blushing. She suspected that her avoidance of physical intimacy since Allen had assaulted her was putting a strain on Anna, even if she wouldn't admit it. "I was thinking—well, I was thinking maybe I was ready to…"

Anna shook her head and walked to the couch, picking up her laptop and a file. "Some of us can't leave our jobs at the office, unfortunately. You're welcome to hang out, if you want, but I have early patients tomorrow morning."

Mack took the hint and saw herself out. Sex could wait, she knew. Anna had been patient with her, and she could return the favor.

Mack, having rearranged her schedule accordingly, threw herself into Jess' trial. She met with Jess on a semi-regular basis, familiarizing herself with the facts. Three years earlier, Dorothy Johnson, an eighty-five-year-old mother of three and grandmother of eight, had been raped and murdered while home alone one February night.

The murder was discovered when Dorothy's daughter Eleanor called police to report that her mother hadn't sent her a good-morning text and requested a welfare check. The dispatcher scoffed at the idea that one missing text warranted police involvement, but it was a slow morning and the officers arrived on scene to find Dorothy's battered body cooling on her kitchen floor.

Two weeks before the murder, Dorothy had called to report a burglary. She had come home from the weekly bingo party at her sister's nursing home and found that her iPad, which normally lived on her kitchen counter, had been stolen. Despite the slashed window screen and a broken window the patrol officers found in the guest bedroom, Dorothy's son Eddie told the Property Crimes detective, who followed up a few days later, that he thought his mom had just misplaced her tablet. Everyone agreed that Dorothy's memory had been fading in recent years.

Police couldn't find any fingerprints from the burglary, or any evidence that the window had been broken on purpose. Dorothy did live on a golf course, after all. Maybe a stray ball had broken the window, and Dorothy really had just misplaced her tablet. Dorothy was confused but apologetic, content to buy a new iPad and move forward.

But just two weeks later, police returned to Dorothy's home to find a bloody crime scene that could not be explained away. In addition to the blood, there were a number of pieces of physical evidence that told a terrifying story of Dorothy's final hours. A bingo card sat on the kitchen counter, and the crime-scene investigators almost missed the bloody thumbprints—Dorothy's own, analysis revealed—that had been used to complete the board. Police assumed that the killer had dipped Dorothy's thumb in her own blood to make the prints, but there was no hint as to the reason behind this macabre act.

Dorothy's purse and jewelry box were found in the bedroom, empty. Even her wedding ring had been taken—apparently violently, given the bruising on her finger.

Mack pored over the reports and recordings until she felt like she knew Dorothy and her family. The photos of Dorothy before her murder even reminded Mack of her own grandmother, Lela Mae. They were both short, stout women with meticulous white perms and a penchant for appliquéd shirts. The autopsy report suggested that, although Dorothy's death had been near instantaneous from a single gunshot behind her right ear, the elderly woman had suffered terribly in the hours before her death. Cigarette burns checkered her arms, legs, and chest, and superficial cuts made intricate patterns across her skin. Blood had dripped and splashed around the house.

Mack had never seen a case with this level of violence. It seemed clear that Dorothy's killer must have been someone she knew. Strangers rarely inflict such terrible wounds unless they are true sadists. Textbooks would suggest this kind of killer had killed before and would kill again, but there were no unsolved cases matching this M.O. The police initially focused on Dorothy's friends and family. Perhaps one of her bingo friends—one of the men, almost certainly, given the violence—had been rebuffed romantically and reacted badly. Maybe a delivery guy noticed her home alone and sensed an opportunity, although, other than the purse and jewelry box, there was no indication that the killer had stolen anything from the house.

The rape kit eventually resulted in a full DNA profile—both from the vaginal swabs and from saliva left on Dorothy's breast. When it was run through CODIS, the profile had hit to Francis "Frank" Jefferson, a three-time loser who got out of prison six months before Dorothy's murder. His most recent conviction had been—interestingly—a home invasion. Police hadn't found any link between Frank and Dorothy. When they interviewed him, he denied knowing her or ever visiting her home. He doubled down on that story when confronted with the photos and the DNA results and accused the police of planting his fluids at the scene. That story was enough to arrest and charge him for Dorothy's rape and murder. Dorothy's iPad was never recovered, even when they executed a search warrant on Jefferson's home. Based on the belief that Jefferson had entered and committed the burglary to case the house for his later crime, he was charged with that offense as well. Mack had done more with less, but this would be a tough case.

CHAPTER FOUR

It had been a very long day. What was supposed to have been a quick meeting at Tucson PD with a group of homicide detectives had taken a turn when a tall, good-looking guy interrupted Mack's presentation—for November, her topic was charging standards for domestic violence homicides, just in time for the holidays—with a loud yawn.

"Sorry," he said, not sounding sorry in the least. "I'm just tired from a late night at a crime scene. You know, where I was *detecting*? Doing my *job*? Not telling other people how to do *theirs*?"

"Oh?" Mack asked. "I get your frustration. Do you want to tell me about the case last night?"

The guy folded his muscular arms over his chest and leaned back in his chair. Mack mirrored his posture against the podium. She looked around the room, hoping for a friendly face. She hadn't taken much notice of the group when she'd come in, halfway through her first coffee of the morning and still waking up, but now she noticed the sea of frowns facing her.

In a back corner, slouched against the wall and scrolling on his phone, she noticed Craig Caldwell. She didn't know Craig well, had never worked a case with him, but he'd been partners with Dave Barton for many years and they'd attended a few social events together. When Dave had promoted to sergeant, he became Craig's supervisor, and Mack wondered if their friendship had been negatively impacted by the change in the power dynamic. The tall, clean-cut detective had always made female attorneys swoon, but he had been married for twenty years to his childhood sweetheart. Mack had found him to be professional and pleasant, but cold. He wasn't one of the cops who would call her out of the blue with his legal issue du jour. In fact, Mack couldn't think of any prosecutors Craig was known to be close to.

"Detective Caldwell," she said. "Were you on scene last night? How about you help your colleague out."

He shook his head without looking up. Mack resisted the urge to roll her eyes. It was too early for macho bullshit posing, and she was impatient to wrap up. She had lunch plans with Jess and a presentation at a nursing home in the afternoon.

"No need," the yawning detective said. He looked her up and down, and Mack felt self-conscious in her severe bun and slim-cut gray suit. "I could explain, but I'm not going to. You don't do trials anymore, you wouldn't understand."

Mack set her computer remote down and stared at the detective, her mouth a thin line. "Why don't you step out?" she suggested. "Get yourself some coffee? Because I heard about last night from the prosecutor on scene. Heard you all know who did it but didn't have enough to keep him in custody and had to let the guy go. So you go fuel up, and I'll keep doing my *job*, which is to help *you* all get convictions, rather than catch-and-release policing. 'K?"

Mack heard a chorus of angry whispers and let her shoulders drop. She shouldn't have been so hard on the guy. She didn't recognize him, but based on what she knew of the case, it had been a brutal scene. A toddler, dead at his father's hands, but not enough evidence to prove it—at least not yet. That would be enough to make even the strongest cop a little testy.

"Look," she said, hoisting herself to sit on the table at the front of the conference room. "We're on the same team. I know it doesn't always feel like that. But we are. I spent almost six years trying sex crimes, okay? I know how hard family cases are—on you, on the victims and their loved ones, and on us, too. Let's work together to get the best results we can. Deal?"

The guy stood up, his chair scraping loudly against the floor. He left the room without another word. The remaining members of his unit filed out after him. Mack tried to catch Craig's eye as he left, but he studiously avoided looking at her.

Mack stared at the twenty remaining detectives, many of whom now had their arms folded across their chests, grim expressions on their faces. She wasn't sure where things had gone wrong. Her good relationships with law enforcement had always been one of her favorite things about being a prosecutor.

"Let's—let's just wrap up, okay? I'll reschedule with your lieutenant, and we can reconvene another time."

Mack had picked up soup and scallion pancakes on her way to Anna's house and sprawled on Anna's couch in the dark with a beer and a marathon of *The Real World* on television, waiting for her. By the time she heard the psychologist's key in the lock, though, the food had gotten cold.

"Hey!" she called. "I brought dinner, but I don't think it's any good anymore."

Anna sighed. "I texted you I had something come up and to eat without me. See?" She picked up her phone and scrolled to her texts. "Shit. I typed it, but never sent it. I'm sorry."

Mack shrugged and sat up. "It's okay," she said. "I wasn't really very hungry, anyway. I had a really hard day."

Anna laughed scornfully. "A hard day?" She crossed the room to stand in front of the television, and Mack could see how tired she looked. Her dark brown linen suit, freshly ironed that morning, was wrinkled now, and her hair had lost its volume. "What constitutes a hard day in your job? A senior citizen got scammed? You worked past three?"

Mack took several deep breaths. "I don't really want to talk about it," she said. "I was looking forward to dinner and a movie with you, but maybe I should just head home."

Anna approached the couch. She cupped the back of Mack's head and leaned in, kissing her lightly on the cheek. She smelled like Greek food, sweat, and hints of Dolce and Gabbana Light Blue perfume. Mack wrinkled her nose.

"I'm sorry," Anna said. "Thank you for bringing dinner. I bet we can warm it up and it will still be delicious. Why don't I hop in the shower and then you can tell me about your hard day? I can give you a foot rub and we can watch *Diamonds Are Forever*, okay?"

Mack's heart was beating louder than normal. She had been looking forward to telling Anna about her experience with the detective that morning, and a foot rub sounded incredible. She had been wearing heels almost every day recently—every time she had a presentation to give. Her feet were killing her. But the last thing she needed was more conflict.

"I'm going to go," she said. "But I'll leave the food. We can catch up tomorrow. Maybe we'll both be feeling better. That sound good?"

Anna rubbed the back of Mack's neck gently and leaned against her, Mack's forehead bumping her stomach. "I'm really sorry," she said. "Things are…crazy at work right now. Today was Bring Your Romantic Partner to Therapy Day, and those are always hard. It's important they have those appropriate outlets for their sexual behavior, I get that, but most of the partners were with these shitbags when they committed their crimes, and they just accept whatever lie they're told because 'he loves me,' or 'he's changed.' They never change."

Mack felt Anna's hands clench into fists around her hair. The pressure hurt, but she didn't want to interrupt. It had been like pulling teeth to get Anna to talk to her lately.

"They've just gotten better at lying. Sometimes I hate these guys. And their women just make me so angry. I could have done anything with my life, and *this* is where I wound up? But I'm sorry. I shouldn't take it out on you. You get to have hard days, too. How about we go out tomorrow night? Go try that new hot pot restaurant you saw? Maybe find some live music somewhere?"

"That sounds nice," Mack said. She stood and grabbed her purse. "I'm still going to go, but *that* sounds nice. I'll see you tomorrow."

The next morning, Mack found a dozen orange tulips in a vase on her desk. A folded piece of notebook paper served as a card. *Jess let me in*, it read. *I hope today is a better day. xx Anna*

CHAPTER FIVE

One Wednesday night in early November, Jess suggested happy hour, and Mack said yes without thinking. It had been weeks since she'd spent any time alone with her friend. It seemed like Jess and Adam were quickly getting serious, while Mack and Anna were still trying to regain their rhythm as a couple.

She called Anna before she left the office, to let her know their plan—a couple beers and sandwiches at Bisonwitches, downtown. She wasn't surprised to hear her girlfriend sigh. Early in their relationship—their *first* relationship—Anna's sighing had driven Mack nuts. But she had come to realize that it was a psychologist's trick, a subconscious way of stalling for time. Still, it didn't hurt to confirm.

"Is everything okay?" Mack asked. "We didn't have plans tonight, did we?"

"No, but I was hopeful I'd get to see you tonight, and I'm a little frustrated that you're spending time with Jess instead. I thought we could continue our Bond festival. I think we're up to *Live and Let Die*."

Mack leaned back. Her temper flared, and she resisted the urge to toss back a callous response. "I'd love to see you tonight," she said, "and watching a movie sounds great, *after* happy hour. My friendship with Jess is important to me, too."

"Shouldn't you choose your girlfriend over your friend?"

Mack ran her fingers through her hair. It had been another difficult day, and conflict with Anna was the last thing she needed. She'd started the morning with a presentation to Tucson Police's Violent Crimes units, talking them through the district attorney's new expectations regarding independent review of police-involved shootings. It was a sensitive topic, and she wasn't exactly shocked by the amount of pushback she received, but it still stung. She tried joking around with officers she'd known and worked with before but was met by stony stares.

"I'm not choosing anyone," Mack said. "I don't ever want to choose either of you over the other. This seems like a pretty extreme response to something that isn't a big deal, Anna. Jess asked if I wanted to grab drinks, you and I didn't have plans. If we *had* had plans, I would have said no to Jess."

"Oh," Anna said, and Mack could hear the psychologist's professional mask slip into her voice. "Well, thank you for letting me know that my reaction seems extreme. I'll try to temper it. Help me understand what you're saying: whoever asks you first wins? Can I go ahead and just reserve you every night after work, then?"

Mack couldn't tell if the question was rhetorical but knew the wrong answer would only fan the flames. She looked up and saw Jess standing in her doorway, briefcase slung over one shoulder and gesturing toward the parking lot. She leaned forward and held up one finger. Jess came fully into the office and sat down.

"I'd love to come watch the movie after dinner," Mack said. "But it sounds like maybe the moment for that has passed. Jess just got here, so I'm going to head out. Why don't you text me if you want me to come over later?"

Anna hummed noncommittally into the phone and ended the call. Mack slumped in her chair.

"You okay?" Jess asked. "That sounded tense."

Mack forced a smile. "Bitches be crazy," she said, grabbing her purse. "I'm starving. Let's go."

They drove separately to the restaurant, and the waitress delivered their beers—they were Miller Lites, but who could argue with the three-dollar happy hour special?—before Jess returned to the phone call in Mack's office.

"I know I only heard the tail end, but it seems like maybe there's some tension?"

Mack continued peeling the label from her beer bottle. "I'm not sure," she said. "I really like Anna, most of the time, but lately it doesn't really feel like she likes me so much."

"What do you mean?" Mack could tell that Jess wanted her to look up from the label, which she was now tearing into progressively smaller pieces.

"Well, like, I love doing stuff with Anna. We have fun hiking, and we've been going to the gym together, and we love concerts and movie nights. But it seems like everything has to be on her terms, you know?" Mack looked up at last. Jess was being compassionate, and Mack wanted to sink through her barstool and let the earth swallow her whole. Instead, she started shredding her napkin. "Maybe she doesn't even see me as an independent person, just as, like, a sidekick. It wasn't that way before, when we were sort of dating, or when we were friends in between, and so I'm having trouble adjusting. I don't want to be anyone's pity project, but especially not hers. It seems like when I want to spend time with her, she backs away, and when I go do my own thing, she resents it."

"Okay," Jess said. "So, what was it like before, when you were sort-of dating?"

Mack ran her hands through her hair and rolled her shoulders. "It was more like we were really good work friends, first, and then one of the things we liked to do together was have sex. We had a ton of fun together, but the 'relationship' part of it was never that serious. And then we stopped having sex, and we wound up just friends."

"And now? Are you...?" Jess paused and raised her eyebrows.

"No. I—I don't feel ready. Which is really stupid. You know, when Allen attacked me, I was unconscious for a while, and I don't know if he—well, if he *raped* me or not. I just can't bring myself to ask for the rape kit results, because mostly I just don't want to know. Knowing wouldn't change what happened, and it certainly wouldn't make me feel better, even if the answer is no. Even if he did—I don't know...do whatever—I wasn't there for it. It didn't even really happen to *me*. It's not like our victims, who know exactly what these shitbags do to them. So it feels like I should be fine, because if I wasn't even raped, then where's the trauma, right?"

Jess put her hand on Mack's, stopping the destruction of the napkin. "No," she said. "We're not doing that. We're not playing 'is this trauma valid?' The reality of what happened to you is *terrible*, Mack, whether or not rape was part of it. Don't devalue the very real horrible thing that happened to you. You get to have whatever response you have to it. If you never want to have sex again—I mean, for your sake, I hope that's not what happens, but I'm just saying—then that's fine. Is Anna giving you a hard time about it?"

Mack finished her beer. She'd ordered a Jayhawk sandwich—two chicken breasts with cheese and honey mustard—and it would cancel out the impact of a second drink. She gestured to the waitress for another round. She'd still be fine to drive to Anna's, if that's how the evening unfolded.

"You know," she said, after taking a long drink of her fresh beer. "We've reached my limit for emotional processing today. I appreciate your kind words and support, but I'm going to decline to answer that question."

Jess smiled and dug into her taco salad. "Okay," she said through a mouthful of lettuce. "Whatever you need, champ."

Mack laughed. "Thanks, sport. Let's talk about you instead. How are things going with Adam?"

Jess smiled even wider. "Really good. It's still new, I know, but I like this guy. I feel like I know him really well, which is a weird thing to say, but, it's like…when we're talking I feel like I know what he's going to say before he even says it. And he's emotionally available in a way that I'm not used to from men."

"My understanding is that men don't do emotional intelligence."

"Exactly! We're actually spending Thanksgiving with my parents, and it was his idea."

"Whoa!" Mack said. "That's a big step."

"They haven't met a boyfriend since I was in high school. I can't tell who's more nervous: Adam or them."

Mack looked at her, waiting. She sensed a hesitation behind Jess' words. "But?"

"But nothing!" Jess exclaimed.

Mack rolled her eyes, not caring that Jess would see.

"Okay, there are buts."

Mack smiled. "Go on."

"Weird stuff," Jess said. "Stupid stuff, really. But, like—okay, here's an example. I'm pretty sure he doesn't have a license."

"He can't not have a license," Mack said. "This is a city you have to drive in to get around. What do you mean?"

"I know! But I've never seen him drive. Like, he takes an Uber when he comes over. And if we're going out, we take my car, and I drive. It's not that I mind, even. I'm a strong, independent woman, and I'm happy to do the driving. But I've asked him about it—a couple times, actually—and he always has excuses. Like his car is in the shop. I mean, that happens, but if they're keeping it for two weeks they give you a loaner, right?"

Mack nodded.

"Or he says he wants to drink when we go out, which is a totally valid thing, too, right?"

Mack nodded again.

"But it's weird. I just *feel* like he's lying to me about the whole car thing. And ultimately, who can care? If he doesn't have a license, so what?"

Mack leaned forward and took a bite of her sandwich while she considered that. "Is it possible he just can't afford a car and he's embarrassed about it?" she asked.

Jess played with her salad. "Maybe. I don't know. I'm trying not to focus on that. You know, that's that thing I always do, where I find the slightest reason to write someone off and then it's over. I'm trying not to rush this—to let it evolve and see where it goes. I *really* like him, Mack."

"That's very sweet. You know I'm happy for you."

"Thanks. I think this is the first time a guy has ever liked me as much and as quickly as I like him. He brings me flowers, takes me out to dinner, the works!"

Mack felt a twinge of jealousy. "I'm a little surprised you were free tonight, actually."

Jess shrugged. "You and I haven't seen each other in ages. And, Adam picked up a shift last minute, so it seemed like perfect timing."

"Ah," Mack said, stung by the realization that she had been Jess' plan B.

She felt her phone buzz in her pants pocket and read a new text from Anna. *I was a jerk. Can you please come over after dinner? I'll make popcorn and apologize in person.*

Mack smiled, and decided she would pick up ice cream on her way over to her girlfriend's house. Ice cream fixed everything.

CHAPTER SIX

Mack gasped for breath, far past her comfort zone. Her feet pounded the pavement. Her lungs and calf muscles ached with her efforts. Her ribs—technically healed but still tender—throbbed. No matter how hard she pushed, she couldn't quite keep up with Anna, whose shorter legs seemed unaffected by the pace she was setting.

Finally, just as Mack was ready to collapse, Anna slowed to a walk. She tousled her short brown hair, damp with exertion, and took deep recovery breaths. Mack dropped to her knees on the grassy lawn next to the running trail. She felt like she was going to puke.

"You'll feel better if you stand up," Anna said. She leaned side to side, stretching her obliques.

Mack pulled her shoulders back and felt her spine pop. "I'm out of shape," she said. She took a long drink from the water bottle Anna offered her. "Am I dying? It feels like I'm dying."

Anna wiped her face on her gray running tank top. "You haven't been out since you got hurt. It's only natural that it's hard to get back into it. You're far from death."

Mack rose unsteadily. "You keep going," she said, hands on her hips. Her T-shirt, soaked in sweat, was itchy against her back, and her sports bra felt much too tight. "But I'm toasted. I'll wait here for you when you're done."

Anna consulted her Fitbit. "I'm okay. We've only done a smidge over three miles, so I'll probably come back out this evening, but we can quit for now."

They walked slowly back to Anna's Infiniti. It was a beautiful Saturday, with the cloudless blue skies that had lured Mack to Tucson in the first place and a slight nip to the air. When Mack woke up feeling restless, Anna had suggested a run. It had been a long week of presentations at a series of interchangeable nursing homes, trying to convince the residents that their grandchildren probably weren't calling from Thai prisons in need of Apple gift cards. By Friday afternoon, Mack had been vibrating with unspent energy.

After their run, she desperately wanted a shower. They had plans to meet a friend of Anna's for lunch, and there was a new female spy movie out that Mack had suggested for the afternoon. Now, though, she was reconsidering the rest of the day. She had pushed herself too hard, too fast.

"What if I never get back to where I was?"

Anna hummed under her breath and considered the question. One of the things Mack loved about her girlfriend was the psychologist's careful, measured approach to the world, but sometimes her unwillingness to just respond drove Mack crazy.

"I don't think one run is enough to justify that kind of assumption," Anna said finally. "There's no reason to believe you're incapable of building back the stamina and strength you had before you were attacked. You've been medically cleared and should have no lasting damage from the injuries to your ribs. You couldn't run ten miles when you first started running seriously, but you built up to it. You just need to give it some time."

"But what if?"

Anna came to a stop at a red light and looked at Mack. "Then you'll find other ways to take care of yourself. You'll try yoga, or swimming, or you'll buy a Peloton. Maybe you'll become a weightlifter and bust out of all your suits."

Mack smiled half-heartedly. "It's not just running, though. *Nothing* is like it used to be. I keep the lights on all the time—my electricity bill is a nightmare—and I jump at the slightest noise. I bought a keychain with a big spike on it. I mean…I just…it feels like I'm just waiting for the other shoe to drop."

Anna put her hand on Mack's knee and squeezed it gently.

Mack shifted away and crossed her legs. "Too sweaty."

"You've been through a major trauma, Mack, and it's been less than six months. Go easy on yourself, okay? And maybe go easy on me, too. I'm just trying to help."

Mack leaned her head against the cool glass of the window and pulled out her phone. She scrolled through her messages, looking for something to distract her. She wanted a concrete answer. She wanted to know *when* she'd be back to her old self, able to outrun her girlfriend, never the one who had to turn back early. Able to walk through her home in the dark without breaking down. She was tired of waiting. She wanted to feel better. She wanted her body to be ready for anything, to resume a normal life. "I'm not sure I'm up for lunch after all," she said. She was itching for a fight. She missed the way it felt to argue.

Anna released one of her signature psychologist sighs. "I'd really like it if you came," she said. "But if you need to rest, that's okay. There'll be plenty of opportunities for lunch."

Mack rolled her eyes, grateful for her sunglasses. Anna had been exceedingly respectful of Mack's need to rest, both in the days following the attack and since they'd officially gotten back together. Sometimes, Mack thought Anna was too accommodating. She wanted to be pushed a little bit. She wanted Anna to help her live up to her potential, not just hold her hand and murmur platitudes.

Sex Crimes had required sixty-hour weeks of Mack at least three times a month, but she found herself adrift in her new position, which barely needed thirty hours a week from her. She filled her free time through the holidays with movies, books, long hikes—alone or with Anna, when her girlfriend was free—and even an occasional midday nap. She looked casually into taking piano lessons, something she'd given up as a child and always regretted, but the first person she called was only available at the same time as her regular speaking engagement at the Tucson Public Library and she didn't try anyone else. Each Tuesday, a new group of elderly patrons would shuffle in and squint at the projection screen as Mack explained how to avoid internet and telephone scams. She had memorized the speech and, after the first six times, she could have recited it in her sleep.

In short, Mack was bored.

Anna had gone home to California to spend Christmas and New Year's with her parents and siblings. Mack's mother had come to Tucson for a long weekend over Christmas. It was the first time they'd spent the holiday together in years. Even though Mack was raised Jewish, they had celebrated Christmas when she was a kid, to fit in with the other families in the neighborhood. Mack fondly remembered going to K-Mart every December 26 to buy discount ornaments for the next year. Mack had agonized over spending four days alone with her mom, worried what they'd talk about for that long with no one to serve as a buffer, but she'd been pleasantly surprised at how well it had gone. It was their fifth time seeing each other in a year, which was the most time they'd spent together since Mack had left for Dartmouth. Now that she wasn't so consumed by her job—could leave work at work and engage more fully with the world around her—they'd had a lovely time.

In the full swing of the new year, her spats with Anna had been increasing, sometimes even erupting into full-scale arguments. She couldn't tell if Anna was frustrated with her or just mirroring Mack's mounting frustration with her whole entire life. Anna's days, and most evenings, were filled with the rotation of patients, evaluations, and reports that she'd been juggling for as long as Mack had known her. She didn't have Mack's luxury of free time, and Mack worried that the novelty of having her around was wearing thin.

The second Friday in January, Mack was half dozing in the hammock on her back patio, half listening to a true-crime podcast and half sipping from a leftover seasonal stout, when Jess called, asking if Mack and Anna wanted to meet at Paradise that night. Adam was working, and Jess wanted to stop in and say hi to her boyfriend.

"Boyfriend, huh? I don't know that I've ever actually heard you use that word before."

"Sure you have," Jess said. "You've just never heard the word *my* paired with it."

Mack laughed and looked up at the play of the late-afternoon sun on the mountains. Anna was in Mack's living room, writing a report. She had plans with friends later that evening, and Mack hadn't seen Jess outside of work in close to a month, what with the holidays, her focus on Anna, Jess' focus on Adam, and the upcoming Frank Thompson trial. She'd been planning on a little home spa night while Anna was out, but she supposed that her face mask could wait.

"Two drinks," she said, "and then I turn into a pumpkin."

CHAPTER SEVEN

Anna agreed to swing by Paradise for a drink with Jess and Mack on her way to meet her friends, so long as they drove separately.

"Is it okay if I only stay for one drink?" Anna asked.

She didn't care how long Anna stayed, she was just excited that they were going together. Spending an evening out with her girlfriend was one of her favorite things to do.

"Explain it to me again. Why does Jess have to date the bartender at the lesbian bar?"

"Umm, he's very cute? You'll see." Mack looked at Anna, beautiful in black pants and a leather jacket, hair styled in artful disarray, makeup done to perfection. Then she looked down at herself: ancient jeans and a blue Oxford shirt. She shrugged off her discomfort. Anna was meeting up with a group of colleagues at a fancy wine bar downtown, while she would be spending the evening in a dive bar. It was okay that they didn't match.

Anna rolled her eyes. "How cute could he *possibly* be? She must be desperate, huh?"

"I don't think she's desperate at all. He's a nice guy; you'll like him. He seems to be really good to Jess, so I'm cool with him. I think he even dropped the L bomb last week. She didn't come right out and tell me, but I'm reading between the lines. It's important to me that we spend time with them." She had been resisting the urge to push the two of them together, aware that each woman had her reasons for distrusting the other.

Anna hummed under her breath. "I just don't feel like Jess likes me very much," she said. She ran her fingers through her hair, rearranging it, and Mack recognized the vulnerability in the gesture.

"It's not that she doesn't like you," she said, putting her hand on Anna's hip and pulling her into a hug. "She just worries about me. It literally does not matter who I might ever choose to date. I could go out with Mother Teresa and she'd still worry. She was the youngest in her family, and I think she sees me as her chance to be a big sister. She likes you more than she likes most people."

Anna smiled and leaned in to Mack's shoulder. Mack pulled her even closer, enjoying the way the petite woman fit against her. The tentative peace Anna and Jess had struck after the Allen attack was holding, but Mack knew that too much push in either direction could disrupt the balance.

"I get jealous, sometimes," Anna said, her voice muffled against Mack's shirt.

"Hmm?" Mack asked. She was focused on the way Anna's hand felt, rubbing small circles on her back just above the waistband of her jeans.

"You spend all your time with her," Anna said. "I'm worried she doesn't like me and will convince you to break up with me. I know it's stupid. But it seems like, sometimes, when things happen in your life, you tell her before you even talk to me. You do all your processing, and by the time you tell me, it's not even a conversation. You've already done the work and I'm just batting cleanup. I'm a psychologist, but you talk things through with your lawyer friend, instead of me. And I'm worried you'd rather be with her than with me."

"Not even a little bit," Mack said. She could feel her muscles tensing and struggled to remain calm. "Jess is basically my sister, so what you're worried about would be incest, and incest is a felony punishable by up to two point five years in prison. Also, it's gross."

Anna laughed and kissed Mack's neck. "Okay," she said. "I believe you. Rationally, I know it's healthy for us to have friendships and interests outside our relationship and everything, but sometimes my lizard brain kicks in and I just want you all to myself."

Mack relaxed. Her relationship with Anna was fine. Her friendship with Jess was fine. Everyone just needed to stop worrying. She had enough time and energy for everyone, especially since it wasn't like her job took up most of her life anymore. She wanted the two most important people in her life to be able to spend time together without hurt feelings, and maybe Anna's agreeing to go for a drink was a step in that direction, even though Anna was being kind of harsh about Jess' dating choices.

Jess was already at the bar when they got to Paradise. The place was quiet, no karaoke that night. Despite the low-key vibe, Jess was dressed up, wearing a silky tank top and very tight jeans. Her hair was down and meticulously curled. Mack knew that Jess' hair was naturally stick straight, just like hers. She could only imagine how long it must have taken to give it so much body.

"Looking pretty good for your evening at the lesbian bar, huh?" Mack asked, giving her friend a one-armed hug. "You trying to tell us something?"

Anna laughed. "It's a bold choice."

"You ladies know me." Jess waggled her eyebrows. "All attention is good attention."

Adam was behind the bar, drying glasses and keeping one eye on Jess and the other on the dozen patrons scattered around the room. Jess was right—he really was cute. His dark brown hair had grown out some, revealing curls that, paired with his wide smile and the dimple in his left cheek, gave him an undeniable charm.

"Have you met my girlfriend Anna?" Mack asked him. "I don't think she's been in since you and Jess started dating."

He reached across the bar to shake Anna's hand. "I've certainly seen you before, but I don't think we've met. You'd be hard to forget!"

Anna blushed and Mack smiled, pleased. She pulled Anna flush against her and kissed her temple. "Ain't that the truth!"

Anna fumbled with her purse, pulling out a credit card and offering to buy a round before she had to move on.

"Be careful, though," Mack said. "She prefers cocktails with at least four ingredients."

Adam laughed. "No Miller Lite here. Got it."

"Oh, for sure," Jess said. "She's definitely the bougiest of the three of us. Vodka cocktails, all day long."

"Can I see some ID?" Adam asked. He winked, and Anna blushed an even deeper red.

"I'm well over twenty-one," she said, handing over her license. "But I'm flattered."

Adam laughed, glancing at the license and handing it back. "It's policy," he said. "Rocky catches me handing out liquor without checking and it's" —he drew a finger across his throat— "for me."

The three women laughed.

"Please don't get him killed," Jess said. "Not tonight, anyway. We've got big plans once his shift ends. I managed not to bring any work home this weekend, so we have all night and all day tomorrow. This'll be the first time we'll have thirty-six uninterrupted hours for ourselves."

Mack blushed and felt herself begin to relax. This was fine. Jess and Anna could get along fine. Adam might be just the thing their dynamic needed. He would take up a lot of Jess' time, which would make Anna happy, and he clearly made Jess happy. Mack pictured the four of them double dating, maybe even taking couples' vacations. Her thoughts were interrupted by Adam sliding a highball glass across the bar to Anna.

"Try this," he said. "I've been fiddling with this recipe I got in Charleston last summer. Vodka, aperol, little of this, dash of that."

Anna looked hesitant but sipped the drink. "This is delicious!"

Mack rubbed Anna's back under her jacket.

Adam smiled. "I'm glad you like it. This one"—he pointed at Jess, who stuck her tongue out—"has no imagination. She never wants to try anything new."

Anna took a longer drink. "She's wrong for that. Feel free to treat me like your personal guinea pig. Try any experiments you want."

By the time Anna was ready to leave to meet her friends, Mack and Jess had switched from beer (Mack) and wine (Jess) to vodka sodas. They were laughing about an old case, when an angry mother had thrown a sex toy at Jess across a conference room table. Adam, looking on, seemed horrified by their casual approach to the oddities of their work. Anna kissed Mack's cheek as she rose from the back table they'd commandeered. Mack grabbed Anna's wrist and pulled her closer, circling her arms around her waist.

"I'll see you tomorrow?" Mack asked.

Anna smiled. "I have the whole day free. You want to go for a hike? Call me when you get up, and we can figure out a plan. Looks like you might wind up sleeping in a little, so I'll probably head to the office first thing."

Mack pushed a lock of Anna's hair behind her ear and kissed her.

"Bye, babe," Anna said. "Be safe!"

"Another round!" Mack called to Adam. "This one's on your girlfriend!"

CHAPTER EIGHT

"Well, don't you look like shit," Roxanne Bailey said as she walked into her office, noting the disheveled blonde sprawled on her couch. "Long night, Pumpkin?"

Mack groaned in response. She moved her head, tentatively, side to side. Pleased with the results, she tried sitting up. That was too much, and she sank back into the cool black leather, covering her head with her black North Face fleece. "Long *year*," came her muffled voice. She could feel the seam of her Oxford shirt digging into her left armpit. The right leg of her jeans had ridden up, and her ankle was cold. She wondered where her shoes were.

"It's only January," Rocky said, settling into her desk chair and taking the cap off a bottle of water.

"That should tell you how long it's been!"

Rocky rolled her eyes. "But seriously, folks. Why don't you start by telling me why you're asleep in my office at ten o'clock on a Saturday morning? You haven't spent the night in my office in at least five years."

Mack groaned a second time and pulled the fleece off her head. She sat up, wincing as her head pounded. "Is it ten already? Shit."

Mack and Rocky had met the night of Mack's twenty-third birthday, back when Rocky was a bartender at one of Scottsdale's lesbian bars. They had hit it off immediately. An odd pairing, the pretty femme law student and the butch bartender ten years her senior, but Rocky had recognized something in Mack and taken the younger woman under her wing. In return for free drinks and a shoulder to lean on, Mack had loyally followed Rocky as she changed jobs between several bars in Phoenix and Tucson before finally buying Paradise two years earlier. Mack always got the sense that maybe Rocky wanted something more than loyalty out of the deal, but Rocky had never said anything and Mack had never asked.

Rocky sipped her water and watched Mack rub her face.

"I crashed here when the bar closed last night," Mack said. "Adam let me in. He's a nice guy."

Rocky frowned. "I'll have to talk to him about that. He can't just be letting people sleep in my office, doesn't matter who."

Mack waved her off. "He knows we're tight," she said. "And besides, he's officially Jess' *boyfriend*, now. So this is one of the perks of being friends with the bartender's girlfriend, I guess."

Rocky was wearing black slacks, a white button-down shirt with one too many buttons undone, a skinny black tie, and a pinstriped vest to round it out.

"You're looking very Shane today," Mack said.

Rocky snorted. "That might almost be a compliment."

"No almost," Mack said. "You look good. You get some sun?" She was curious about her friend's outfit, which seemed out of place for a Saturday morning. She wondered if Rocky hadn't made it home the night before, and what it might mean that her chest was suddenly tight with jealousy.

"What's going on, Mack?"

"Can I have some aspirin?"

Rocky dug through a desk drawer and emerged, victorious, with two caplets. Mack swallowed them gratefully and looked at her watch, trying to calculate how much longer she needed to spend making small talk before she could get away.

"Mack," Rocky said again. "What are you really doing here? It feels like it's been months since I've seen or heard from you."

Mack shrugged and considered the question, weighing how honest to be. "Jess and I were here late and I didn't feel like taking another Uber. I didn't really intend to stay overnight, just sleep it off a bit and head home. I definitely thought I'd be gone before you got here."

"Why not call Anna?" Was Mack imagining the slight bite to Rocky's tone? She and Anna had never spent much time together. Anna didn't like Paradise, really, choosing instead to frequent more upscale bars. Although neither Anna nor Mack had ever said anything to Rocky about Anna's preferences, Mack always suspected that she knew what they were and took them personally. Mack's own appearances at the bar, sporadic at the best of times—mostly between trials—had steeply dropped off since she and Anna had gotten back together.

"She had plans with friends. It's not a big deal. I've certainly slept in worse places." That was mostly true. She knew that Anna would have detached herself from her group of psychologist friends and picked her up if she'd asked, but Mack hadn't wanted to disturb her. She was tired of feeling so dependent on her girlfriend, especially as Anna seemed to be growing increasingly annoyed at her.

Rocky watched her intently.

"How are things going with her? You guys have been back together, what, like four months now?"

Mack again considered the question before answering. She was surprised Rocky knew how long she and Anna had been back together, and tried to remember if she'd actually told her, or if Rocky had learned about the resumption of their relationship some other way. "Things are good. Well, you know, as good as they can be considering…" She trailed off, gesturing vaguely around the room.

"Considering what?"

"Considering I still can't bring myself to have sex, I hate my new job, and I'm about to start a month-long trial, I guess." Mack flopped back, frustrated, and ran her hands through her hair. Rocky could always be counted on to push her past the point of casual small talk.

"Ah," Rocky said. "What's up with the new job?"

"It sucks."

"I get that. I didn't even realize you wanted to leave the DA's office. Where are you now?"

Mack slumped back against the couch and wondered if she had gum in her purse. Her mouth tasted like she'd been chewing on shoe leather. Old shoe leather.

"Oh, I'm still at the DA. I'm in this new position where I don't do trials. I'm just a performing seal, promoting the DA's pet criminal-justice initiatives. But now I've got the chance to do a trial, with Jess, and that's a whole other set of problems." Mack gestured vaguely. "Don't worry about it. It's not important. It's just one more thing that isn't going the way I want it to. If there was just *one* thing going well, maybe I'd feel better about the state of everything else."

Rocky scooted her desk chair closer and put her hand on Mack's knee. Mack resisted the urge to back away.

"I only ask because I worry about you, you know."

Mack shrugged, uncomfortable. "Thanks, Rocks. You've always been a pal. But I'm fine. Things with Anna are fine, and this work stuff will pass. I can survive anything for a year, right?"

Rocky took a long drink of her water, finishing the bottle, and tossed it into the recycling bin. "Mack knows best," she said finally.

They sat in tense silence as Mack plotted the quickest way out of the conversation. She was about to make an excuse and get up when her phone rang. She looked at the screen, surprised to see Sergeant Dave Barton's name.

"Dave," she said. "Long time no talk."

"Hey, Mackenzie," the gruff officer said. "I need you to come downtown."

"Downtown?" Mack got up, gathering her fleece and purse from the floor and glancing apologetically at Rocky. What perfect timing.

"Yeah," Dave said. "I need to talk to you. At the station."

"Is this on the—what was his name—the Valenzuela case?" Mack asked, wracking her brain to think of other cases they'd had in common before she went on leave.

"No, it's"—Dave hesitated—"it's something else. Just get down here, and I'll explain."

Mack heard Dave hang up and looked at her phone, confused.

Rocky waved her off. "It's fine. We can catch up another time. You go solve crimes."

Mack smiled, grateful for the escape route Dave had provided, and made her exit.

CHAPTER NINE

Mack swung her old blue Saab into the visitor lot and walked slowly into Tucson Police headquarters, mindful of her still-aching head and upset stomach. She couldn't count the number of times she'd taken this exact route, but the familiarity of it was not comforting. She puzzled over why Dave wanted her to come in on a Saturday morning. She was sure they had no cases together—Steve Andersen had long since been sentenced and shuffled off to the Department of Corrections, and all of her other cases had been reassigned when she'd gone on leave.

She approached the receptionist. "Mack Wilson, ADA. I'm here for—"

"She's here for me, Liz." Dave Barton came through the security door. He must have been waiting for her. The short, muscular police officer looked tense, despite being dressed casually in jeans and a black polo. His head looked freshly shaved, and he was surprisingly tan for midwinter. Mack wondered if he and his wife had gone to their timeshare in Belize for New Year's Eve.

"You'll need to sign in," the receptionist told Mack, gesturing toward a law-enforcement visitor log.

"Not that one, actually," Dave said. "She'll use the civilian one."

Mack cocked her head and looked at him, taking the proffered notebook and entering her name, address, and phone number, along with the date and time. "Is this not an official visit, Dave?"

Dave was silent. Once she finished writing, he handed her a blue-and-white sticker with VISITOR printed in large block letters and gestured her through the door.

"Really?" she asked. "A visitor badge? What are you afraid I'm going to do?"

Dave didn't respond.

They walked quietly through the twisting halls toward the depths of the building. As they passed a holding cell, a sudden pounding made Mack jump.

"It's okay," Dave said. "Just someone coming down from PCP. He's been doing that all morning."

Mack's heart thudded wildly. She was not reassured.

Dave guided her into an interview room. He paused in the doorway, and Mack almost bumped into him. Annoyed, she glanced around the room. There was a flashing red light on the video camera in the corner of the ceiling. They were being recorded. Dave hadn't warned her about that. Whatever was about to happen, it would be preserved for whoever wanted to watch it. Mack would have to be careful what she said.

It was not, she noticed, a so-called "soft" room, where police interviewed children, victims, and other civilians. It was a hard room, a suspect interview room. Mack wondered if they were meeting someone there, possibly a suspect who wanted to talk to a prosecutor, seeking a better deal in exchange for information, but the room was empty.

Dave gestured to a chair, and Mack sat. She tilted back, noticing that the chair's legs were uneven—a tactic, designed to make the person sitting there uncomfortable. It worked. So did the flickering fluorescent light overhead. Mack felt a trickle of sweat run down her back.

"You going to tell me what this is about?" she asked. "The theatrics are impressive, but I'm starting to lose my patience, Dave. You called me on my personal cell phone on a Saturday morning, and I happily came down here to meet you, because we've worked together for a long time and I know you wouldn't drag me in for no reason. I think we know each other well enough for you to do me the courtesy of—"

"Do you know this girl?" Dave interrupted. He sat in the chair across from Mack and opened a manila file, sliding a photograph across the table.

Mack studied it. She recognized the setting—had seen enough other pictures just like it. The girl on the medical examiner's cold steel table was young, a teenager. She had probably been pretty, in a bland kind of way. Straight red hair, shoulder length, that clashed with the green sheet tucked around her just below her shoulders. She wouldn't have driven high-school boys wild but would likely have grown into a lovely woman. No visible injuries.

"She looks familiar, but I can't place her. Doesn't help that she's…you know. If I did know her, it wouldn't have been like this." She looked up and met Dave's eyes. He was watching her intently. "Dave, what is going on? Why am I being recorded? Why aren't you telling me what's up?"

"We found this girl stuffed inside a Rubbermaid tub in the desert this morning."

"Okay," Mack said. She felt like there was some fact just out of reach, something that would make this whole situation make sense. "That's terrible. I'm so sorry. But *I'm* here because?"

"She didn't have any ID, any credit cards with her name on them, anything like that. The only thing she had was your business card." Dave tossed a plastic evidence bag onto the table. Mack recognized her own handwriting. "With your cell number written on it."

CHAPTER TEN

Dave's words hit Mack like a physical blow. She leaned back, focusing very hard on resisting the need to vomit.

"Are you telling me that I'm a suspect, Dave? Do I need a lawyer here?"

Dave studied her across the table, and she studied him right back. He looked exhausted, with pronounced circles under his eyes and five o'clock shadow across his jaw. The slightest hint of something like regret flashed in his eyes.

"I can't tell you if you need a lawyer, Mackenzie. You know that. But I do need to advise you of your rights." He fished a laminated card out of his pocket, even though he and Mack both knew the words by heart. "You have the right to an attorney—"

Mack shoved her chair back and puked into the room's trash can.

Dave's chair scraped against the floor, and soon enough he was rubbing her back, whispering into her ear.

"It's gonna be okay, Mack. Trust the process. Give me a minute, huh?"

Dave stood and left the room, and Mack closed her eyes. A dead girl with her business card in her pocket. Her mind raced. The girl must have been murdered, even though the picture didn't show it. They wouldn't have brought Mack in like this for a natural death, or even an overdose. Plus, if it wasn't murder, what was the girl doing in a plastic bin?

Mack gave out cards all the time. It was one of the main things she did in her new executive position. She'd even had new cards printed, because her old ones still said she was in Sex Crimes.

She flipped the evidence bag over. A Sex Crimes card. That didn't narrow the timeline much; she could have given it to anyone any time during the last six years. The card had her cell number on it, but she did that all the time, too—kept a bundle of cards with her number on the back in her purse, so they'd be handy.

A vague memory of a crowded bar pushed into Mack's consciousness. She leaned against the cinderblock wall. She suspected she knew who the girl was, or at least how she'd gotten that card. The list of questions in need of answers was much longer than the list of answers she could provide. Who was she? How had she died? Who had killed her? Why was Mack being considered as a suspect?

The door opened. Her face betrayed nothing as Dave came back into the room, carrying two bottles of water. He set one on the table.

"Have a drink," he said.

"No, thanks," Mack said, stubbornly.

"Mack," Dave insisted. "Mack—*have—a—drink*." He flicked his gaze up toward the video camera. Its red light was no longer blinking. Whatever happened next would not be recorded, which could help Mack get the information she needed. It could also allow the police to claim that she'd confessed. She needed to tread carefully, especially since there could still be someone watching them from the monitoring room on the other side of the two-way mirror.

Slowly, Mack uncapped her bottle of water and took a long drink. The water washed away much of the foul taste in her mouth.

"I'll waive my rights," she said. "You don't need to read me the card. I'll talk to you. But you have to give *me* a little information, Dave. You have to tell me what's going on."

"If anyone asks," Dave said, "the camera cut out after you threw up. Just a glitch. These things happen all the time." He noticed Mack looking at the mirror. "No one's back there. Anyone associated with the case is still on scene. As far as they'll know, you invoked and no more interview. I got the footage I needed, and no one needs to know what we discuss from here. I don't really think you killed anyone, but some of my colleagues aren't as willing as I am to give you the benefit of the doubt."

"Why?" Mack asked, honestly stymied. She thought she had a good relationship with Tucson Police. She'd certainly worked hard for them over the years and had generally gotten them the results they wanted.

Dave grimaced. "Honestly, Mack, I don't understand it myself. Homophobia? Sexism? Some 'us-versus-them' mentality because you guys in the DA's office have cracked down on charging aggravated assaults against cops? Some of the guys are LDS, and they don't like how you handled the Andersen case. They don't love your new approach to training, either. They think you're too focused on policy. There's a whole lot swirling around you right now. It's been building in the last few months, but I haven't paid much attention until this. I think you—and this dead girl—are at the unfortunate confluence of a whole lot of factors."

Mack thought about that. "Well," she said. "Shit, then."

Dave smiled, but it didn't reach his eyes.

"And you swear there's no one in the monitoring room?"

"If there was someone, you think I would've aired TPD's dirty laundry? In front of a murder suspect? I mean, you can look if you want, but I promise you no one is there."

Mack believed that Dave had always been straightforward with her. Even during the Andersen case, he'd told her when he disagreed with her. He'd never pulled any punches, and she had no reason to doubt him now. "Why are *you* interviewing me? Why not one of them?"

"I volunteered, Mack." Dave leaned against the wall, his arms folded across his chest. "I probably shouldn't've, but I said I could get you to talk, and no one argued. I don't think anyone else really wanted to do it. They'd rather sling mud behind your back than confront you to your face, and I didn't want one of those bozos to strongarm you into saying something you couldn't deny."

"Dave, I swear to you, I had nothing to do with this girl's death, and I will do whatever I can to help you figure out what happened to her. But you have to help me, too. You have to tell me what you know."

"I believe you, and I'd appreciate your help. Lord knows we're gonna need to catch a break on this. It's the kind of case that's destined to go cold, you know?"

Mack nodded. Bodies that had been dumped almost always resulted in cold cases, because it was rarely possible to prove who had dumped them. Even if the suspect had the best motive in the world, police officers couldn't rebut the age-old story: "Sure, Detective, I fought with my wife/father/neighbor, but then I just walked away. Whatever happened next wasn't me!" Despite the popular perception that there were cameras everywhere and Big Brother was always watching, the reality of homicide cases, in Mack's experience, was that proximity was half the battle. She had never heard of a case that was cracked through surveillance footage. Once criminals caught on that their cell phones included GPS trackers, they started leaving them at home or turning them off when they crimed around town.

"I'll give you what we have," Dave said. "It's not much. This seems like a crazy thing to say, but—"

"It can't be crazier than literally everything else you've said since I got here."

"Just wait. Right now, you are officially a person of interest in a homicide case. You are sitting in an interview room where the video camera cut out shortly after you started puking. Your office will know about this by this afternoon, if they don't already. We need to get you out of here. The easiest way to do that is to clear you. The easiest way to do *that* is for you to have a good and verifiable reason for your cell number to have been found in a murder victim's possession. Who is she, Mack?"

Mack studied the photograph. "You don't have any ID? No clues?"

"So far, nothing."

"She looks familiar, I just can't place her for sure. What *do* you have? Can I at least see more pictures?"

Dave took a slim stack of photos out of his file and placed them on the table. Mack recoiled. The first one showed a large plastic bin—the kind Mack's mom used to store winter clothes in the attic. The lid was off, and the girl was folded inside it. Mack used to fold herself into her mom's bins the same way. She'd pull the lid over herself and pop out, shouting "Boo!" This girl couldn't do the same.

The second photo showed the girl stretched out on the desert floor beside the bin. She wore a black leather jacket over a black spaghetti-strap tank top. Her jeans were unbuttoned and unzipped and pushed down to her thighs. No underwear, no shoes. Again, Mack got the strong sense that she'd seen this girl before. The context danced just on the edge of her memory.

"Cause of death?"

"Autopsy isn't scheduled until Monday. No visible injuries, nothing that leaps out. Some weird things about the body, though."

"Like what?"

"Well—and remember, I'm just a cop, so what do I know—but she wasn't stiff. She flopped right out when we dumped the tub."

"So either she got found too quick to be in rigor…"

"…or she was out of it already. And we know the tub wasn't there Thursday."

"How do we know that?"

"It was found by a young woman. Beth Shankar. She was over at Tanque Verde this morning early, going hiking."

Mack knew that area, had hiked there herself on a number of occasions. If she hadn't had so much to drink at Paradise last night, she might have wound up there this morning with Anna, who liked the convenient parking.

"She goes a couple times a week, and when she went Thursday morning, the tub wasn't there, so it got her attention today. It looked like it was in good condition and had just been dumped, so she thought she'd check it out. I guess she thought maybe it fell off a truck or something. I don't know, I can't imagine opening a random bin I found in public, but that's her story. Looked inside and got more than she bargained for."

Mack's eyes widened involuntarily. "That's horrific."

Dave didn't respond.

"What else?"

Dave motioned to the first photo, which showed the girl's hands on the floor of the tub, next to her feet. "See how her palms are on the bottom of the bin? She's kind of leaning forward on them?"

Mack nodded.

"We'd expect there to be blood pooling, right? From the pressure? The big purple bruises?"

This was Homicide 101. Gravity caused blood to pool at the lowest point of a dead body, because the heart was no longer beating, in the two to four hours following death. There'd be matching bruises on the soles of her feet and her buttocks—any place her body weight had rested.

Dave pulled out a photo showing her hands. They were unblemished.

"It can take a while for that to develop, right? Maybe she was found before it started?"

"Maybe," Dave said. "But how quickly could a body be found under these circumstances and have it still be coincidental, right? I mean, surely she wasn't found immediately after she was dumped."

"Where was the business card?"

Dave pulled out another photo, this one showing a small pouch with Rosie the Riveter's image on it.

"This was in the back pocket of her jeans. She was using it as a wallet. It's weird, though. She didn't have any credit cards, any ID, anything that could be used to identify her. She had some cash, your business card, and a bunch of prepaid Visa cards."

Mack considered that. It was possible that this girl didn't carry anything that showed her name or address. Mack's own wallet was overflowing with identification, but she wasn't a dead teenager. It was also possible that someone could have gone through the pouch and removed anything that could have identified the victim. For that matter, someone could have planted the business card.

"Okay," she said. "But if the killer took her ID, why not take the cash and the Visas? If they were trying to incriminate me, why not plant something more incriminating than my business card? Has anyone looked up the prepaid cards? Sometimes they're registered."

"Already thought of that. None of these are registered. None of them have much money on them—they were all originally in the hundred-and-fifty-dollar range, and now they're either empty or almost so."

"Any records of the transactions?"

"Nope. When you use them without registering them, they're untraceable."

Mack's mind raced with possibilities, and she forced herself to slow down and take a deep breath. "Okay, what about this? She looks really young, right?"

"Very."

"What kind of young girls often have prepaid debit cards? Usually a lot of them."

"Sex trafficking victims."

"Exactly," Mack said. "What if we assume that johns were paying her with gift cards? But she wasn't handing them over, right? She still had them in her pouch. So either she didn't have a pimp, or she was holding out on him."

"A great motive to get rid of her," Dave said. "Girls this young, they're not working on their own. She must have had someone behind the scenes."

"We've seen it before," Mack said. "Girl stops earning, she gets taken out. We've never seen anything quite so…calculated…as this, but we've certainly seen girls beaten out of the game, even killed."

Mack pulled the photo of the girl's face closer. She had seen this girl before. It was dark. And loud. She was sweating and her heart was pounding. They had spoken. They had spoken about—

"I think I know who this is," Mack said.

This time, she didn't make it to the trash can. She vomited all over Dave's jeans.

CHAPTER ELEVEN

It came back to her in a rush. That night at Paradise, back in September. Her first time in a bar in months, and she was immediately overwhelmed by the smell of old beer and the twinkling lights. She'd gone to meet Anna to celebrate their decision to officially get back together at the bar where they'd had their first date, but Anna was running late. She had a patient who showed up late, and she'd stayed to do the session. Mack got a cider and was standing at the bar when she felt a hand on her elbow. Her heart raced at the unexpected touch, and she jumped. Turning, she saw a girl—the dead girl—who was clearly underage. Mack looked around, wondering if Rocky was pranking her. Why was there a child in the bar?

But then the girl leaned close to her, and Mack had to focus on what she was saying to avoid looking down her shirt. She knew better than to stare, but she was one drink in after two dry weeks and her head buzzed. The girl said she'd buy Mack a drink—she'd recognized Mack from the television coverage of the Andersen trial and needed someone to talk to. She was having a "situation" with a coach and didn't know what to do. She was jumpy, anxious, and

Mack heard something in her voice that made her think the girl was on some sort of uppers. "Pressure of speech," Anna would call it. The mention of the Andersen trial didn't set Mack at ease. Just the opposite. She didn't have the mental energy to hear another disclosure from another victim, especially one who would accost her at the bar while possibly on drugs. She'd gotten disclosures while out in public before—most of her colleagues had—but she couldn't face it that night.

She grabbed a card out of her wallet and pressed it into the girl's hand, urging her to call during business hours. She steeled herself to offer some vague words of support and encouragement, but the girl disappeared into the crowd without another word. Then Anna arrived and Mack promptly forgot the strange encounter.

Dave went to change his pants, and when he got back to the interview room Mack told him about that night, aware that her explanation didn't make her look like the compassionate, victim-oriented prosecutor she tried to be.

"Paradise has security cameras," she said. "We should be able to get the footage from the owner. She's a friend of mine."

"Do you remember when this was?" Dave asked. "Best-case scenario, it's been almost three months. Most places don't save their footage that long, if they save it at all."

"I should know," Mack admitted, "but I don't. Anna would. Dr. Lapin. You know her. She and I are…well, she's my girlfriend. She paid the tab that night. It'll be on her credit card bill."

"Okay," Dave said. "Let's call her, and your friend who owns the bar, too. I've worked with Dr. Lapin. But Mack, I'm not sure this actually absolves you. I mean, what is that footage going to show?"

Mack stood and paced the small room. She finished the bottle of water Dave had given her and concentrated on the disconnected memories she was starting to piece together.

"Best case, the footage shows me walking in. It shows the girl approaching me, and me brushing her off."

"Are you sure? You sure it won't show *anything* suggesting any kind of preexisting relationship? Or interest on your part?"

Mack blanched. "It might…it might show me walking after her into the restroom. Depending on where the camera is. But Dave, there's a perfectly reasonable—"

Dave cut her off with a raised hand. "I can't help you if you're not honest with me, Mack."

Mack's mouth was very dry. "I'm giving you everything I know. I went into the bathroom to splash some water on my face. She scared me when she talked to me, and I needed to collect myself. You know how much of a toll the Andersen trial took on me—on all of us. You can't tell me that, if someone came up to you when you weren't expecting it and brought it up, you wouldn't have a reaction."

"That may be true," Dave said. "But if I got spooked and someone wound up dead, I'd have to face the consequences. So do you."

Mack ran her fingers through her hair. She was frustrated. Did Dave believe her or not? The recorder wasn't running, but if she said something that wound up being used against her, it would be her own damn fault. If anyone knew better than to talk to the cops, it was Mack. "It's not like that, Dave. I wasn't following her, really, but I think she was right in front of me. We didn't talk in the bathroom, and then she left. She didn't say anything else to me."

They stared at each other. The silence between them was overwhelming, and Mack fought the urge to fill it with excuses.

"You gave her your cell number. Did she ever use it?"

"I'm sure she didn't. You can subpoena my phone records. I never heard from her after that night."

"Subpoenaing *your* phone records doesn't give me anything unless we figure out *her* phone number."

Mack knew he was right. Without a number to cross-reference, Mack could claim any number of things. How many defendants had she heard suggest looking at their own phone records? It was an easy offer to make, because the police could never really follow up.

Mack was getting tired and was starting to confuse herself. Her hangover was back in full force. She yawned and blinked, fighting to push through and find a path to exoneration.

"Have you checked missing person reports yet? She's young. Maybe someone filed on her. That might help us get a better sense of when she died."

"Not yet," Dave said. "But it's on the list. Figuring out who she is, and letting her family know, are my first priorities."

Mack and Dave were usually on the same team, but this was far from an average case. Dave's first priorities might include letting this girl's family know what happened, but Mack's was saving her own skin.

"What happens now?" she asked.

Dave just looked at her. "What do you mean?"

Mack slumped into the seat, losing the battle against the weariness that was settling over her. "Am I under arrest, Dave? Do I get a phone call? Can I at least have some clean clothes?"

He stood. "Go home," he said. "Get some sleep. You're going to need it. You have an uphill fight ahead of you, I think. You're going to need some resources on your side, because you've got some powerful adversaries. These guys...well, like I said, I don't really understand it, but it seems clear they're gonna work pretty hard to pin this on you. You'll have to work even harder. I'll help as much as I can, but you're going to need a team."

He walked her out, taking back her visitor pass as he held open the security door for her. "You okay to drive?"

She smiled but didn't answer. She might rest a minute in the parking lot, just to give her nerves a chance to settle, but she was okay. She was always okay. She was ready for battle.

CHAPTER TWELVE

Mack sat in her car, reeling from the turn her day had taken. She had to snap out of it. Get organized. Get moving. Dave was right: she needed a team. She was reluctant to disturb Anna, who might be at work, but Jess never minded a call—regardless of the time of day.

Mack couldn't identify the music in the background when Jess picked up, but Jess explained that she and Adam were having a late lunch at her favorite Ethiopian restaurant. Mack was happy for her friend—really, she was—but she had a favorite Ethiopian restaurant? Jess barely tolerated Mexican food until she started dating. They agreed that Jess would call back later, when she had time to chat, and Mack let the happy couple return to their injera love fest.

Anna picked up on the third ring, and Mack could picture her in the small office where she worked between sessions with patients and on Saturday afternoons. her work wardrobe, and winter meant wool, often in rich jewel tones. Her built-in bookshelves overflowed with everything from textbooks and binders full of research to literary fiction and romance novels. Anna would be at her desk, sleek black wood and metal, meticulously clean. A green-shaded library lamp would be on in lieu of the fluorescent overheads, which gave her headaches, and her hair would be glinting in the soft light.

"What's up, Doc?" Mack asked, hopeful that Anna wouldn't hear the strain in her voice.

Silence. Mack could imagine the pursed lips that accompanied Anna's "I smell bullshit" face. Since they'd resumed dating, Mack had mostly resisted the urge to call Anna "Doc," and it had been a mistake to use the word now. She explained the situation as succinctly as she could, starting with that night at Paradise. She hadn't mentioned the girl that night—had forgotten about her as soon as she'd seen Anna walk in. She'd been on the verge of a panic attack, but Anna's soothing presence had been enough to set her at ease.

"…so now I'm calling you," Mack finished.

She was met with silence. Anna had asked only a few clarifying questions, largely leaving Mack to ramble through the convoluted story. Now that she was done, though, there ought to have been some kind of reaction.

"Are you still there?" Mack asked.

Anna cleared her throat. "Yes."

"Well, what do you think?"

Anna hesitated, and her silence turned suddenly oppressive.

"I think—Mack, I think approximately sixty percent of my income comes from the Tucson District Attorney's Office, largely as a result of the work done by TPD. And another thirty percent comes from the Pima County Adult Probation Office. That adds up to about ninety percent of my livelihood, and it sounds like that livelihood is now at risk, since the police are apparently investigating my girlfriend for murder."

"What does that have to do with anything?"

"Mack, I—I'm sorry. Listen, you will get through this, and everything will be fine. I have full confidence in your ability to rise above any challenges unscathed. I know this must be terrible for you, but I—I can't be involved."

"Anna, you can't possibly think that I—" Mack stopped when she realized the call had ended. She slumped back against her car seat, shocked. Had she just been dumped? She replayed the brief conversation in her mind. It certainly sounded like a breakup.

Mack tried to decide who else she could call, and realized there wasn't anyone she could really trust. She scrolled through her contacts. Peter Campbell would probably know about the investigation soon, if he didn't already. If what Dave had told her was true, one of Campbell's church buddies—someone high-ranking in the department—would surely notify him. She considered drawing the sting—calling him herself before he heard the news from someone else.

She remembered an ADA who had been fired for having been solicited by a prostitute. He hadn't taken her up on her offer, had told his boss as soon as he got to work the next day, but even the suggestion of sordid behavior had been enough to end his twenty-year career. No, drawing the sting was out. It was just possible the story wouldn't get out, and she might be able to skate through all this without the office ever knowing.

Maybe she needed to hire counsel. She definitely needed a drink. And some Advil. Of the fifty or so defense attorneys in her phone, minus the public defenders, she wasn't sure there were any she could really open up to. The Tucson legal community was minuscule, and the gossip was fierce. She remembered how quickly everyone had found out about Benjamin Allen, and then her identity was being protected as the victim of a crime. Suspects had no such protections. Even attorney-client privilege wouldn't keep her safe from the rumor mill.

She paused over Linda Andrews. Linda had represented Allen, had known about his obsession with Mack and hadn't told her, claiming privileged communication. If Linda felt like she owed Mack a favor, maybe she could be trusted.

Mack kept scrolling. Linda was a terrible defense attorney. Mack would rather have no one on her side than someone that useless.

The Saab had become uncomfortably warm in the midday sun, so Mack started the engine and shifted into gear. Her phone buzzed. A notification from her work email. Michael Brown, accelerating their monthly status meeting two weeks to Monday at lunch. No mention of the reason, but the timing was too perfect to be coincidental.

This is all just great, Mack thought as she pulled out of the visitor lot and headed home to wait for Jess' call. *Here I was, looking for something to fill my time. Ask, and I have received.*

CHAPTER THIRTEEN

Jess finally called Sunday night, sounding breezy and chatting easily about her weekend until Mack interrupted to explain why she'd called the day before. Jess immediately sobered.

"Of course you didn't kill anyone," she said. "This is some homophobic bullshit, and we're going to take care of it. We need to get you an attorney and hire an investigator. I don't have a ton of money right now, but I'm sure between the three of us we can put together a retainer."

Mack was grateful for the support but hesitated to mention that Anna wouldn't be contributing. Eventually, though, Jess asked what Anna thought about the situation, and Mack didn't see a graceful way to lie.

"She, um, well, I think we're not seeing each other for a while." Mack chewed on her thumbnail. She had the sudden urge to get up and leave the room but fought against it. She couldn't outrun this.

Mack heard Jess' sharp intake of breath.

"It's okay," she said. "I mean, I know I've been a lot, with the Allen stuff and all. She just didn't have room to take this on, too. It doesn't mean she's not a good person."

"Respectfully," Jess said, "that's *precisely* what it means. This has nothing to do with her, and if she can't support you through it... well, frankly, you're better off without her. I hope she chokes on a chia seed."

Mack didn't laugh. She reached out a hand for the beer she'd opened and set down, untasted, on her coffee table, but changed her mind. Anna had picked out the table. It was fine, but its open, boxy design was more rustic than the one Mack had really wanted. That one had a glass top and Anna had emphasized how much of a pain it would be to keep it clean. Mack hadn't cared enough to make an issue of it. She'd assumed that Anna would be spending as much time using it as she would and was happy to let the other woman make the choice.

"You don't think, I mean, I need you to know that I—"

"Again, of *course* you didn't kill anyone, Mack. You don't like to kill cockroaches. You don't like to eat meat because it comes from dead animals. And, hey, even if you *had* killed this girl, I would stick by you, because I'm sure you would have had a good reason. But you obviously didn't, and anyone who knows your heart knows that."

Mack sniffed. She hadn't even noticed she was crying, so great was her relief at receiving the unqualified support she'd been looking for since Dave had upended her world the day before. This time, she did pick up the beer and drained it in one long swallow.

Monday morning, Mack was uneasy, and her unease warred with her hangover over which negative feeling would carry the day. She woke up to find a text from Rocky asking how the rest of her weekend had gone. That was casual enough—nothing to raise alarm bells—but it still set Mack on edge. She liked Rocky, but she wasn't sure she trusted her ability to be discreet. She didn't need anyone finding out from her friendly local lesbian bar owner that she was a murder suspect. Her thumb hovered over the screen. What she wanted was to delete the message without responding. If she started a new life, somewhere far away, she'd never need to talk to Rocky again.

Instead, she sent a brief response. She typed and deleted four different versions, trying to adopt an authentically breezy tone. She finally settled on *Just work stuff piling up. Thanks for checking in though!* She pressed send and locked her phone, not waiting to see if Rocky would respond.

Mack hated lunch meetings under the best of circumstances. She didn't like smelling other people's food. She didn't like hearing them chew. The idea of eating a salad while casually talking about rape and murder repulsed her.

One of her mentors had told her about the time she was called out to a murder scene from a fancy Italian dinner. The victim had died from a shotgun blast to the head, and his brain matter on the ground resembled her meal. The story was presented as an amusing anecdote of life in the trenches, but Mack had never looked at spaghetti the same way again.

Today, given the high stakes and her nerves, the best Mack could manage was a granola bar and an unsweetened iced tea. She hoped the caffeine would cut through the headache gathered just behind her eyes.

Charlie Waters was at one corner of the conference table, talking quietly with two women associated with Campbell's re-election campaign. All three were drinking coffee, no food in front of them.

Michael Brown, looking polished and smug with his slicked-back hair and suspenders over a French-cuffed white shirt, had opted for takeout from the deli down the street. A turkey sandwich, it looked like, and Mack's stomach rumbled at the sight of it.

Campbell had brought his lunch from home—a family-sized can of chicken, a can opener, and a fork. Mack assumed he'd just forgotten crackers or vegetables, *something* to pair with the chicken, but realized—based on the lack of reaction from anyone else in the room, all of whom were probably used to eating with Campbell—that this was his whole meal. She shuddered, wondering how she could keep her stomach calm as she watched a man eat four servings of canned chicken. Then the smell hit her, and the question became even more pressing.

"Before we get to our first agenda item," Campbell said between bites, "we have something to resolve." He had tossed his tie over his shoulder to keep it from getting chicken juice on it. His precise haircut and expensive navy suit looked out of place in the drab government conference room.

Everyone nodded. Mack wondered what exactly they'd heard, and how they'd heard it. Michael had a brother who was a cop, she knew, and she wondered if they were close enough for him to have been the source.

"Mackenzie," Michael said. "You are currently considered a person of interest in a homicide case being investigated by Tucson PD. Assuming that crime is eventually solved, it will be prosecuted by this office. Given the inherent appearance of impropriety, aside from any actual conflict, why do you think you shouldn't be placed on administrative leave pending the outcome of the investigation?"

Mack hadn't expected him to be so blunt. Admin leave—a fate worse than termination, in some ways, since she could be kept hanging, unpaid, for months. Still, they seemed to be giving her a chance to talk them out of it. Maybe cooler heads would prevail. She opened her mouth to respond, but Campbell raised a hand to stop her.

"I am deeply concerned about these allegations," he said. "Especially since they concern the Community Liaison I personally selected. At best, Ms. Wilson, you are alleged to have engaged in some highly inappropriate contact with a murder victim. At worst, well…" Campbell trailed off, finally looking at her for a response. Mack took a deep breath and dove in.

"Although I believe it goes without saying, Michael, Mr. Campbell, let me start by saying unequivocally that I did not commit any crimes related to that girl's murder—or any crimes at all, actually. In fact, it's not just that I didn't commit any crimes. I was approached by a member of the community, responded appropriately, and cannot be held responsible for what happened to her after our interaction ended."

Mack explained, once again, the night at Paradise when she and Jane Doe had met. She explained the trauma she was dealing with at the time. Trauma caused, as they all knew, by her position as a prosecutor. They faced her, remaining carefully neutral, and the room was silent except for her voice and the sounds of eating.

"This is no different than the type of situation our patrol-officer partners run into all the time," she said. "A 911 call goes out and officers arrive at the scene of a domestic dispute. By the time they get there, the couple has patched things up, or one of them has left the area. The officers pass over their business cards, ask the victim to call if anything else happens, and go on to their next call. Then, after they leave, the fight reignites and someone winds up dead."

"It's not exactly the same, though," Michael said, "since in your analogy we know who killed the victim. In this situation, we still have no evidence to suggest the killer's identity."

"Respectfully, Michael, that's bullshit and you know it." Mack immediately regretted swearing in front of the district attorney, who looked horrified at what he was watching unfold, but she was in too deep to pull back now. "There is no evidence—less than no evidence—to suggest that I killed that girl. If there was any credible evidence, even if it wasn't enough to land me in jail, I would have found that my security badge mysteriously didn't work this morning when I tried to get into my office. I wouldn't have even gotten to my office. I would have been met at the front door by an investigator with a box of my stuff—which would include, of course, the *numerous* awards I've been given for my service to this office and this city. The idea that I, with no criminal history—not even a minor in possession charge as an undergrad—would suddenly graduate to *murdering* a victim disclosing abuse is ludicrous."

"I think what we need to consider," Campbell interjected, "is the appearance of impropriety."

"The only people who see that appearance are in this room," Mack retorted. "No one out there in the world believes I killed this girl."

Michael cleared his throat. "Actually, sir, I have information from the department that a number of police officers believe that Ms. Wilson is the likely offender in this case, and further investigation will result in charges against her."

Mack rolled her eyes. "I'd love to have the names of those officers, Mike. And I'll bet you the detective actually investigating the case won't be on the list. We have credible evidence to suggest that our Jane Doe was a sex-trafficking victim." That might be stretching things a bit, since all they had was a hunch based on the prepaid debit cards in her purse. "I'll do whatever you want. A polygraph—"

"I hardly have to tell you, Ms. Wilson," Campbell said, "that polygraphs are not admissible evidence."

Mack gripped the arms of her chair more tightly. "I'm not going to be tried for this murder, sir, so the admissibility of a polygraph doesn't concern me. My point is: I will do anything it takes to convince you and TPD that I had nothing to do with this case."

The room fell silent. Michael picked up his phone, but Mack kept her focus on Campbell. She knew that, whatever decision got made, he would be the one to make it.

Campbell took one final bite of canned chicken, and Mack felt something within her release. Then he raised the can to his lips and drank the juice. Horrified, Mack gagged, trying to keep her face neutral.

"I think," Campbell said, lowering the empty can to the table, "that it's too soon for absolution. For now, Ms. Wilson, you are officially placed on administrative leave. When and if there comes a time when you can demonstrate your innocence in this matter with evidence, rather than mere assertions, we can revisit your role in this organization."

Mack's stomach dropped. She felt the warm sting of tears gathering and a lump in her throat that foreshadowed a panic attack.

Campbell looked at her, his blandly handsome face impassive. He looked no more invested in her fate than he would be if they were talking about the weather. Mack realized that he'd come into the meeting already knowing the outcome. This was a convenient time and place to eat his chicken.

Mack didn't argue as a security guard helped her to her feet. He held a box with her purse and a few other odds and ends from her office. Not, she noticed, her laptop or work phone. Numbly, she followed him to the door.

CHAPTER FOURTEEN

Mack spent the next two weeks mostly on her couch, moving blearily between sleep and old seasons of reality television. The rules were well-known around the office: an employee on administrative leave was required to remain at home during normal working hours, absent specific permission to leave the house. The employee was prohibited from speaking to anyone else who worked for the District Attorney's Office, which meant that Jess was taking a big risk the few times she called Mack to check in. Their conversations were brief. There wasn't much to say.

She hadn't told her mom. She'd practiced telling her in the mirror, had drafted emails only to delete them unsent. Her mom would be supportive—that wasn't the issue. Mack just didn't want to admit what was happening. The only people who knew were part of her day-to-day world. Admitting to her mom, who hated talking about her work before the Allen assault and *really* hated it after, that she was a suspect in a homicide would make the whole thing real in a way Mack wasn't prepared to face.

She could have gone hiking or running either before or after work hours, but neither activity held any appeal. She knew she'd feel better with a regular sleep schedule, three healthy meals a day, and some exercise, but she couldn't bring herself to make any of that happen. She could have watched movies, read, or taken up a new hobby. She *could* have told her mom, who would happily have come for an extended visit. Instead, she felt stuck in limbo, holding her breath and anxiously waiting for whatever would come next. She hadn't even gone grocery shopping. She was living off the meager contents of her pantry, whatever she could get delivered from the local Chinese restaurant, and her well-stocked liquor cabinet.

Every couple days, she would pick up the Sabrina Fisher file. Maybe this was an opportunity to get some work done after all. She flipped through the pages, searching for something no one had seen back then. Nothing. Frustrated, she tossed the file back onto her coffee table and went back to reality TV.

It was close to midnight, and Mack was deep into a bag of honey-mustard pretzels and an episode of *Survivor*, when her phone buzzed. An email alert, on her personal account, from an address she didn't recognize: *DBTPD2016@gmail.com*. She opened the message, but it was blank. There was an attachment, though, titled "autopsy." She opened that, hoping that Dave Barton was using an unconventional method to contact her and she wasn't inviting a virus onto her phone.

A quick glance at the attachment proved that Dave was indeed the sender, and Mack responded to the email with a quick "Received." She had reviewed autopsy results before, but never for a death that impacted her so personally. She started with the toxicology report. Jane Doe had tested positive for THC, the psychoactive metabolite of marijuana, as well as GHB—gamma hydroxybutyrate—a club drug that could be used recreationally but was also a popular choice as a date-rape drug. Mack had seen cases involving GHB-facilitated rapes before. It was a popular choice because it came in a clear liquid that could easily be slipped into someone's drink and was cheap and easy to obtain. GHB was known to be a disinhibitor that could cause relaxation and increased sex drive. Too much, though, could cause drowsiness, dizziness, and memory loss, and an overdose could result in blackouts and unconsciousness. Mack had even seen cases where girls had died, though their rapists hadn't meant to kill them.

Mack wondered if Jane Doe had taken the GHB for fun or if it had been administered by someone else. She paged through the report, looking for evidence of a rape kit.

Jackpot: scrapings from under her fingernails, swabs, and even a vaginal aspirate. This test involved flushing the vaginal canal with sterile water and collecting what came out, in hopes of finding foreign DNA. Preliminary results: sperm. It would take time to get a profile, of course. Mack wondered whether that would show one contributor or more than one. So far, nothing had disproved her theory that the girl was a sex-trafficking victim. Multiple DNA profiles could help confirm that. Even before the results came in, however, the sperm could help. Mack needed a fact to hang her innocence on, and maybe the sperm was it. Maybe she could spin it that the killer *had* to have been a man, which, therefore, would exclude her.

The most interesting thing about finding GHB in the tox results was that it only stayed in the body a few hours. This meant that Jane Doe had died relatively quickly after being drugged. She'd had cases where they only knew GHB was used because the rapist had eventually admitted to it. Even though the victim had been tested less than six hours after the rape, the drug had already been metabolized.

The GHB hadn't killed Jane Doe, though. Mack turned to the medical examiner's notes, looking for cause of death. The results were preliminary, and she flipped between the document and Google, trying to figure out what exactly the medical examiner's findings meant.

The girl had been stabbed once in the chest, but it looked like that wasn't the cause of death, either. She hadn't been hit in the heart or lungs, and no major arteries were severed. Blood had seeped into the surrounding tissue, and that took time. The medical examiner had prepared slides of the tissue and examined them under the microscope—and that's when things got *very* odd. Jane Doe's blood had apparently expanded, damaging the tissue. The ME speculated that she had been frozen for some time and then thawed. That was the only thing that could account for this specific type of tissue damage.

Mack started to see the light. She'd heard of killers storing bodies in freezers. She wasn't sure what the pathology was—and didn't feel like she could ask Anna, under the circumstances—but it didn't seem all that different than keeping any other souvenir. The possibility of freezing helped explain two things Mack had wondered about since she'd seen the pictures in the interview room: the size of the Rubbermaid tub and the negligible amount of decomposition suffered by the body.

She flipped to the vital-statistics section of the report. The girl was five foot even, and one hundred and two pounds. Age estimated at sixteen. Tiny. Yet the tub she was found in had plenty of room to spare. Why use something unnecessarily bulky? It would be harder to move and harder to hide. If he'd pulled her right out of the freezer, however, he would have had to put her in a container that would accommodate whatever shape she'd frozen into. As she thawed, sometime between the hiker's trips to the trailhead Thursday and Saturday, she came to rest in a more natural position.

Three days in the Arizona desert, even in January, would normally cause some pretty advanced decomp, especially in a closed plastic container. Mack had noticed how pristine the girl looked in those photos from the scene, though. Almost like she was sleeping. Decomposition was caused by bacteria breaking down the body's tissue, and heat accelerated that process. If she'd started from frozen, she wouldn't have decomposed at all in the freezer, and once she was out, decomp would be slowed way down. In fact, even the medical examiner sometimes stored bodies in cold conditions for weeks before conducting autopsies.

Finally, Mack looked at the photos attached to the report. There, at the base of the girl's neck, was a barcode tattoo. The barcode was fake; there was no way to read it with a scanner, just a series of random lines. Mack had seen these before, and they always meant that the bearer of the tattoo was being trafficked. They were a mark that traffickers put on their property. Jane Doe's killer was likely to be the man who was trafficking her, but Mack also knew that men using sex workers and sex-trafficking victims could often turn violent, so the girl's clients couldn't be ruled out.

She sat back in her desk chair, heart pounding. They had been assuming that months had passed between Mack's meeting Jane Doe and her death—and that she had been killed and promptly dumped in the desert. These results meant that those assumptions couldn't be counted on. It was very possible that Mack had been the last person to see Jane Doe alive.

Except, Mack realized, for her killer.

CHAPTER FIFTEEN

Mack pulled a pad across the desk and started a to-do list. The autopsy results didn't clear her, but they did give her some ideas for further action.

First, they needed to identify the girl. Missing person reports might help, but they weren't a guarantee. The sex-trafficking angle might provide a faster route to success. Somebody had to take her photos to the Track—the area of Tucson in which the most sex workers were on the streets. By showing her picture to other sex workers, it might be possible to get a line on who she was. Hopefully, they could even find out who was trafficking her. That would be a solid lead.

Even more crucial than identifying the girl was identifying her killer, but there was nothing Dave or Mack could do to speed up the DNA results. Those would take weeks if they were lucky, and months if they weren't. Mack doubted that anyone keeping a body in a freezer was a first-time killer. That might mean that his profile was already in CODIS, if he'd been sloppy before. If he was as neat as he appeared to be, though, he might not be in the system.

Mack considered her situation. To get herself off admin leave, she needed to demonstrate to the district attorney that she hadn't killed Jane Doe. If the police arrested someone else, that would prove her innocence. Maybe she didn't need to identify *the* killer, so long as she could identify *a* killer.

It was time for reinforcements. She created an anonymized and encrypted ProtonMail account and used it to email Dave and Jess, requesting a meeting that evening. They both quickly replied with thumbs-up.

By eight o'clock, Mack was restlessly wandering her living room, waiting for her team to arrive. She had debated serving snacks and drinks but decided against it. She had beers in the fridge if anyone wanted one.

Jess arrived first, wrapping Mack in a firm hug as soon as she came in the door. They hadn't seen each other in person since Mack's meeting with Campbell and subsequent removal from the office. Just by being there, Jess risked losing her own job. Mack was so grateful for her friend's willingness to help her, it almost hurt.

"Have you talked to Anna?" Jess asked, kicking off her Nikes and padding to Mack's couch. Her oversized sweatpants declared her allegiance to the University of Michigan, where she'd gone to undergrad and law school, while her Spoon concert T-shirt was almost threadbare.

"Not since she said we had to stop talking. A few weeks ago, I guess? It's hard to keep track of time, you know? Anyway, I haven't reached out."

"You shouldn't have to reach out. You're in crisis, and she's a grown-up."

Mack shrugged, uneasy. Despite her own growing anger at her girlfriend—her *ex*-girlfriend, now, she guessed—she was uncomfortable with Jess' disdain. She still wanted Jess to like Anna for reasons she couldn't explain, not even to herself.

"I saw her today," Jess said, picking flakes of nail polish off her thumbnail. "She was testifying in the trial I'm second chairing."

Mack was taken aback. How odd that her best friend might have a more up-to-date look into her relationship status than she herself had. She cleared her throat. "How—how did she seem? How is she? Did you talk to her?" She wondered how Anna looked. Mack had lost almost seven pounds, and she wondered whether Anna was also suffering from the breakup.

Jess shrugged. "She wouldn't make eye contact with me and only talked to the first chair. Which was fine with me, frankly. I have nothing to say to her. I hope she feels bad about what she did—and, if she does, I'm certainly not going to absolve her."

There was a firm knock on the door, and Mack went to answer it. Dave had the hood of his Marines sweatshirt covering his face, and Mack saw that he'd parked down the street.

When the cop came into the living room, Jess laughed. "Real James Bond look you've got going there, Dave."

He grunted and leaned against Mack's kitchen counter. "I talked to Dr. Lapin," he said.

Jess looked confused. "Why?"

"She was able to give me the date of that night at the bar," Dave said.

Jess rolled her eyes.

"Good," Mack said. She took the slip of paper Dave handed her, Anna's neat handwriting surprising her. For some reason, she'd assumed Dave meant they'd talked by phone.

Dave cleared his throat. "Maybe you could follow up on the camera footage?"

"Sure," Mack said. "I'll talk to Rocky this week." She couldn't look away from the date on the slip of paper. That was the night she and Anna had celebrated getting back together. It would have been their anniversary, if their relationship had lasted. But now, it was less than six months later and she felt further from the psychologist than she'd ever felt before.

"Jess," Mack said, trying to shake off thoughts of Anna. "Do you think Dave should talk to Adam? That's Jess' boyfriend, Dave. He was bartending that night, I think. Maybe he noticed something about the girl. Or could say when I left the bar, or something."

"I'll have him call you," Jess said to Dave.

"Perfect," Dave said. "Anything he can contribute would be super helpful. Even if it's just vouching that Mack stuck around after the girl left. It's a little…unorthodox…that my objective witness would be my suspect's best friend's boyfriend, but this whole case is unorthodox, I guess. Speaking of which, I want you guys to have these." He pulled two cell phones out of his pocket and handed one to Mack and one to Jess. They were cheap Android smartphones, nothing either woman would have used willingly.

Jess looked at hers with a puzzled expression. "What's this for?"

Mack found her way to the contacts list on her new phone and found only two listings: D and J. "I think," she said. "Dave doesn't want us to communicate using our personal or work phones?"

"I don't know anything for sure," the detective said, "but I'm hearing things around the station, and I don't like what I hear. I'm not saying your phone *is* being tapped, Mack, but I can't rule it out. Any number that Jess and I would use to reach you would be registered to us, right? So let's just start using these burners and not worry about it."

"Okay," Mack said. She swallowed hard and cleared her throat. "Okay. Good, then. Good thinking, Dave. Let's move forward. You've both reviewed the autopsy report?" She waited for their answering nods. "Good. We're here because we agree on some fundamental facts. At least, I hope we do. First, I did not kill Jane Doe. Second, Jane Doe was definitely murdered. Third, in order to get off admin leave, I have to prove to Campbell that I did nothing wrong. Unfortunately, we all know it's almost impossible to prove a negative, right?"

Jess and Dave nodded again.

"So I propose that we don't prove I didn't kill Jane Doe. Instead, we prove that someone else did kill Jane Doe."

"That seems like a really complicated way of saying 'solve the case,'" Dave said.

Jess laughed. "You're not wrong," she said. "But I actually don't think that's what she means. Is it?"

"You are correct, sir," she said. "It's not. For police to *solve* a case like this—I mean, unless there's a complete DNA profile and it hits in CODIS or someone comes into the station and spontaneously confesses—is basically impossible. This is a perfect example of a cold case in the making, and we don't have time for it to go cold."

"I don't understand," Dave said. "Are you suggesting we frame someone for murder?"

Jess winced. "No, not framing anyone," she said. "I think Mack is suggesting a SODDIT defense, right?"

"Yes," Mack said. "I'm suggesting we put together a plausible explanation for an alternate suspect. Some Other Dude Did IT.

Defense attorneys do it all the time, and they invent their 'other dudes' out of whole cloth. I'm suggesting that we look carefully at the evidence and find an actual, identifiable, other dude. Find enough evidence to lead to an arrest, even. I think that if we can go to Campbell with a suspect in custody, that'll be enough to get me back to work."

"That sounds like a frame to me," Dave said. He crossed his burly arms over his chest. "And I don't frame people."

Jess snorted. "Cops frame people all the time," she said.

Dave stood up. "Not me."

They were losing him, and Mack couldn't do this without him. Prosecutors didn't investigate crimes. She had some ideas, but she couldn't even direct an investigation ethically, let alone conduct one herself. Even if she knew how to do it, what would she have to show for it? Nothing. She needed an indictable case, which meant Tucson Police had to have whatever she had. Dave was her ticket to getting off admin leave. She glared at Jess, who quickly composed herself.

"Easy, guys," Mack urged. "Most cops don't frame people. I know you, specifically, don't frame people, Dave. I think Jess just got carried away. Right?"

Jess nodded reluctantly.

Dave sat back down on the couch, but he still looked unhappy.

"Again," Mack said. "I'm not suggesting we make up or plant evidence. I think we need to move away from that word 'frame.' We're not going to pin this on an innocent man. But it seems pretty clear from everything we know that Jane Doe was a sex-trafficking victim, and sex-trafficking victims aren't surrounded by innocent men. I think it's likely that the evidence in this case, once we develop it a little bit, could point to a bad guy. If he's not actually the specific bad guy that killed her, well, he's still a bad guy. We'll still be getting *a* bad guy off the streets."

"I like it," Jess said at last. "We do just enough to draw Campbell off Mack, and we clean the streets in the process. We probably won't find enough to convict, but the SODDIT defense never results in a conviction of the other guy. We just need to establish reasonable doubt about Mack, and for that, we just need probable cause to arrest the other dude."

Dave considered that, and his face eventually relaxed. He uncrossed his arms and leaned back against the brown leather. "What are the chances that the rape kit comes back with a mixed profile?" he asked.

"Pretty good, I'd say," Jess said. "In fact, I'd bet money on it. And it's likely that at least one of the contributors will be a felon, right?"

"Right," Mack said. "So, we have a goal: identify a felon with his DNA inside a murdered sex-trafficking victim and develop probable cause from there. Now, let's talk specifics."

"The first step," Dave said, "is ID. We have to figure out who the girl is. I'll start with the NCMEC database." He was referring to the National Center for Missing and Exploited Children, which served as a central list of missing kids. "I can use my department access to review entries, starting in Arizona and widening the scope as necessary. Nothing suspicious about that. I'll set the search parameters to include children reported missing in the last year, to start, since we have no way of knowing how long Jane Doe was on the street before her death."

"Then once you find potential candidates," Jess said, "we can review them."

"If we find one that looks like a good match, Dave, you can do a DNA test to confirm," Mack added.

"Are we sure the hiker isn't the killer?" Jess asked, looking again through the crime-scene photos spread across Mack's coffee table. "I mean, her story seems pretty weak."

Dave shook his head. He wasn't sure, so he'd re-interview her, in hopes that either she'd incriminate herself or maybe provide additional information that could help identify the killer.

Mack thought the idea that the hiker was the killer was a dead end. Although she herself was fairly strong for her height and weight, she didn't think she could have lifted that tub. Unless the hiker was some sort of female Hulk Hogan, she suspected she couldn't do it, either. Perhaps that was an avenue for clearing Mack, even—prove that only a man could have disposed of the body.

Heartened by these options, and by the support of her team, Mack sent Dave and Jess back into the night.

CHAPTER SIXTEEN

Over the next week, Mack heard nothing from Dave and grew increasingly anxious. Maybe he'd had second thoughts about helping her. Maybe his boss had found out and intervened. Maybe—and this was worst possibility of all—he'd found something that further implicated Mack, and he hadn't just changed his mind about helping her, he'd become convinced that she was guilty. She didn't know what she'd do if she lost Dave's confidence. The more anxious she became, the less she felt like she could pick up the burner phone Dave had given her and reach out. She was paralyzed by catastrophic scenarios she couldn't help but imagine.

Before Jess had left Mack's house the night of the conference, they had agreed not to speak until there was something to report. Despite Jess' firm belief in her innocence, despite the burner phones, Jess was worried they might get caught communicating in violation of the administrative-leave rules. Mack understood the concern, though it meant cutting off her emotional support and only source of news about the office. If Mack cost Jess her job, though, she didn't know how she'd live with herself.

"Besides," Mack had said. "This will give me a chance to really dig in and spend some time with myself. I've been thinking about wallpapering my living room. Maybe something in a nice bright yellow."

Jess had given her a pained smile but didn't argue.

At least she could help with the Frank Jefferson trial, Mack thought, before remembering that the file was in her office. She didn't want to ask Jess to bring her a copy. If talking to someone on admin leave could get her fired, surely smuggling her a case file would be worse. Mack's review of the witness interviews would have to wait.

There wasn't much Mack could do on her own to forward the investigation. One evening, she bought a plastic tub, approximately the same size as the one Jane Doe's body had been found in, and loaded it with one hundred pounds of books. She had been right—she couldn't lift it, although if she strained she could scoot it across the floor. She wasn't sure how much that would help her, if push came to shove and she wound up on trial for murder, but it might make a nice courtroom demonstration. Mack swallowed hard against a sudden lump in her throat. She really, *really* hoped it would never come to the point where she would need courtroom demonstrations.

On Thursday, Mack headed to Paradise as soon as her leave requirements allowed. She caught Rocky in her office wearing jeans and a sweatshirt and looking ten years older than she had the last time Mack had seen her. Mack wondered what was going on but didn't have the energy to ask about someone else's problems.

Rocky smiled when she saw Mack, but even her smile looked stressed. "Hey, Pumpkin. Long time, no see."

Mack nodded and came into the office. She sat on the couch, looked around the dingy room, and saw the surveillance monitor set up in one corner.

"Do you remember the night Anna and I came in to celebrate getting back together?" she asked.

Rocky sat back in her ancient desk chair. "I do."

Mack handed her the slip of paper with the date Anna had written on it. "This was the night. Do you by any chance still have surveillance footage? It's a work thing."

Rocky squinted at the piece of paper and studied Mack carefully. "You have a work thing that involves surveillance footage from my bar? I haven't heard anything about crimes happening here."

"No, no. It's not a crime. I'm just hopeful you have the video, so I can show my boss what I was doing here."

Rocky studied her some more. "Help me understand," she finally said. "Were you doing something you weren't supposed to be doing? Is this about Anna?"

"No." She bit the side of her tongue and looked at Rocky. She wondered how little she could get away with telling the other woman. "There was a girl here that night. She came up to me at the bar. We didn't talk much—she freaked me out, to be honest, so I kind of shrugged her off, and she left pretty quickly. I don't know why she was looking for me, or how she found me, or anything, but she knew who I was. Anyway, she wound up getting murdered."

"Murdered?"

"Yeah, murdered, and the police want to see your surveillance footage from that night, to see if it matches my version of events. So I'm hopeful that your system preserves footage that long and you can give me the video."

"Why didn't the cops come to me directly?" Rocky asked. "I always cooperate with law enforcement."

"Well, that's a fair question. I'm working with a detective to clear this up, and we thought it might be easier if I talked to you myself. But if you'd rather I have him call you, I can do that." She got up.

"No," Rocky said. "I guess it's fine." She gestured for Mack to join her at the monitor. She looked at the slip of paper and typed something into a search bar. "Here's everything from that night," she said. "The system automatically breaks it up into fifteen-minute increments. What time did you get here?"

Mack thought back to that night. She'd eaten dinner at home—leftover fried rice from the Chinese delivery place around the corner. After, she showered and did a little work before heading out. Anna was supposed to meet her at Paradise around nine. "Not late," she said. "Maybe quarter to nine? Let's start at eight thirty, to be safe?"

Rocky scrolled through the series of videos. "This is weird," she said, stopping and looking back at Mack. "There's, like, two hours of footage missing. Eight forty-five to ten forty-five."

"Seriously? That's the exact time I need to see. I wasn't here very long. Anna and I had a couple drinks and then went back to her house to keep celebrating. The karaoke was too loud for us. So the girl must have been gone by nine or so, at the latest. What happened to the footage?"

Rocky clicked and typed. "The system didn't malfunction," she finally said. "Someone—someone deleted those time codes."

Mack stared at her, dumbfounded. "*Why?* Can you tell from the program? Or can you at least tell who did it?"

Rocky looked steadily back at her. "That morning I found you in here, hungover after spending the night on my couch. Are you sure you didn't do more than just sleep, Mack?"

Mack counted to ten, slowly, inside her head. "Are you—are you asking me if I deleted surveillance footage, using a system I don't understand, only to come looking for it months later and pretend to be outraged that it's gone?"

"You're good with computers," Rocky said. "You've done trials on computer cases. It's not that I don't trust you, Mack, I just need to know what I'm dealing with here. If you deleted the videos, you can tell me. We'll figure out what to do about it."

Mack's eyes widened. "This is unbelievable. Any number of people could have deleted it, Rocky. You have, what, like six bartenders? Another ten waitresses? Security? It's not like your office is locked, *anyone* could get in here. The cameras aren't hidden—even customers can see them and guess where you keep the system."

"That's not a denial."

"No," Mack said. She walked to the door. "This is a denial: I didn't delete anything. And fuck you for thinking I might have, Rocky."

Days passed without Mack speaking to another person. She spent most of her time spiraling on her couch, staring at the blank walls, trying—usually unsuccessfully—to sleep. She couldn't focus on anything but her increasing anxiety. She would pick up a book and read the same sentence four times before giving up. She left the television on most of the time, just for the noise, but couldn't bring herself to sit down and watch anything. She knew she should call her mom, but she couldn't bear the idea of lying, and telling the truth would be even worse.

Even online shopping had lost its appeal. The first few days, Mack entertained herself making lists of possible home improvements. She even ordered tools and materials online, wound up with everything she needed to patch drywall and re-grout her tile, and wondered if Jess and Adam had been dating long enough to ask for his help with a bathroom demolition and rebuild. By the time the boxes arrived, however, she had lost interest, and the pile sat by the door and began to collect dust.

Mack tried not to think about Anna, but thoughts of the psychologist crept in uninvited during both her waking and sleeping hours. She flowed from anger to hurt to outrage to a willingness to forgive and forget and back again. She missed Anna's easy sense of humor, her ability to find the upside to any situation, no matter how grim. She was sure that if Anna were there, she'd be learning to knit or reading her way through the modern American canon or even just cooking vegetables every night for dinner, instead of eating bowls of microwave popcorn on the couch.

In her nightmares, she chased Anna through endless corridors, found her mutilated body at the bottoms of mineshafts, and flew through the air toward a falling Anna who was always just out of reach. Mack woke up panting and stumbled to the master bathroom. Resting on the cold tiles until her back ached was the only thing that could bring her heart rate down to normal.

Without the surveillance footage, there was no way to prove what had happened at Paradise that night. Without proof, she risked losing Dave's support. She enabled audio notifications for the burner phone Dave had given her and waited.

Eight days after the meeting at Mack's house, Dave finally sent the two women the text message they'd both been waiting for.

Need to meet, it said. *Progress made. 9pm, same place.*

Jess got there first and wrapped Mack in a tight hug as soon as she was in the door. Mack started crying.

"Sorry," she said, sniffling, as she pulled away. "I don't—I don't even know why I'm—"

"You don't ever have to apologize," Jess said. "I know this has been a really lonely time."

Jess brought Mack up to speed on the Frank Jefferson case as they waited for the third member of the team. By the time Dave showed up at Mack's door, Mack had stopped crying.

"You really think parking up the street and wearing that stupid hoodie is really going to keep anyone from knowing what you're up to?" Jess asked. "Anybody following you could figure out whose house this is in fifteen seconds. They're the police. Figuring things out is their literal job. And it's not like anyone else would be following you."

Dave shrugged sheepishly. "I drove my wife's car, too," he admitted.

Jess laughed. "Well, that makes you look suspicious as hell!"

Mack gestured at them to sit down, and hesitantly told them that the surveillance footage from Paradise had been deleted. Dave studied her across the coffee table.

"You can reach out to the owner if you want," Mack said. "She'll cooperate. Maybe you can tell who deleted it, or at least when it was deleted. Best-case scenario, I'll be able to prove I wasn't there when it was deleted. Which I can say with confidence, since I wasn't there when it was deleted."

Jess bit her lip. "This doesn't look good," she said finally.

Mack knew how it looked. "Do either of you have anything else you want to say about it? Now's the time to chicken out, if you're going to." She glanced from Jess to Dave, trying not to look as worried as she felt. She knew she had nothing to hide, but they had to make their choices. She couldn't—*wouldn't*—force them to stay.

Dave pulled a manila file from under his sweatshirt. "We can come back to that," he said, "but I have some updates. I don't have the DNA confirmation back yet, but I'm pretty sure I've found our Jane Doe. I was also able to re-interview Beth Shankar, the hiker who found the body." He reached into the file and pulled out a photograph. "We all know it can be hard to compare autopsy photos to live photos, but luckily, we have an eyewitness right here in the room. Mack, is this your girl from Paradise?"

Mack studied the photo. A high-school cheerleader, red hair slicked into a high pony. Pretty, but forgettable. "I can't be sure," she said. "Her hair is different, and I never saw the girl at the bar smile. I think so. Maybe?"

Dave handed her a second photo. "What about this one?"

There was no hesitation. "This is her." The girl in the photo had the same hairstyle—a blunt bob, choppy bangs—and the same angry look in her eyes she had had that night at Paradise. She was even wearing the same black leather jacket.

"These photos were taken six months apart," Dave said. "The first, about four months before she ran away, and the second, about two months after she ran away. She came home to see her sister."

"Have you talked to the family?" Jess asked. "When was she reported missing?"

"Not yet. I wanted to confirm that this was the girl before I upset her mom unnecessarily. I'll set it up. Missing since August, but it seems like there's an asterisk on that date. I don't have all the details, but I'll get them in the interview."

Mack felt an ache in the back of her throat. This girl, this vibrant, angry girl—who had so recently been a happy, smiling cheerleader—was dead.

"What's her name?" she asked, her voice thick.

"Morgan Packer."

Mack felt Jess and Dave watching her as she studied Morgan's photos. She could imagine this girl at a football game, even dating the quarterback. But she could also imagine her curled into the bottom of a Rubbermaid tub, and she shuddered before putting the pictures back on the table and looking up.

Jess cleared her throat. "You re-interviewed the hiker?"

"Anything useful there?" Mack asked.

"Maybe," Dave said. "Beth Shankar, age thirty-three. She works at Raytheon, some sort of tech job. She tried to explain it, but it was over my head. I don't think she's the killer. She's just a slip of a woman, almost as small as our victim."

"Plus," Mack said. "I just feel like this is a man's crime. I think pulling focus away from 'a woman could have done this' would definitely be in my best interest."

"Fair point," Dave said. "Anyway, the last seven months or so Beth has gone hiking at Tanque Verde every Thursday and Saturday. A neighbor—she thinks his name is Joe but no last name—recommended the trail. She thinks he's cute. They run into each other at the mailboxes and chat. He asked if she liked hiking, and she said yes. She didn't, really, but hoped he was leading up to asking her out. He wasn't. He told her this trail was great and he went twice a week—"

"Thursdays and Saturdays," Mack and Jess said in unison.

"Bingo. She's never seen him there but keeps going in hopes of 'running into him.' At some point, she decided maybe she does like hiking after all, and started going just for fun, but still on those days. Just got into the habit. She's a big fan of thrift shops, and when she saw that pristine Rubbermaid tub, she thought maybe it fell out of a truck or something and would have something cool in it. I think she was just nosy, but that's me editorializing. Anyway, she opened it, and you know the story from there. She says she was traumatized, hasn't been back, hasn't seen Joe."

"Do we know where Joe lives?" Jess asked. "I'd be interested in what he has to say."

"We've got nothing," Dave said. "It's a big apartment complex with central mailboxes. Without a last name, I don't have anything to go on. Beth didn't have his number or a clear idea of what unit he lived in."

"What's his description, at least?" Mack asked. "Joe might not be his real name. He might not even live there at all, he might have been setting her up."

"I don't agree," Jess said. "I think that's too far-fetched to be real. Why Beth?"

Dave considered the question. "I think I'm somewhere between you two," he said finally. "He might've set her up. The whole thing definitely sounds suspicious. But I agree with Jess that a setup sounds crazy. Anyway, her description of him was pretty useless. 'Ruggedly handsome,' but no other details, really. White guy, somewhere between twenty and forty, average to tall, some facial hair."

Mack groaned. "So roughly forty percent of Tucson's residents?"

"Roughly," Dave said.

Mack went into her kitchen and grabbed a pumpkin porter left over from the fall out of her refrigerator. She gestured an offer to Jess and Dave, who declined. "I don't know," she said. "I agree that a setup sounds crazy, but Beth's whole story is crazy anyway. Cute guy asks her out of the blue if she hikes, recommends a trail, gives her specific information to help her find him, then never shows? Cute guys know they're cute. He was using his looks to get her to the hiking trail. But, why did he want her there if he wasn't going to meet her? He wanted her to find Morgan."

Mack felt sure that Beth *had* been set up. The only way the chain of events made sense was if Joe—whoever Joe turned out to be— had wanted Beth to go looking for him, and then find something else. He knew she would look. He might have played the same game with other women, just to make sure someone would find the tub.

"We do have one very important thing," Mack said. "This is our first description of the killer. Handsome white guy. That helps."

"Mack..." Jess started, but Mack raised a hand.

"Joe's the killer," she said. "Mark my words."

CHAPTER SEVENTEEN

Given that Mack had positively identified Jane Doe as Morgan Packer, they decided not to wait for DNA results before talking to the girl's family. The lab anticipated at least a three-month turnaround, given their backlog, and Mack wasn't sure she could last that much longer on admin leave. The Motor Vehicle Division records indicated that Morgan's mother and older sister lived in Oro Valley, a suburb just north of Tucson. Dave arranged to meet them at the family home the following evening after work.

"I want to come with you," Mack said.

Dave crossed his arms over his chest. "I don't think so."

"It's not a good idea, Mack," Jess said. "There's no gray area here on whether you'd be breaking the admin leave rules."

"Of the three of us," Mack said, "who here actually met Morgan?" She raised her hand. "Just me? Okay. How about this one. Of the three of us, who here is wearing a rut in the carpet because Morgan's murder has landed them on admin leave?" She raised her hand even higher. "Still just me? Okay. I get to come."

"*No*, Mack," Dave said. "There is no valid reason for you to come on this interview."

Mack let her hand drop and sank into the couch. "Of course there is. I've prosecuted child-sex-trafficking cases, I've met the victim, and I'm great with families. My perspective could prove very important, and, if you fill me in on everything after the fact, then my perspective can't change the course of the investigation."

Jess and Dave exchanged a long look. Dave rubbed his head and nodded.

"I'm so glad you see it my way," Mack said. "Now, what should I wear? Are we going for a cop look? Casual?"

"Cop," Dave said, at the same time Jess said, "Detective chic. Polo and jeans."

Mack understood. If she and Dave looked more or less like a matched set, it would help avoid questions from the family about her presence.

Dave picked Mack up at home, and their drive northwest was quiet, both of them thinking ahead to the coming interview. Mack wondered how much, if anything, Morgan's family knew about the life she had been leading before her death.

"You know," Dave said at last. "I haven't heard from that bartender yet. What's his name...Adam? Do you know what the holdup is?"

Mack shook her head.

"I need to talk to Jess about it."

Mack's phone buzzed. A text from Rocky. A fourth text from Rocky, actually, each offering increasingly infuriating apologies. Mack knew she'd have to respond at some point. Rocky obviously felt guilty for suggesting Mack could have deleted the surveillance footage, and Mack knew the right thing to do was patch things up and move forward. Their friendship had never been deep enough for Mack to expect Rocky's unwavering loyalty the way she had expected Anna's. She wasn't in the mood to let bygones be bygones, though. Not yet.

Before she knew it, Dave was pulling into the driveway of a neat adobe home nestled in the foothills below Catalina State Park. When the door opened, Mack did a double take. The young woman framed in the doorway was a dead ringer for Morgan.

"Yeah," she said in a dull voice. "We look—looked—just alike. People always called us the twins. I'm Robin. Come on in." Robin turned away from the door and led them to a living room that would have been cheery under other circumstances. It was crowded with overstuffed brown leather furniture and had metallic art shaped like the sun, a cactus, and a family of quails on the walls.

Morgan and Robin's mother—whose name, Mack knew, was Fern—sat slumped against the arm of the couch. It was clear that both women knew why Dave and Mack were there.

"Mom," Robin said, gesturing Dave and Mack to matching armchairs. "The police are here."

The older woman hardly acknowledged her daughter's words, but her eyes were fixed on Dave. He swallowed hard, twice, and got down to business. Fern confirmed Mack's identification of Jane Doe as Morgan Packer. Morgan, sixteen, had been a high school junior. She was young for her grade, but she'd always been a high achiever. She'd wanted to be a veterinarian and had been aiming higher than an Arizona state school, much to her single mother's dismay in contemplating tuition bills. That was the main reason Morgan had started cheer as a freshman: she wanted another extracurricular, in addition to her after-school job at a local vet clinic, hoping for scholarships.

Things had taken a turn at the end of sophomore year, when Morgan went from enthusiastic and upbeat to sullen and withdrawn. Fern and Robin had both asked what was going on with her and tried to talk to her. Morgan, the baby of a close-knit group of twelve cousins, had only receded further into the world she was building on social media, but then deleted her accounts altogether. Frustrated, Fern had resorted to using tracker applications and demanding access to Morgan's texts, but she hadn't gotten to the root of the change in her daughter.

She was using a burner, Mack thought. *Whatever happened sophomore spring, she couldn't risk Mom finding out about it. That time period is the key to this whole thing. We figure out the spring, we figure out why she ran. We figure out why she ran, we figure out why she died.*

"Any boyfriends?" Dave asked.

"Mom and I talked about—well, we thought maybe Morgan was gay." Robin looked uncomfortable at her words. "She never, like, came out to either of us, but it seemed like, well, I don't know, it just seemed like she wasn't interested in boys like I was when I was in high school."

"Would it have been a problem, if Morgan was gay?" Mack asked. Maybe they were getting somewhere, finally. Lots of teens ran away when faced with homophobia at home.

"She could've brought anyone home," Fern said, her voice thick with what Mack imagined were hours of tears shed since Dave's call. "And it would have been fine. So long as she was *home*. I think she knew that."

Robin had been particularly hard-hit by Morgan's about-face. Twenty-three and in the first year of a master's program in education at the U of A, Robin had adored her kid sister. Despite the seven-year age difference, they had always been close. Robin had never viewed Morgan as a burden and had happily pulled her little lookalike on adventures in her old red wagon.

"I was home from the dorm last summer and one afternoon I found my wallet open on my dresser. Some money was gone, and my license. The only person who could have taken it was Morgan, but she denied it when I asked, and I didn't want to push her too hard. She was so prickly by then. It was only like sixty bucks, and they didn't bat an eye at the MVD when I said my license got stolen. I didn't know why Morgan wanted it, I've never heard her say anything about drinking or going to bars, but I figured she probably had a good reason. I was sort of even glad I could help her with something. By then, she wasn't letting anybody in."

Fern turned to face her daughter, and Mack was struck by how strong the family resemblance was. "I didn't know that," she said. "When was that?"

"End of July?" Robin said. "Maybe a week or two before she left the first time."

"The first time?" Dave asked.

Mother and sister explained that, although Morgan didn't really live at home after she ran away, she'd come home sometimes—through October, at least. Fern would return from work and find Morgan in the kitchen, a spread of snack food before her on the table and a load of laundry in the washer. She wouldn't stay long, just a couple hours. Her family would encourage her to stay, would offer family therapy or individual therapy or drug counseling or whatever services would help Morgan feel comfortable enough to return for good.

"Was she using?" Mack asked. She recalled the autopsy results, which had shown marijuana and GHB use in the hours before the girl's death.

Fern and Robin looked at each other, unsure how to respond. Finally, Robin spoke. "I only saw her twice after she left in August, but I think so. She was doing this thing where she, like, clenched her jaw? I don't really know how to explain it."

Dave and Mack were familiar with this behavior, common among those who used uppers—usually methamphetamine. Morgan hadn't had the pockmarked skin and rotting teeth that indicated long-term use, but if she'd only been using for a short time, she wouldn't, necessarily.

"Do you have any idea what caused the shift in Morgan?" Dave asked. "Or what caused her to leave home in the first place?"

Fern hesitated.

"Anything you think could be important," Mack said. "Please, tell us. It might help us figure out what happened to her between August and...and her death."

"She had cheerleading camp that summer," Fern said. "And she came home one day all worked up. She wouldn't tell me what happened, just that there was some trouble with another girl and the coach. I asked a couple times, but that's all she'd say."

She gave Dave the names of the girl, Sophia Baar, and the coach, Jeffrey Mayer, and promised not to let either of them know that the detective might be calling. Fern seemed exhausted in a way that Mack recognized from the countless mothers of victims she'd met over the years. Only mothers, though. Mack had never met a father who carried that same bone-weary weight.

The conversation seemed to be drawing to a close when Fern asked, "You're that lawyer, right?"

Mack cleared her throat and ran her hands through her hair, which hung limply around her shoulders. "I'm a lawyer, yes."

"The one who was in the Andersen trial," Fern said.

Mack was immediately uncomfortable. Morgan had also mentioned Andersen during their brief interaction. Mack wondered if the family had ties to the case. "Yeah," she said. "I was one of them."

Fern smiled, and her pain was so clearly visible that Mack recoiled against the shock of it.

"Morgan and I watched the Jeannie Bea show every night," Fern said. "Morgan always talked about how great you were. We were so impressed with you, so young and so powerful in the courtroom. She even talked about maybe doing what you do, instead of becoming a vet."

"Thank you," Mack said. She wondered if her encounter with Morgan at Paradise hadn't been the coincidence she'd thought. She wondered if the girl had sought her out to disclose, before being pushed away by Mack. She felt a rising tide of guilt, her throat aching.

Dave and Mack requested permission to look at Morgan's bedroom and then excused themselves. The room was still preserved the way the girl had left it. At first glance, it was a typical teenaged girl's room—pinks and purples forming the background for cheerleading awards, band posters, and framed photos that showed her taking care of animals. Mack hadn't seen any evidence of pets in the house, so she assumed they were from the vet clinic.

"What do you think of the social-media thing?" Mack asked. She was surprised there was no computer in the room. Maybe Morgan had taken it with her.

"I assume she had some secret accounts after she deleted the ones her mom knew about."

"Will we be able to find them?"

Dave shrugged, not looking away from the dresser drawer he was sorting through. "Hope so. It's hard to imagine there wouldn't be traces of the trafficker on them, right?"

Mack's thoughts exactly.

The girl's desk was immaculate. A rack for necklaces and earrings occupied one corner, and a photo of Fern with her two daughters in happier times stood next to it. Otherwise, the surface was empty.

Mack began opening drawers and sorting through stacks of class notes, magazines, and other teen detritus. After ten minutes or so working silently—and finding neither a burner phone nor anything else that could shed light on the mysteries Morgan had left behind her—Mack uncovered a crumpled sticky note at the back of the desk's bottom drawer.

"Dave," she said.

The detective turned away from Morgan's closet. Mack spread the small piece of orange paper out on the desktop. *See me after school.* Signed with a heart.

"I've got to talk to that coach," Dave said. "If he didn't give her this, maybe he'll know who did."

CHAPTER EIGHTEEN

They decided that Dave should talk to Sophia first, before the coach, and he arrived at Canyon del Oro High School bright and early the next morning. He had agreed, after much pleading on Mack's part, to call her from the school and keep his phone on speaker and with her muted. Nothing on the recording would show that Mack was listening in. He called her once he was in, telling her he had flashed his badge at the secretary and commandeered an empty classroom.

Sophia came in, accompanied by the principal, who had pulled her out of homeroom and walked her down the hall. Dave reassured her that Sophia wasn't in any trouble, and the principal returned to her office.

Dave confirmed later that Mack's mental image of Sophia—based only on her voice—was accurate. The petite, bubbly senior was wearing her cheer uniform that day, in preparation for an afternoon basketball game. She was tan even in the dead of winter, and her strawberry blond hair was in a tight bun, not a strand out of place. Mack suspected that this was a girl used to getting what she wanted, from both teachers and other students.

Sophia told Dave that she'd met Morgan the summer after eighth grade, when they'd both attended a pre-high school cheer orientation meeting. Sophia's older sister had been the team captain, and Sophia fully expected to assume the same position. Preferably by junior year.

Unfortunately, Coach Mayer hadn't seen Sophia as a leader. He'd favored Morgan, who was only doing cheer to make her look well-rounded on her college applications. Even at that first camp, though, Coach had singled Morgan out for special attention. By junior year, it was clear to everyone—players and assistant coaches alike—that Morgan and the coach had grown too close.

Despite their initial tension, Sophia and Morgan had become friends during the intervening two years, and the other members of the squad encouraged Sophia to talk to Morgan about their concerns. After summer cheer camp one afternoon late the previous July, Sophia called Morgan. They met at Riverfront Park. Sophia picked it because it was off the beaten path for both of them and she believed they wouldn't be interrupted. From the moment Morgan joined Sophia at a picnic table, she was ready to fight.

"I think she knew what was coming," Sophia said. "And she was already pissed about it. She just kept telling me I didn't know what I was talking about, that her relationship with Coach was special, that he was training her to cheer in college. She said we were all just jealous, because we knew we were never going anywhere."

Morgan had stormed off before Sophia had the chance to bring up specific incidents members of the team had told her about. One girl thought she'd seen Morgan and the coach kissing in the locker room after an away game. Another swore she'd overheard Coach Mayer tell Morgan he loved her.

"Do you know if Morgan had a second cell phone?" Dave asked.

Sophia hesitated. "I'm not sure. Sometimes I'd see her with a phone that wasn't her normal one, but the one time I asked her about it she said she'd borrowed it from her mom. That sounded kind of, like, weird. I mean, who borrows their mom's phone? But she and her mom were always really close, so maybe it was true."

"What about social media?" Dave asked.

"Mmm, she deleted her socials in like, July, I think?"

No one spoke for a minute, and all Mack could hear was Sophia cracking her gum. She wondered if Dave was taking notes.

"She didn't start new accounts?" Dave asked. "Doesn't *that* seem weird?"

"I'm not sure," Sophia said. "I'm not sure she would have, like, friended me after I talked to her, anyway. I can ask around, I guess? And call you if I find anything?"

Dave agreed to that, and started to bring the interview to a close, when Sophia volunteered that Morgan had shown up for the beginning of the new year in August, but within a week had just stopped coming. Sophia texted her, asking if she was okay, but never heard anything back.

Sophia didn't make the cut for the new phone number, Mack guessed. *Morgan was pissed about the intervention.*

While Dave waited for the principal to bring Coach Mayer to the classroom he had staked out, he and Mack discussed Sophia's information. They agreed that, if she was telling the truth, then at least a dozen girls and three assistant coaches had suspected the Mayer and Morgan were having an inappropriate relationship. Mack was disappointed that no one had thought to tell Morgan's mom or sister. They were discussing whether they should pursue an investigation into the school for potential failure to protect when they heard a knock at the door. Mack immediately muted herself and turned to her laptop, googling the Canyon del Oro cheer squad. Unlike her mental image of Sophia, the picture Mack had formed in her mind of Coach Mayer was proven incorrect. Where she had expected the coach to be a young, attractive athlete, what she found was a short, slightly paunchy nerd on the wrong side of thirty.

Victim selection was key to a successful predator, and something about Morgan must have stood out for Jeffrey Mayer and made her a compelling target, but Mack wondered what the appeal had been for Morgan.

The coach already sounded nervous as he introduced himself to Dave and asked the standard question about why they were meeting. Dave explained that he was free to leave at any time. This was just a voluntary chat. Mayer agreed, seeming more at ease, and Mack's spidey sense came to life immediately. The primitive creature that lived deep inside her and was in charge of recognizing danger unfurled its wings and stretched, responding to something in Mayer's tone.

"Tell me about your relationship with Morgan Packer," Dave said in his most neutral and inviting tone.

"M—Morgan Packer?" Mayer said, stumbling over the name. "I'm not sure…"

"She was on your cheer squad until she stopped coming to school in August."

"Oh, *right*, yes. Morgan. Well, um, she was a fine cheerleader. I didn't know her very well, of course. Quiet girl, shy. Never seemed to fit in, but then I make it a rule never to get to know my girls all that well. There's so much risk now, you know?"

Dave waited, silent. Mack knew this technique. Make the silence so uncomfortable that the suspect rushed to fill it with incriminating information.

Thirty seconds went by. A minute. Mack was ready to confess something herself, just to make it stop. But Mayer didn't crack.

"That's a good policy," Dave said finally. "What brought it on?"

"It's just always been my way," Mayer said.

"The problem with that, Mr. Mayer—"

"Please, call me Coach. Everyone does."

"The problem with that, *Coach* Mayer, is that I have some information suggesting that you actually knew Morgan Packer very well. Well enough that it could cause some real trouble for you."

"Information?" Mack could hear the nerves creeping into his voice. "Morgan wasn't close to any of the other girls, so I don't see what—"

Dave interrupted. "I interviewed Sophia Baar."

There was a long pause, and again Mack itched to fill the silence.

"Sophia had a grudge against Morgan," Mayer finally said. "Everyone knew it. She was mad because of her perception that Morgan was getting special treatment."

"I don't think so," Dave said. "I think Sophia told me the truth. I think you're desperate to make this go away, Coach, because the school already suspects something, and any hint of scandal will get you cut from the program here. Then you're screwed. Schools don't hire coaches who rape their athletes."

Mayer gasped. "Is that little bitch saying I raped her? Because she's a liar and a drug addict. That's why I kicked her off the team in the first place!"

"You kicked Sophia off?"

"No, Morgan. Well, I was going to kick her off, but then she quit coming. And now she's lying. I never raped her."

Mack heard a thud—paper hitting a desktop. *The photos.*

"Morgan isn't saying anything," Dave said. "She's dead. Murdered."

There came a keening sound that Mack realized was Mayer beginning to cry. She couldn't tell if he was faking it. Maybe he was really surprised, but maybe he was performing grief for Dave in hopes of getting himself out of trouble.

"Did you kill her, Jeff? Were you afraid she was going to tell?"

"I—I could never. I loved her. She wasn't a bitch or a liar, I just panicked when you threatened me. Morgan always put my job first. When you said I raped her, I just—I reacted without thinking. Everything that ever happened between us, she wanted it. She started it. It was *all* her idea."

"I'd like to hear all about it, but first, I need to let you know what your rights are."

Mack fist-pumped as Dave read Mayer his *Miranda* rights. Whatever came next, it would stand up in court. Maybe Mayer really had killed Morgan, and Mack could be back at work the next day as if nothing had happened.

The story came out in fits and starts. At first, the relationship between Mayer and Morgan had been appropriate, at least on the surface. Mayer was attracted to the petite redhead from the first time he saw her, but she was only fourteen, so he resisted the urge and focused on making her the best cheerleader she could be. He thought she might be his ticket out of Oro Valley, out of the home he shared with his mom after an expensive divorce and bankruptcy.

During the spring of her sophomore year, though, the situation changed.

"She came on to *me*," Mayer said. The sound of him hitting the table came through the phone and startled Mack. "She said she'd had a crush on me since cheer camp. She wouldn't pretend to be interested in boys her own age, because she wanted me. All the boys were interested in her, but she wouldn't have anything to do with them."

It was her idea for Mayer to buy her a burner phone. He didn't understand why, at first, but she had explained it would keep their relationship safe from prying eyes like her mother's and sister's.

"She said that her family would never understand, they'd think it was wrong, what we were doing. I—I'd never had this kind of a connection with a student, but she seemed to know exactly what she was doing. She said I shouldn't tell anyone, because I'd get in trouble. She said no one would understand or love her like I did. So I did what she wanted."

Mack was struck by the familiarity of Mayer's words. She'd heard these justifications before. Countless girls had told her that their abusers had said these very same things to them, trying to convince them to stay in abusive relationships. She wondered whether Mayer was making this up on the spot, or just twisting things he had said to Morgan to paint himself in the best possible light.

"We were in love," Mayer insisted. "Morgan was helping me. When we got together, you can't even understand how broke I was. A good dinner was *two* packs of ramen noodles. But Morgan helped me afford to get out of my mom's house. She wanted me to go back to school. Said if I finished my degree I could be a real teacher, not just a coach. At first, she gave me what she was making at the vet clinic, but that wasn't enough."

"You know, I looked you up," Dave said. "That's some car you're driving. Fully loaded F-150s aren't cheap."

Mayer scoffed. "She hated my old beater. If we were going to be together—*really* together—I had to get something she'd be proud to ride in. The payments…they just put me further behind. That's when"—he sniffled—"that's when she had the idea to start charging men for, you know…for doing it with her."

The level of cognitive distortion driving Mayer's version of events was insane. Mack could barely listen to him. She wanted to hang up and just get the highlights from Dave later, but she needed to know firsthand if Mayer killed Morgan.

"Morgan," Mayer said, after a long silence, "found an article online describing how much money the right girl could make doing sex work. I tried to talk her out of it. I said I could get a second job, but I guess she was stronger than I was. I would never have forced her to do anything, let alone something so degrading as sex work, but she wore me down. She asked me to be her muscle, make sure that none of her customers got violent."

"What'd you say to that?" Dave asked. Mack could hear the revulsion in his voice. No matter how many times they heard these stories, it never got any easier.

"I was just happy to help keep her safe."

Mack rolled her eyes. *You fucking liar.*

The story continued.

"Morgan started turning tricks in July, and by August I could afford a tiny studio apartment downtown. It was a longer commute for me to get to school, but she was happy to be in the city. She ran away from home, stopped going to school, and started staying with me full time.

"I was thrilled, you know? It was like we were a real couple. She called me her hubby, and I called her my wife. Just to each other, of course, but still. I encouraged her to go back to school, to graduate and go to college. I wanted her to live the rich, full life she deserved. But she loved me too much to leave. We were like Romeo and Juliet."

"Two problems with that, Coach," Dave said. "Romeo wasn't twenty years older than Juliet, and Juliet wasn't the only one who died."

Yeah, Mack thought. *You were a Romeo. A Romeo pimp, more like. You convinced her you loved her, and she did whatever you told her to do.*

"What about the tattoo?" Dave asked. "We've seen those barcodes before, but always on working girls. Their pimps pick them out."

"I saw it online," Mayer said, "but I was *not* her pimp. I never forced Morgan to get the tattoo. Didn't even ask her. I just showed it to her, one night when we were getting ready for bed in that shitty little apartment downtown. I wasn't suggesting anything— just showing her how crazy some people are. We laughed about it together. I never thought she'd do anything that stupid, but it turned out she liked the idea of marking herself as my property. She swiped her sister's ID and used it to get the tattoo."

Yeah, right, Mack thought. She didn't believe Mayer's story for a second. She'd never once met a sixteen-year-old who wanted to be someone's property, but she'd met plenty of men who wanted to own a young girl. Unfortunately, she didn't know how she could disprove Mayer's claims. They could canvass every tattoo parlor in town, but there was no way an artist would remember a basic tattoo they'd given six months earlier. Even if they found the right artist, they still wouldn't be able to prove that Mayer had forced her to get the tattoo. The barcode was a dead end.

"When Morgan disappeared in October, I was happy about it. I thought she'd gone back to her mom's house. She'd begun using marijuana—and then other drugs, too—and I worried that she shouldn't be staying with me anymore. She needed to go home. A girl needs her mother. And besides, the drugs were eating into the rent money."

Besides, Mack thought.

"But she wouldn't listen to me. She'd visit sometimes—like when we fought about money—but then she always came back."

"And then she went missing," Dave said.

"We were fighting. I—I slapped her, once. She was spending all this money on weed and whatever else she was using, and we were fighting. She said it was her money, not mine. She didn't seem to understand that it was our money, same as the money I earned at school. Everything was for the two of us. Then I came home one day from work to find her phone on the bed. I never saw her again. Not at school, not at home, not on the streets."

Mack wondered if he was relieved to have gotten all this off his chest. His story was bullshit, of course, but he didn't know they knew that. From Mayer's perspective, Mack figured he was congratulating himself on skating through the interview with nothing worse than a few bumps and bruises. He'd twisted things to turn himself into the victim and blame Morgan for everything that had happened. He wouldn't realize how stupid his story sounded until the victim behavioral expert testified at trial.

Dave asked for the burner phone, and Mack was hopeful that they could use it to prove she had never called or been called by Morgan.

"I smashed it," Mayer said. "Broke it into pieces against the bedroom wall. I was so angry she left—she didn't even tell me she was going. I threw away the pieces."

The burner was a prepaid Boost Mobile phone. Mayer couldn't give them the number, because he'd deleted it. The asshole had an answer for everything. Mack's limited experience with Boost told her that, without a phone number, there was no way to get call records. They could seize his phone and search it—if they could get into it—but she expected that he really had deleted the number. Mayer was an idiot, but he was probably too smart to have left such an obvious loose end.

"Is that everything?" Dave asked. "Nothing else you need to tell me?"

Mack heard Mayer crying. "I didn't kill her," he said. "I loved her."

Chair legs scraped across the classroom floor.

"Jeffrey Mayer," Dave said. "You're under arrest for sex conduct with a minor and sex trafficking. Stand up, sir, put your hands behind your back."

The call cut off. Mack considered Mayer's fate. He'd admitted enough—even with his distorted view of events—that he wouldn't get out of prison until he was a very old man. But he'd adamantly denied killing Morgan, and Mack was inclined to believe him. Morgan was his meal ticket. Mack suspected that, if they looked at Mayer's bank records, they'd find that Morgan had been bringing in big money. Even if she'd threatened to leave him, threatened to expose him, Mack couldn't see him sticking her in the freezer or dumping her in the desert in a Rubbermaid tub. It would have been a crime of passion, not a calculated single stab wound. Mayer was the type to claim self-defense—they'd struggled for control of a gun, he wouldn't have known how it went off, and he would have had no memory of how she wound up dead. He would have called 911 himself and begged the EMTs to save her.

No, Morgan's had been a careful murder—a murder with a purpose, planned and premeditated—and Mayer wasn't that kind of guy. He would pay for his crimes, but that wouldn't get Mack off the hook. There was still work to be done.

CHAPTER NINETEEN

Mack was sprawled on her couch, napping under a fuzzy blue blanket she'd snagged at a white elephant exchange the previous Christmas. It was Valentine's Day, and she was planning to spend the evening with reality TV and takeout Thai food. Alone again, naturally. Jess was busy with Adam, who had swapped shifts with another bartender to take her to Vivace, an Italian restaurant and fancy by Tucson standards, up in the foothills. The judge had continued the Dorothy Johnson trial because Noah Gardener, Frank Jefferson's defense attorney, had filed a motion saying he needed more time to complete an investigation. He hadn't specified what exactly he was investigating, and Jess hadn't asked. The longer it took for trial to begin, the more likely it was that Mack would be back at work and able to try it with her.

"The motion is very dumb," Jess had said during their brief call. She hadn't wanted to linger—despite the burner phones, she was breaking the rules to have any contact at all with Mack, let alone to talk about cases. "We have DNA, and Jefferson's story makes no sense. What on earth could Noah be 'investigating,' other than a hitherto unknown identical twin to explain away the DNA?"

It felt so good to laugh. There hadn't been much cause for laughter in the last month.

Mack hadn't heard from Anna in almost five weeks, not that she was keeping track. At week three, she had changed the contact in her phone from "Anna Lapin" to "No Thank You," but then she changed it back at week four. If Anna reached out, Mack didn't want to be reminded of her own pettiness. A box of the psychologist's stuff was collecting dust by Mack's front door—shirts, toothbrush, some books, and other belongings that were inevitably left behind when two people stopped sharing a living space.

She jerked awake to the sound of the burner buzzing on her coffee table, *D* on the screen. She answered, her voice thick with sleep. "'Lo?"

"Check your email," Dave said and hung up.

The DNA results were in.

Mack scrolled through the charts to the summary. The sperm fraction of the vaginal aspirate showed a mixed profile, with at least three contributors. Given that sperm only lived in the body for a maximum of two days, it seemed likely that Morgan had still been working, right up until her death. Even if one of the profiles was a match for Mayer—a safe assumption—that left two or more other men unaccounted for. One of the profiles didn't hit on anything in CODIS, so there was nothing to be done with that.

One, though, popped on two cases and was linked to a felon named Ron Simon. The more recent case was a drug conviction, just a year old, for meth possession up in Phoenix. When Simon was convicted, he would have given a DNA sample in response to the standard court order requiring DNA from felons to be entered into the national database. The older hit, though, was from an unsolved sex assault from 1999 in Tucson.

Simon's profile, which had been entered on the meth case, had apparently not been run against the open-unsolved backlog, so his connection to that investigation had slipped through the cracks, as so many did. Dave had helpfully attached the police report on the old case for Mack's review.

The victim, Eileen Travis, had been a very young sex worker—though the reports from back then labeled her a teen prostitute—and had been brought to the ER by a friend on the Track after a client had pushed her out of his car without paying her and taken off. The friend had gotten a partial license plate, but not enough for law enforcement to do anything with. Now here Simon was, seventeen years later, back in Tucson and raping another sex worker. This time, a minor.

This might just do the trick. Excited, Mack reached for the burner to text Jess and Dave but found that Jess had beaten her to the punch. They'd be there in an hour.

Restless, Mack got up and began cleaning her living room just to burn off some of her nervous energy. She folded the blue blanket, fluffed and reorganized the pillows, and looked down at her grubby sweats. Should she change? What did you wear to turn your life around?

Simon looked like a prime suspect in Morgan's death. Mack knew that the DNA analyst would hedge her bets on the stand, wary of overstating the facts. Even with that caution, though, Simon couldn't have left that DNA sample any earlier than about three days before Morgan died, and likely more recently than that. Rapists escalated. His last known rape was before Morgan was even born, and yet his interest in sex workers had persisted. He was a meth head, and meth was a disinhibitor—it wouldn't have made Simon kill, but it might have lowered his inhibitions and allowed him to act on the same urges that had resulted in him beating the shit out of Eileen back in the nineties.

Mack called up OSINT, the open-source intelligence website she used for research on defendants, potential jurors, and witnesses. There was nothing law-enforcement specific about it, it just collected publicly available data and spat it back at anyone who asked for it. OSINT was used by people in all kinds of fields who wanted more information than a standard "getting-to-know-you" conversation typically provided. She typed in Simon's name and scrolled through the results, looking for the *right* Ron Simon. Finally, she found the guy she thought she was looking for. A home address in a low-rent part of town, an old pickup truck, and several photographs. Simon was a big, grubby-looking guy who appeared to like expensive guns and cheap women. He worked in a butcher shop, one of the ones with the big old-fashioned freezers inside. *Perfect.*

Mack paced her living room, waiting for her team to arrive. She didn't know if Simon had raped Morgan by force or through sex trafficking, and she wasn't sure it mattered, from a strictly legal perspective. Either way, he was looking at substantial prison time if the case went to trial. On a personal level, she vowed that Simon would pay for the harm he had perpetrated against the teenager Mack had grown quite fond of since her death. Once upon a time, Morgan had been bright, charming, and on a good path for the future. If not for Coach Mayer's intervention, she could have turned out like Mack—driven, devoted to her work, *alone on Valentine's Day, on administrative leave, a suspect in a homicide case*. Okay, maybe ending up like Mack wasn't a consummation devoutly to be wished, but anything would be better than winding up in a Rubbermaid tub in the middle of the desert.

CHAPTER TWENTY

Mack was told that Dave got to Simon and Son's Meats early the next morning and found the butcher opening up. Simon grudgingly relocked the door and accompanied Dave to the station for an interview. This time, Jess was present in the video monitoring room, and she was the one who had Mack's burner, muted, on speakerphone. Mack, frustrated by her inability to be more actively involved in the investigation, was grateful to both of them for including her. Listening to a description of the interview later—over a beer or lunch—would have been more than she could take.

Jess texted her a photo of Simon so Mack could picture the large butcher as he sat across the table from Dave in the sterile interview room. Simon was in his fifties, and his methamphetamine addiction had taken a toll on his skin and teeth. His stained white T-shirt stretched thin over his stomach. He leaned back in the chair, apparently immune to its wobbling legs and the flickering overhead light. Mack wondered if he'd spent a lot more time in interview rooms than his two priors suggested.

As Dave went through the demographic questions and read Simon his rights, Mack was struck by the butcher's casual tone. He seemed completely unfazed by having been accosted outside his workplace at six a.m. and dragged into the police station. Mack was used to a wide range of reactions from men in this position, but "mildly inconvenienced" was one she hadn't encountered before.

Things started to get interesting almost immediately. Dave asked Simon to confirm his prior felony conviction, and expected that to be a pro forma question, as did Mack, but they were both surprised when Simon responded with, "Nope, not me. Never been convicted of anything."

Dave took a beat to recalibrate. Mack heard papers rustle.

"This isn't you?" Dave asked, and Mack knew he must be showing the prior paperwork to Simon. "Not even this packet from the Department of Corrections? Looks like you ended up there after a probation violation."

"Nope, I never went to prison."

"This sure looks like your picture on this prison pack, wouldn't you say?"

"Big world. Lot of faces look alike."

"Alrighty then," Dave said. "Let's move on, then."

He began to lay out the basics of the unsolved sex assault, without mentioning the DNA results.

"Nah," Simon said. "I never had to pay for sex. Certainly never raped no prostitute."

OMG, Jess texted, *his shirt rode up and he's scratching his belly. It's exceedingly gross.*

Mack shuddered, glad she couldn't see it.

"Okay," Dave said. "What about *this* girl? Do you know her?"

There was a long pause before Simon spoke. "This picture doesn't look like it's from ninety-nine."

"No," Dave said. "This is a different case."

"Like I said, I never paid no girls for sex. Not back then, and not now."

"The thing is, Ron, we have your DNA inside both these girls. So, tell me how that happened. Did you have sex with them?"

"Well, either you're lying, or your DNA is wrong. I never seen this girl before. I don't have sex with hookers, regardless of whether or not they're charging for the privilege. Believe it or not, I get plenty of tail without having to resort to pros."

Silence, and Mack desperately wanted to see what was going on. Was Dave rethinking his approach? Was he waiting Simon out, hoping he'd break? Simon didn't seem like the type to feel the need to fill a long silence.

A loud smacking sound. Dave hitting the table. Mack heard chair legs scraping but couldn't tell if Dave was standing or Simon was backing up to avoid the burly police sergeant.

"Listen to me very carefully," Dave growled. "I know you had sex with these girls, you son of a bitch. I'm not lying about the DNA, and the DNA isn't 'wrong.' Why don't you just go ahead and tell me your side of the story, so I can walk out of here thinking you're just a man that pays for sex, not a man who rapes little girls."

Mack had never known Dave to play bad cop before, and she was struck by how natural it seemed on him. She was surprised, having always thought of Dave as a gentle man.

"Nothing wrong with paying for sex," Dave said. "That way, you don't have to buy the bitch dinner, right?"

Simon hummed noncommittally.

"The problem," Dave said, "is that when I leave here and you go to jail—because you're definitely going to jail today, whatever you say—your new roommates will either hear that you're just a guy who took shortcuts or…well, you know."

"Okay!" Simon said. "I recognize this one. I don't know what you're talking about with the case back in ninety-nine, but this girl, I recognize. I thought she was eighteen. I swear it. Gimme a lie detector. You'll see."

"How do you recognize her?"

"I saw her one time, back in the fall, last year."

"Saw her?" Dave prompted.

"I—you know, I—I paid her. One time! That's it!"

Simon explained to Dave that he found Morgan, who he knew as Morgana, on Craigslist. He'd just broken up with his long-term girlfriend and was feeling lonely. He was surfing the personal ads, looking for a prostitute, and Morgana's ad stood out. Her photos weren't grainy mirror selfies—someone else must have taken them.

"She looked young, sure," Simon said. "But the ad said she was eighteen."

It was clear that she was working with someone, he went on, and that she'd been doing this for a while. She looked like a pro. So he called her and went to meet her at the motel where she operated, and that's all there was to it. When he left, he saw a tall, good-looking guy waiting around outside and assumed that was her pimp. He tried to call her again, a week or so later, but no one picked up.

"Do you still have the ad?" Dave asked.

"No," Simon said. "But I probably still have the number in my phone."

Silence for a while, then Dave reading a series of digits out loud. 520, a local number. Something about it sounded familiar to Mack. She shuffled through her papers until she found the one she was looking for—Mayer's biographic information. *Jackpot.* The number on Morgan's Craigslist escort ad was Mayer's phone number. That was a dead end on getting Morgan's number, but evidence that Mayer had been actively trafficking his teenage girlfriend. They'd known that his supportive-boyfriend story was bullshit, but now they had an actual fact to contradict it, rather than just a feeling. Mack wrote a note to make sure Dave recognized the connection and told Mayer's prosecutor about it. Whoever had the case, they'd want to know. Mack would.

"Why are you talking to me about this girl, anyway?" Simon asked. Mack was surprised it had taken him this long. Most guys, that was the first thing they wanted to know—why were the police interested in them? She picked up her personal phone to text Anna and ask what that meant. She was halfway through writing the text when she realized she couldn't send it—since she and Anna were apparently no longer on speaking or texting terms—and set the phone down.

"Why do you think?" Dave asked.

A long silence.

"Why do you think I'm asking about her?"

"I—I—I—" Simon stammered. "I'm not sure. Maybe she's saying I didn't pay her. That's the only thing I can figure, but I don't know why she'd lie about that. I paid her what we agreed on. Right there in the room."

Mack could imagine Dave milking the silence that followed for all it was worth. At last, he spoke.

"Girl's dead, Ron. I think you killed her."

"Hey! Hold on!" Simon shouted. "I never killed no one. I've been straight with you. I didn't kill that girl back then, and I didn't kill no one now. You look at my record, you'll see I never killed no one."

Mack heard chair legs scraping against the floor. Dave's parting words were faint as he moved away from the microphone. "You'll understand if I don't believe you, right?"

Dave kept Simon cooling in the interview room while he and his team drafted a search warrant for his home, and Mack went back to pacing her living room, intermittently straightening a pillow or a pile of papers as she waited for the results of the search. She wanted to go for a run, just around the neighborhood, but the terms of her administrative leave confined her to the house during work hours. Her second choice would have been a beer, but per the employee handbook she had been issued on her first day, she couldn't drink during business hours either. She was too keyed up to read or take a nap.

As the hours passed with no news, her anxiety swelled. She turned on an episode of *The Bachelor* she had paused halfway through the previous evening, but she couldn't focus. Maybe the judge had denied the warrant request, though Mack knew there was ample probable cause to believe that evidence pertaining to Morgan's murder might be found in Simon's possession. Maybe the judge had granted the warrant, but they hadn't found anything in the search. Almost six weeks had passed since Beth found Morgan's body, and anything could have happened in that time. Maybe they had found something, but it was so terrible that Dave hadn't been able to break away. Another body, perhaps. They might have even found a live victim and were getting her emergency medical treatment.

Mack slumped onto her couch. These were the kinds of spirals Anna had been so good at talking her out of, at helping her find a firm grip on reality with which she could pull herself back from the edge. In her absence, Mack would have to do it herself. She looked at her watch. Four hours had passed. Depending on the complexity of the warrant application, the duty judge reviewing it, and the state of Simon's house, it could be another three or four hours before

Mack heard anything. That was just the way the system worked: slowly. Mack felt her heart rate slow. She concentrated on taking deep breaths. Four count in, five count hold, four count out. By the time she reached breath nine, she was asleep.

She awoke to the sound of her doorbell. Her living room was dark, her head was pounding. She glanced at her watch. It was almost two a.m. She shuffled to the door and peered through the window to see who could be there so late. It was Dave, two Circle K coffees in his hands. She let him in and he handed her a cup, still hot, and leaned down to take his shoes off.

"It's okay if you want to keep them on," she said.

"Not after walking through that pigsty." He padded in his socks toward the couch. "I don't even want to sit on your furniture, but I'm too tired to stand."

"You want me to put a towel down?" Mack asked.

Dave blinked at her, confused. "Actually, that would be great."

When they were settled and Mack's offer of a snack had been refused, Dave told her about the search. Simon's house, less than ten minutes from the Tanque Verde trailhead where Morgan had been found, wasn't exactly a hoarder home, but it wasn't far off. He lived alone, and he clearly wasn't focused on neatness. There were stacks and stacks of paperwork for the police to sort through. Most of it was uninteresting—twenty-year-old tax documents, user manuals for appliances that had since been discarded, and similar garbage. At the bottom of one pile in the bedroom, however, they had hit the jackpot. The pornography jackpot.

"Bad stuff," Dave said. "Kids, torture porn, all kinds of stuff. Stuff even I've never seen before. Perfect fodder for Dr. Lapin. She'll have a field day with this guy."

Mack flinched. She didn't think Dave knew all the ins and outs of her history with Anna. She guessed she would have to get used to it; when she went back to Sex Crimes, Anna was bound to come up often. She was the main expert used in cases with a forensic psychology component.

In addition to old-school pornographic magazines, they found over twenty-five thumb and external hard drives, along with three computers. All of the eight drives they previewed contained additional pornography. None of it was straightforward adult pornography, either. When it came to anything sexually deviant, Simon was a connoisseur. One of his computers was downloading files from BitTorrent when police entered, and Dave read her a list of the file names. Mack blanched, unprepared for how graphic the titles would be. She had tried a number of child-porn cases and knew that file names often contain accurate descriptions of the contents of the file, but she had to ask Dave to stop giving examples. She was already convinced. Ron Simon was one sick fuck.

In the garage, they'd found a chest freezer. This was more consistent with the position in which Morgan's body had been found than the walk-in freezer at the butcher shop would have been. Also incriminating was the fact that the back wall of Simon's garage, directly behind the chest freezer, was lined with shelves filled with Rubbermaid tubs. Dave pulled out his phone and scrolled through photos for Mack. They weren't the exact same kind of tub as the one Morgan had been found in, but they were close enough for Mack.

"You know," Dave said. "I think we actually solved the case. I think Simon really did kill her. What do you think?"

Mack considered the evidence they'd gathered. The story as they knew it was simple. Morgan had been a good kid—smart, responsible, close to her family—until something happened at the end of her sophomore year. She had gotten involved with her cheerleading coach, and Mayer had convinced her to run away from home and live with him. Then he got her hooked on drugs, forcing her to do sex work so that he could pay his bills. During her three months with Mayer, she returned home periodically to do laundry and see her family. In September, she went to Paradise. They didn't know whether she'd gone looking for Mack or if that was a coincidence. Either way, she tried to talk to Mack but was turned away. In October, she ran away from Mayer, but she hadn't gone home. Maybe she found another trafficker to work for, they didn't know. At some point, though, she met Simon. He drugged her, killed her, and stored her in his freezer, before eventually discarding her.

Mack scratched her cheek. There were so many things they didn't know, and would probably never know, about Morgan's life. When had she left Mayer, and under what circumstances? Actually, *had* she left Mayer, or was she still working for him when

Simon came into the picture? When had she died, and where? The answers to those questions would help all the other pieces of the case slip into place, but Mack knew that, without a confession from Simon, they could never be sure.

"Why'd he drug her?" Mack asked. "Did he drug her, or did she take the GHB herself?"

Dave scrolled through more photos from the search. Mack saw piles of what she would call trash but what Simon would probably call his important belongings. Stacks of old newspapers lined the walls. A folding table covered in old cell phones. Not even smartphones, from what Mack could see. Just old Nokias and Motorolas from the early 2000s. Dave stopped when he got to a picture of the bathroom counter and zoomed in on a pickle jar filled with discarded needles.

"We don't know what these are. Maybe meth, possibly his own. But we're going to test them, and hopefully we'll find GHB residue. As to the why, well, that's up to the prosecutor, isn't it?"

Mack considered how she would present the case if she were the prosecutor. The evidence was totally circumstantial, but she'd won circumstantial cases before. She'd lost some of them, too, though. Simon would have zero jury appeal, so it would all come down to argument. Would she be able to sway a jury without a smoking gun, or would a defense attorney prevail on a cop-out argument, asking the jury simply to hold the State to its burden?

She thought about possible ways to bolster the case. If the needles showed GHB, that would be helpful, but convincing the crime lab to analyze all of them—instead of just one or two as a representative sample—would be an uphill battle. It would take months to examine all the hard drives and computers, but maybe they'd find something there, evidence that he'd viewed Morgan's Craigslist ad, possibly even something directly linking him to the Tanque Verde trailhead.

The wheels of justice would turn, but they would turn slowly. It could be a year or more before the case was ready for trial. The question was where Mack would be when the time came—back at work, or still on admin leave, twiddling her thumbs and waiting for resolution.

"Did they test the tub for fingerprints? The one Morgan was found in?"

"They tried, but it had been wiped clean."

Mack leaned back against the couch. She was so tired. Her nerves were fried. They had investigated the case and gone where the evidence had taken them. Everything they had pointed to Ron Simon. Still, she wished there was more. Some irrefutable *proof* of Simon's guilt.

"With the understanding that Assistant District Attorneys cannot direct law enforcement investigations," Mack said, rattling off the disclaimer she'd issued hundreds of times. "And the further understanding that I am on administrative leave and wouldn't be assigned to this case anyway…"

Dave laughed, and the exhaustion momentarily lifted from his face. "Get on with it, Counselor."

"It sure looks like you have probable cause to arrest Ron Simon for rape and homicide, dontcha think?"

Dave nodded and smiled. "I'm glad you think so. I do, too. We formally arrested him about forty-five minutes before I got here. I would have come by earlier, but when patrol went in to put the cuffs on him and transfer him to intake, he took a swing at one of them. Clocked the kid pretty good, actually, he'll have a shiner for a good long while. Anyway, they took him down hard, and Simon wound up needing some medical attention. Couple cracked ribs, maybe a little concussion."

It sounded like Simon had gotten a lot worse than he gave, and police officers injuring defendants never played well in front of a jury. Simon wasn't the kind of guy who would have a lot of jury appeal, but jurors could be unpredictable. Given all the media attention police brutality had been getting, Simon's injuries were not going to be helpful. Mack sucked air through her teeth.

"I know," Dave said. "But I saw it go down, and they didn't mistreat him. He's a big dude, and he put up a good fight. Anyway, he's in the ED, but under arrest for murder and a slew of other charges, including the ninety-nine rape, and now the aggravated assaults on the arresting officers."

"How'd you get him on the old case?" Mack asked.

"We found the old victim. I had Detective Caldwell track her down. She's alive and well and happy to prosecute. I talked to James Harris, and he said they'll keep all the cases involving Morgan together, so Simon will go to the same ADA who has the Mayer case, Nan Chin."

Mack let out a breath she didn't realize she'd been holding. Of *course* Dave had been keeping James apprised of the situation. It was a good idea to keep the cases together; that would reduce the number of people Fern and Robin had to deal with and would lead to a streamlined prosecution of the men who had victimized Morgan. Even though Mayer and Simon hadn't committed their crimes together, there was overlap between them, and a single prosecutor would be much more able to keep the cases straight. Mack knew Nan, but not well. She was a few years younger but had a reputation for being smart, dedicated, and great with victims. If it wasn't going to be Jess—and it couldn't be, because it would be an obvious conflict of interest given their friendship—she was glad it was Nan.

There was one final barrier, as far as Mack could tell, separating her from getting back to work. "When is grand jury on Simon?"

"Nan said Monday, I think."

For the first time in almost six weeks, Mack slept easily, without Morgan haunting her dreams.

CHAPTER TWENTY-ONE

Grand jury was set for nine a.m. that Monday, and Mack was waiting by her phone when Dave texted that the jurors had indicted Simon on all counts. She fist-pumped alone in her living room.

Thirty minutes later, Mack's phone buzzed again, this time with an email to her work account. It was Michael Brown, saying that Campbell wanted to meet that afternoon. Mack's stomach dropped. Either all her hard work investigating Morgan's murder was about to pay off, or she was about to get fired.

It wouldn't take much to bring down her career, just Robin or Fern letting slip to Nan that she'd been there with Dave for the interview. All their efforts to keep her out of the reports would be wasted if that happened.

Mack wanted to talk to Jess, to get some reassurance that her head wasn't on the chopping block, but she and Adam had gone to Santa Fe for a long weekend. They would be back the next afternoon. Mack grabbed her phone and scrolled to her text thread with Anna. She didn't want to impose, and Anna had made it clear that she wasn't going to be available to help Mack through this situation, but she was desperate. Donning her psychologist hat, Anna would be able to help her contextualize what was going on and rationally assess what her response to the meeting should be. She typed and erased three different versions before hitting send.

Hey, I know it's been a minute and I'm not sure if I should be texting you, but I wanted to let you know that they made an arrest in the murder. He was indicted this morning. I have a meeting with Campbell this afternoon to discuss getting off admin leave. I'm pretty stressed about it, so if you have some time and could give me a call, I'd appreciate it. Hope all is well with you.

She knew that Anna had enabled read receipts on her phone, so it shouldn't have surprised her when the word *Delivered* on her screen changed to *Read*, yet, when the telltale three dots appeared, her stomach lurched.

After a moment, the dots went away. Mack held her breath, waiting for them to reappear…but they didn't. She sighed and headed for the shower. Whatever was coming, she'd have to face it without help. The very least she could do was wash her hair.

Mack was early for the meeting and sat on a bench outside the executive suite for an agonizing twenty minutes, waiting to be summoned into the conference room. She'd dressed up for the occasion, wearing her Monday trial outfit with her favorite jewelry—pearl earrings and a matching necklace. She knew she looked good, professional and credible, ready for action. No casual observer would see any hint of the strain she'd been under since January.

When she was called in at last, she said a cordial hello to Michael Brown, who glared at her from the far side of the table, and Charlie Waters, who was buried in his phone. Campbell breezed in moments after she was seated. She wondered if he had a camera in the conference room, allowing him to see when everyone was gathered and ready for him, and self-consciously pushed a loose strand of her long blond hair behind her ear.

"So," Campbell said. "We're all in receipt of the Simon indictment. Correct?"

A chorus of nods.

"Ms. Wilson, I appreciate your patience as this matter worked itself out. Can you start back today, or do you need the evening?"

"Start back, sir?" Mack exhaled shakily. She felt like she must have missed some crucial piece of what Campbell had said.

"Yes," Campbell said. "In your absence, Mr. Brown was fulfilling the Community Liaison's duties. Now that you're back, you'll resume them. I believe Mr. Brown had a busy afternoon scheduled today and a full day tomorrow. If you're able to take this afternoon's commitments, I know Mr. Brown will be happy to get back to his own position. If, however, you need a little more time to prepare, he can cover those meetings set for this afternoon and give you the calendar for tomorrow."

Michael glowered on the other side of the table, but Campbell appeared not to notice.

"There's no reason for Ms. Wilson to take over so quickly, sir," Michael said. "I can continue to handle both positions through the end of the week. Give her time to ease back into getting up every morning."

Mack knew she needed to tread carefully. "As you all can see," she said, then paused, suddenly aware that no one was looking at her. Charlie was still busy with his phone, Michael was watching Campbell, and Campbell was staring into the middle space with a perfect expression of a politician's casual disinterest. "As you all can see, I'm here and ready to go. I can absolutely take this afternoon off Mr. Brown's hands and let him get back to his important work."

Mack couldn't believe she was being put back in the Community Liaison position with no discussion. She had started the day on administrative leave because she was suspected of murder, and now Campbell wanted her to be the public face of the office again? It was as though the last six weeks had never happened. Campbell had based his whole campaign on his tough-on-crime stance—no one was above the law—and this was a good example. No one could argue she'd been given preferential treatment, that was for sure. She wondered if that had been Campbell's game all along—parade her in front of the media as the poster child for equal treatment. She suppressed a shudder at the thought.

"This situation hasn't hit the media," Campbell said. "Outside of this office and the Tucson Police Department, there's no reason for anyone to know that you were on administrative leave at all, let alone the intricacies of why that decision was made. Now that the investigation has reached a satisfactory conclusion, I see no reason to dwell on bad memories."

He stood and left the room, apparently confident that she and Michael would coordinate the transfer of duties. Mack sat back, awestruck. The machine ground on, regardless of the people chewed up by the gears.

Tucson Police Department issued a statement that Ron Simon had been arrested and indicted for the murder of Morgan Packer, a sixteen-year-old who had disappeared from her home some months earlier. Simon was believed to have acted alone. The statement was signed by a commander, not Tucson Police Chief Miguel Corrigan himself, and Mack recognized the name as belonging to one of Campbell's biggest supporters on the force. She wondered whether it was really meant for the media, or just to be filed somewhere in case someone later looked back at the situation and questioned Campbell's choices. The whole thing seemed just a little too carefully orchestrated.

Back in her office, Mack sat and looked at her empty desk. Six weeks away from work, and the only thing she'd missed was a handful of phone calls. Community Liaison wasn't a job that accumulated a lot of paper. Mack glanced around the spacious room. She'd never taken the time to finish unpacking her awards, books, photos, and knickknacks. She'd technically been in the job almost six months—minus her six-week administrative leave—and the office looked as impersonal as it had the day she moved in. Mack had gone to law school to be a sex-crimes prosecutor, and it was the only job she'd ever really seen herself holding. Where did that leave her, if she couldn't have it anymore? Who was Mack, if she wasn't *that* prosecutor?

As she sank deeper into the chair and her thoughts, she was interrupted by her desk phone, its ring overly loud in the silent room. It was Jess, welcoming her back to work and asking her to join a party on the second floor. The Dorothy Johnson homicide trial was set to start the following week, after being continued a second time to accommodate the judge's vacation schedule, so Mack wasn't too late to try it with Jess after all.

She went downstairs, still thinking about her empty office, to find that Jess and lead detective Kimberly Watson had commandeered a conference room. Jess liked being able to visualize a case with large diagrams, photos, and maps. It helped her organize her jury presentation for maximum impact.

"Mackenzie," Kimberly said, shaking Mack's hand with slightly too much force. "Welcome back."

Mack didn't know Kimberly well. They'd never done a trial together, and she wasn't sure the other woman had ever served as case agent. Mack looked at her with a critical eye. African American, mid-forties, average height and weight, overdressed for a casual prep session. Mack worried about her jury appeal. Given the circumstantial nature of the case, they needed the jury to like and believe in them. The defense would almost certainly be one of two things: either Frank didn't know Dorothy at all and the DNA was wrong, or Frank had consensual sexual contact with Dorothy and lied to the cops about it. The easiest reason to explain why someone had lied to the cops was to say they were scared. If Mack were Frank's lawyer, she'd take the second option. Arguing that DNA was wrong was risky. It wasn't 1996 anymore—jurors tended to believe in the science when it was there.

They needed to make Kimberly look as non-threatening as possible. Lose the boxy suit and go with something more feminine. Make her look more like a fourth-grade teacher and less like a career homicide detective. If the jury liked and trusted Kimberly, Jess, and Mack, they'd be more likely to like and trust the case they presented—and convict Frank Jefferson of murder.

Jess was examining the eight-by-ten photos of the crime scene that hung on the room's whiteboard. Mack joined her.

"What are you studying so intently?" she asked. Her friend had barely acknowledged her arrival in the conference room, even though they hadn't seen each other since Mack's reinstatement.

"I had a meeting with defense yesterday to discuss exhibits," Jess said. "And something's up. Noah wants to make sure we're marking all these pictures, and they just seem irrelevant to me. I don't understand what his point is."

Noah Gardener, Frank's attorney, was known for being thorough and thoughtful. If he had a reason to use the images in trial, they needed to figure out what it was. Noah didn't have a reputation for playing games, but he wasn't one to lay out his strategy for the other side. It wouldn't be trial by ambush, but they'd have to figure out his plan if they wanted to stop him from scoring points.

The photos progressed through Dorothy's home from the guest bedroom window—where Frank had presumably entered the house first during the burglary and then during the murder—through to the kitchen, where Dorothy's body lay in a pool of blood.

Jess pointed at two photos of the guest bedroom's window. "Look at these."

Mack looked. "What's on your mind?"

"This one shows cobwebs on the inside of the window. See here?"

Mack saw.

"But on this one, no cobwebs."

Mack stepped closer. "You're right," she said. "Do you think law enforcement wiped the cobwebs away and rephotographed? Maybe while trying to get fingerprints?"

"No," Jess said, opening her laptop. "I think these were taken on different days."

Mack looked over Jess' shoulder. She had two files open—one of photographs from the murder scene, and one of photographs from the burglary scene two weeks earlier. In each investigation, the window in the guest room had been photographed. At the time of the burglary, the window screen was slashed and there was broken glass, but there were no cobwebs. Two weeks later, the screen and glass had been repaired, and the window was covered in webs.

They turned to Kimberly. "Did you notice this?" Jess asked.

She looked at them blankly. "I'm not sure what the issue is. Nobody dusted in the two weeks between pictures."

"The point of entry for both crimes was supposed to be this window, and it's clear that the burglar cut open the screen and busted the glass to let himself in," Jess said. "But two weeks later, the killer didn't disturb the cobwebs, the screen is intact, and the window is latched. No one broke this window to get in and commit the murder."

"What's your point?" Kimberly asked.

The police had been subject to mounting public scrutiny over the previous several years, as incidents of police brutality had become more well publicized. She'd known a lot of cops who'd left the force, overwhelmed by the pressure. Kimberly had stayed, and Mack wanted to believe that meant she was the kind of dedicated investigator that the police force needed to be successful—but she was skeptical. The fact that Kimberly didn't understand the enormity of this issue was deeply concerning. She would need even more preparation than Mack had thought.

"One of two things has to be true," Jess said. She was scrolling through the burglary photos, zooming in on details and peering intently at the screen. "The murderer didn't come in through the window—we know that now—so, either we made some assumptions from the burglary, or it was supposed to *look* like he used the window. Which leaves the question, how did he get in? Were the burglary and the murder related at all, or were we just supposed to think they were? Either way, Noah noticed these photos, and I'd bet my own cash money that he has a plan to deal with them. Whatever he's going to say, we don't have anything to rebut it."

CHAPTER TWENTY-TWO

Mack glanced at her computer's clock. Only an hour until she could head home. An hour was only two thirty-minute blocks of time. Each thirty-minute block was only three ten-minute blocks. Each ten-minute block was only two five-minute blocks. So she just had to make it through two five-minute blocks six times. Easy peasy. She could definitely manage not to fall asleep in that time. Even doing that math had taken up...two minutes. She groaned.

She had been up late the night before, brainstorming with Jess about those damn cobwebs and trying to revamp their strategy. They couldn't walk into trial and argue that Frank Jefferson had entered Dorothy's home through that window. Noah would disprove it with one photograph, and that would cost them whatever credibility they'd started out with. But there was no sign of forced entry anywhere else in the house, so either Dorothy let him in herself or someone else did. They had checked the photos and confirmed: the Arcadia door to the backyard was locked, and so were all the other windows.

Jess planned to call Eleanor Johnson, Dorothy's daughter, to ask whether it seemed likely that her mother had let a stranger into the house, but they knew the answer to that already. Everything they'd heard about Dorothy was that she was a cautious, security-oriented individual. Definitely not the type to admit a stranger, especially not a big young guy like Frank Jefferson. Had Frank posed as a repairman? Dorothy might have told Eleanor if she was expecting someone.

Mack hated scrambling this close to trial. This felt like something Kimberly should have checked on early in the investigation, not an issue they had to fix in the hours before jury selection.

She looked up to find Charlie Waters standing in her doorway. The office's lanky public information officer looked permanently rumpled, and that afternoon was no exception. His khakis and short-sleeved plaid shirt needed ironing, and his hair desperately needed a comb. Mack smiled, happy to see a friendly face, but the smile faded when she noted Charlie's anxiety.

"I don't want you to freak out," Charlie said, coming into the office. "It's probably nothing."

"What a terrible way to start a conversation," Mack said.

Charlie threw himself into one of the visitor chairs. "Sorry. It's been a hell of a day. Unfortunately, you're going to hear about this sooner or later, and all signs point to sooner. The office has received a public-records request from KGUN."

"What are they looking for?"

"They're looking for stuff about you, Mack."

KGUN, an ABC affiliate, was known for its hard-hitting investigations into local government agencies. Mack felt her stomach drop. A public-records request on a case was one thing. A public-records request on *her* was something else entirely. She cleared her throat. "What about me?"

Charlie ran his hands through his hair, causing it to stick out even more.

"It's really broad. The impression I get is they're looking for any misconduct across your whole career. They want the normal stuff, like your personnel file, any disciplinary records, and so on, but—"

"There isn't anything to find," Mack interrupted. "I mean, the admin leave thing got expunged, right? When I was reinstated? And I've never been in any kind of trouble at all before that."

Charlie gestured vaguely. "It doesn't get expunged, per se. It's still in your record, along with a copy of the press release formally saying you're not a person of interest and the memo explaining that you were being returned to work because the allegations against you were not proven. But that's not all they're looking for. They want to read all your emails, any documents you've generated that aren't work product, any presentations you've made for trainings you've given. Basically, anything that contains your thoughts or words, they want to see. It's going to take thousands of man-hours to excise work product, and they want us to comply by next week. Impossible, but we'll have to do the best we can. Is there anything I should know about? Do you know what they're looking for?"

Mack blushed and tried to control her breathing as she thought about her illicit involvement in the investigation into Morgan's murder. Her romantic relationship with an expert witness contracted with her office. The off-color emails she'd been known to exchange during trials in an attempt to blow off steam. Any of those things could be the basis for the request, and any of them would result not just in bad press for her but bad press for the office. She was on thin ice with Campbell already—she couldn't afford another misstep.

She swallowed hard. "Can't think of anything," she said, making eye contact with Charlie and hoping he'd believe her. If it was any of those things, though, how would KGUN have found out? Someone must have leaked something.

It came to her in a flash. Michael Brown. Almost had to be. He'd been angry in the meeting when Campbell had reinstated her, but she hadn't thought much about it. Michael was almost always angry. She was sure he would relish any opportunity to get her in hot water.

Charlie tipped his head back, looking at the ceiling. "A friend of mine over at KGUN says they already have enough to run a story, but he wouldn't tell me what the story is. You and Jess Lafayette are about to start trial, right? On that old lady who got murdered?"

"Jury selection starts tomorrow. Do you know when the story is coming out?"

"I'm not sure," Charlie said. "But I bet it's soon, or he wouldn't have called. This is really bad timing, Mack."

"Is there any way we can get a look at the story? I mean, if they're just rehashing Benjamin Allen, that wouldn't be so terrible. Invasive, but comparatively speaking, not so bad."

"I can try," Charlie said, standing. "But no promises. You may want to step aside from this trial, though. Whatever story they're going to run, it's not going to be complimentary. Not to put too fine a point on it," he said, looking at her unopened boxes. "But I wouldn't start unpacking just yet."

Mack followed Charlie out of her office. He turned right, toward Campbell and Michael Brown, and Mack turned left, toward the elevators and Jess.

She found her friend hunched over her laptop, squinting at the screen.

"You may want to consider actually wearing your glasses," Mack said as she sat down.

Jess glanced up, distracted. "Hmm? Oh, I forgot them at home this morning." The brunette finished typing. "You look...kind of green, Mackenzie. What's going on?"

Mack explained.

Jess whistled. "You just can't catch a break, can you?"

"That's an understatement. I think I should back out of the Jefferson trial. I don't want whatever shitstorm is heading my way to interfere. Dorothy deserves your full attention, and you deserve a second chair you can count on to remain employed."

"Absolutely not," Jess said. "You do not have my permission to back out of this case, Mack. I didn't ask you to second chair me because we're pals, or because you need trial practice and I'm giving you a grand opportunity. I asked you because I need someone I can count on, someone who will ride into battle beside me. If we go down, we're going down together, and it won't be because some jackass at KGUN decided to get page views. Jury selection's tomorrow morning, so why don't you go home, get some sleep, and gear up. We've got justice to do."

CHAPTER TWENTY-THREE

Despite the complex nature of the charges and the emotional component attached to any homicide, the facts of Dorothy Johnson's murder were simple. Jess expected their presentation to take only five days. Other than Jefferson's girlfriend, who was expected to give him an alibi, and, unusually, Jefferson himself, no one would be testifying for the defense. Because the trial was anticipated to last only two weeks, tops, picking a jury was easier than it would have been otherwise, and they had fourteen jurors—twelve to deliberate plus two alternates—seated before four on the second day of jury selection. Judge Haberfeld agreed not to impanel them until the following morning, in case someone decided overnight to make up an excuse to avoid participation.

That delay, which some might have called overly cautious on the judge's part, paid off when KGUN's first story went live at six a.m. It was a three-minute segment. Reporter Dan Petrou started with Mack's demotion to Community Liaison following bad decision-making in a high-profile case the year before, then segued into her being put on admin leave when she was named as a person of interest in a homicide case. The main thrust of the story wasn't even about Mack, really, it was a hit job on Campbell for employing a rogue prosecutor, and a challenge to his ability to keep the community safe if he couldn't even protect people from his own subordinates.

It was mortifying, listening to reporter Petrou question Mack's judgment and integrity over footage from the Andersen trial. The worst part was the tag at the end of the clip. "We've uncovered," Petrou said, in his best news voice, "that these are not the only examples of Wilson's unethical and, frankly, appalling behavior. Tune in to the next two installments in this series, coming soon."

Mack clicked off the television. She had been making oatmeal when she turned it on, but now she'd lost her appetite.

The texts, calls, and emails poured in, and Mack finally turned off her personal phone against the onslaught. She had no answers to the questions her friends, family, and other journalists were asking. Mack knew that her mom had a news alert set up for her name, but it was still disconcerting that she knew about the story instantly from her condo two thousand miles away. Her offer to fly to Tucson, though sweet, was overwhelming. The last thing Mack needed was to have to entertain her mother while starting the Jefferson trial and simultaneously dealing with the fallout from Petrou's report.

Rocky's text was more practical than emotional. It just said that, if Mack wanted to talk, she knew where to find her. A kind offer, but one Mack would never accept. If she needed someone to talk to, Jess would be her only option.

Mack wondered if Anna had been watching, or if she'd gone on her normal morning run instead. If Anna had seen the story, she might call, but she might not, and Mack wasn't sure which would be worse. She assumed that their relationship—such as it was—might well form the basis for one of the later segments Petrou had promised. She couldn't decide whether to be grateful or disappointed when her missed calls didn't show Anna among them.

Before the bailiff brought the jury into the courtroom, Judge Haberfeld called Jess, Mack, and Noah into her chambers. The judge, known for her short temper and dislike of surprises, was fuming, and Mack couldn't blame her.

"Did you know this was coming, Ms. Wilson?"

"Not exactly, Judge. I was informed by my office that a public-records request was in the works, but we did not know the content of the story or that it would be released so soon. If I had known, I would of course have informed the court."

That was not the flat "no" that Judge Haberfeld was looking for, and she ignored Mack's attempts to explain further. Jess shot her a glance filled with sympathy and a warning, so Mack sat back, defeated, and let the judge's admonishments roll over her without resisting. Judge Haberfeld had moved to Tucson from Boston in her twenties, decades ago, and Mack usually enjoyed listening to her Brahmin accent. It was different when she was the subject of the judge's wrath, though.

They agreed that the best course of action would be for Judge Haberfeld to ask the jurors if any of them had seen the news that morning. If they had, and could agree to put aside what they'd seen, they could stay. If any of them indicated that they couldn't put it aside, the judge and lawyers would reconvene and decide how to move forward.

Four jurors had seen the story.

"I just don't think I can ignore it," said Juror Six, an older white man who had seemed to want out of jury service the day before, though without success. "I'm not sure this woman should be a lawyer at all, let alone on a murder case. It makes me question the State's whole case, and I haven't even seen any of it yet!"

Two other jurors agreed with Juror Six. They'd found the segment damning and couldn't promise not to hold it against Mack, Jess, or the State's case. The three of them were thanked for their time and released, and the judge and lawyers reconvened. Since the jury hadn't been impaneled, no mistrial was necessary. They just needed to pull a new jury panel and they could start over like the previous two days had never happened.

"Although," Judge Haberfeld said dryly. "I think I'm going to start with Ms. Wilson's recent media appearance. Maybe we can save some time by dealing with it up front."

The lawyers agreed.

At the lunch break, Mack found an email from Michael Brown waiting for her. Campbell wanted to see her, immediately if not sooner. She went from the courtroom directly to the executive suite, where she found the district attorney walking the hall and eating dry-roasted peanuts.

"You wanted to see me, sir?"

Campbell barely looked at her, just gestured for her to walk with him into his office. They sat at a small round table. Mack glanced around, nervous. Neither Charlie nor Michael was present. She'd never had a one-on-one conversation with Campbell, and she wasn't anxious for this to be their first. When he spoke, the fury in his voice was barely contained.

"I assume you saw the news this morning?"

"Yes, sir."

"So did most of the rest of the city. Charlie has been fielding requests for comment from news outlets here and up in Phoenix. There is a petition circulating—and doing quite well, from what I hear—calling for you to resign, and another calling for me to fire you. Why don't you explain, from your perspective, why neither of those outcomes would be appropriate."

She was stunned. A petition calling for him to fire her? Based on a story that promised to be the least bad of a three-part series? She swallowed hard. "Well, sir, the thing about the Andersen trial is just wrong. I mean, Ms. Lafayette had to do closing arguments because I was attacked by Benjamin Allen. But I didn't make any bad decisions, and we convicted him. Everyone seems to forget about the part where he'll spend the rest of his life in prison."

She leaned forward and put her elbows on the table.

"I wasn't demoted—at least, I don't think I was. I guess you'll have to address that, really. And I had no control over being named a person of interest in the Morgan Packer case, nor being put on admin leave. If you'll recall, sir, I fought pretty hard to convince you not to do that, but you made the decision you thought was right at the time. Just like you made the decision you thought was right by bringing me back. You're the elected official—that's your job. If I resign, or you fire me, we'll be adding fuel to the fire. I didn't do anything wrong. I'm a victim of circumstance."

"My Community Liaison was a suspect in a homicide," Campbell said, the words coming out clipped and harsh. "You think that makes you a *victim*?"

"In this case, I absolutely do. Giving them what they want will just make *you* look bad. You have to commit to supporting me, sir, or the media will have a field day. Your administration might never recover. If you make a strong statement, though, calling this attack unfounded victim-blaming, you'll come out looking like an advocate for female attorneys and victims both."

Campbell sat back in his chair and grabbed another handful of peanuts from the open can on the table. He studied Mack carefully. She saw the faintest hint of hesitation in his eyes, but whatever he was about to say was interrupted by Michael Brown hurrying into the office.

"I have your statement ready, Mr. Campbell," he said, sliding a piece of paper onto the table. "It just needs your approval. Ms. Wilson will be boxed and walked, and you can assure the public as to the integrity of your leadership."

Mack started to protest, but Campbell raised a hand, quieting them both. "Ms. Wilson has suggested an alternate approach," he said, looking at Michael. "She thinks I should support her and issue a statement denouncing the story."

"With all due respect, sir," Michael said. "I urge you to rethink that. What if the next story talks about how Ms. Wilson threw up at the police station when she was interviewed? It'll be easy for Petrovich."

"Petrou," Mack corrected.

"Whatever. It'd be easy to spin that into consciousness of guilt."

Mack looked at Michael intently. How did he know she'd thrown up? He shouldn't have been able to watch the video of her interview. It wouldn't have been included with the discovery packet Dave sent to the office after Simon was arrested, because it wasn't relevant. If everyone whose card was found in the wallet of a murder victim got interviewed, there would be hundreds of hours of irrelevant videos to go through. The only reason her name had come up in the first place was bad luck and some police officers who didn't like her. Someone must have told Michael about her yarfing. Probably the same person who told him she'd been interviewed in the first place, which is how Campbell found out about it.

Mack considered what it must be like to be Michael, a prosecutor who had gone his whole career without ever trying a case. Although he held a high-ranking position in the office, he must have known that people talked about him behind his back. It couldn't feel good, being whispered about. Disliked. Laughed at. And then, of course, there was the time, years earlier, when he'd asked Mack out and she'd turned him down flat. Mack wondered if he still carried a grudge about that. Maybe he saw an opportunity for a taste of revenge. Whatever. Her suspicion that Michael had been the KGUN leak was stronger now, but she still lacked proof.

She debated her options. She could call Michael out, notify Campbell that his toady was making independent moves, or she could save her suspicions for later. It sounded like she might be able to save her job without playing that card. Michael needed to know that she knew, but maybe she could get some *quid pro quo* later if she kept quiet now.

"Sir," she said, thinking through her strategy as she started talking, "I think Mr. Brown and I are coming from the same place. We both want what's best for the administration and the office. If you fire me, or if I quit in lieu of termination, the media will never forget it. You'll go down in history as the district attorney who let a murder suspect off admin leave and only fired her when the media demanded it. You'll be like Nixon—they'll never stop asking you what you knew and when you knew it. But if you go the other way—ask Chief Corrigan to issue a public apology to me, and you issue a statement affirming that there is no evidence to suggest wrongdoing on my part and that Ron Simon is in custody for this murder—I think it could wind up being the smartest political move of your career."

Campbell swallowed the rest of his peanuts. He got up and returned to his desk. "I have some calls to make. Mike, do you understand the revised statement I want you to draft?"

Michael looked at Mack, his mouth agape. She smiled broadly, winked, and sauntered toward the office door. Underneath that performance, though, her legs felt weak, and she concentrated on not falling off her heels. "Oh, he understands perfectly," she said, tossing her hair as she headed back to the courtroom.

CHAPTER TWENTY-FOUR

Jury selection took the rest of Monday and all of Tuesday. They started with a brand-new group of one hundred members of the Tucson community, all bright-eyed and eager to get out of jury duty by any means necessary. By the end of Tuesday, though, they had whittled the group down to the fourteen who would hear the State's case against Frank Jefferson. Judge Haberfeld thoroughly questioned the panel during *voir dire* on the issue of the article about Mack, and she was satisfied that the jurors they sat had either not seen the piece or wouldn't consider it.

The clerk called the numbers of the final jurors, and they took their seats as Mack and Jess looked on in dismay.

"I thought we agreed to strike that one," Mack whispered, watching a young Hispanic woman cross the box and take her seat. "She's got major issues with the court system."

Jess adjusted the collar of her chocolate-brown suit. "Too many other weirdos," she whispered back. "We couldn't cut everyone. At least this one seems willing to listen, which is more than I could say for the guy whose son was 'wrongfully convicted' of rape."

Wednesday morning was opening statements. Jess, still focused on how to deal with the cobwebs and the questions they raised, let Mack open. Mack had probably done a hundred opening statements for felonies and misdemeanor DUI cases, but she was nervous as she listened to Judge Haberfeld read her opening instructions.

She pressed her toes into the floor, imagined the soles of her shoes melting through the carpet, and pinched the skin between her left thumb and index finger. An old mentor had taught her these tricks as ways of focusing during times of high stress.

Some of it was the same nervousness she felt before every opportunity to address a jury—that never went away—but there was more to it than that. Between the length of the Andersen trial, her new position, and the two different leaves she'd taken and been put on, Mack hadn't done an opening in almost a year. She felt rusty and hoped the cliché comparing trials to the riding of bicycles was true. Plus, this was her first homicide trial ever, and she was trying it with Jess.

She loved doing trials with her best friend. They had a rapport that made it easy to communicate, and they never had the misunderstandings she experienced with most other prosecutors. Even when they didn't agree about strategy—whether macro or micro—they respected and trusted each other. That respect was a double-edged sword, though. The stakes felt higher. It was even more important to get it right, since, if Mack failed, Jess would be there to see it.

Mack stood in front of the jury and took a deep breath. "Dorothy Johnson loved bingo, her children, and gardening." She was pleased to hear that her voice didn't shake. "Dorothy was eighty-five, but she lived alone, drove herself to bingo, and didn't rely on anyone for help. Dorothy was vibrant and loving and had a great sense of humor." A formal portrait of Dorothy was projected on the screen, and Mack noticed that several jurors were looking at the photo instead of watching her speak. That was fine with Mack, since the more attached they got to Dorothy's kindly face, the harder they'd be hit by the crime-scene photos depicting her brutalized body. Mack hit the button on the computer remote, and the image changed.

"The evidence will show that the defendant in this case murdered Dorothy in cold blood, and that's why you're here today."

Mack avoided the burglary altogether and limited herself to a brief description of the murder and the evidence linking Jefferson to it. "So that's why, when Ms. Lafayette comes back before you in closing arguments, she will ask you to find the defendant guilty of these crimes. Thank you."

Mack sat beside Jess, feeling relieved. She hadn't misstated anything. Hadn't promised anything they couldn't deliver. Her palms were sweaty, and she was thirsty. She checked her watch—it had taken her just under fifteen minutes to summarize the case. Not bad for her first opening statement in a year.

Noah's opening, however, made Mack's look long.

"Thank you for being here, ladies and gentlemen." Noah's white shirt was fraying at the collar, and the elbows of his navy pinstripe suit were shiny with wear. Mack wondered if the outfit choice was intentional, designed to elicit sympathy from the jury. She'd seen that approach before—defense attorneys who wore a Rolex every day, except in trial, when they proudly sported an old Timex. She'd heard rumors that Noah had family money, but she never knew for sure which public defenders were there out of a genuine passion for justice and which just needed to make a living. "You are serving your community by being here today, and so, although I know not all of you are excited to be with us, we're happy you're here.

"So far, you haven't heard any evidence. Nothing Ms. Wilson just said to you is evidence, and nothing I'm saying now is evidence. Even so, the government didn't tell you the whole story."

No argument there, Mack thought. If she'd told them the whole story, Noah would have objected that she was giving them more than was appropriate.

"What Ms. Wilson didn't tell you is that we're here today because the police didn't really take the time to investigate the victim's death. They just pinned the crime on the first guy they could find—my client, Frank Jefferson. You've already heard some things about Frank that sound bad, but you haven't yet heard that there are explanations for those things. Chief among those explanations is that—as challenging as it may be for you to believe this, given the difference in their ages—Frank had a consensual sexual relationship with the victim and, because of that age discrepancy, was embarrassed to tell the police."

Jess and Mack weren't surprised that that was the defense against the DNA evidence, but Mack hadn't expected Noah to state it so plainly in his opening. It seemed like Jefferson would have to testify in order to present that defense, and it was early for Noah to commit to that.

"The government won't be able to meet its burden of proving Frank's guilt beyond a reasonable doubt. At the end of the trial, when you have heard about the half-hearted investigation and have heard Frank's explanations for the circumstantial evidence against him, I will come before you once more and ask you to acquit my client, Frank Jefferson. He is an innocent man, and the government won't be able to prove otherwise. Thank you."

Then they were off and running, calling a series of police officers and crime-scene techs who had played minor roles in the burglary and murder investigations. Each of them presented a necessary link in the chain of custody and allowed Jess to show the corresponding crime-scene photos to the jury, but there was no emotional content to their testimony, and their evidence wasn't generally very exciting. In Arizona, jurors were permitted to ask questions of the witnesses, a measure that allowed them to follow up on threads of inquiry that the attorneys may have left underexplained or not pursued at all. The jurors had very few questions of these context and technical witnesses.

The emotional content that first week was Dorothy's daughter, Eleanor. Mack and Jess had debated calling her, since they didn't really need her testimony. They could easily have started the case with the welfare check without giving the reason for the check, and they knew how rough testifying could be on family members.

Jess' instinct, though, was that Eleanor would help humanize her mother.

"Would you introduce yourself to the jury, Ms. Johnson?" Jess stood at the corner of the jury box, which would encourage Eleanor to look at the jurors when she answered questions.

"My name is Eleanor Johnson," she said, already starting to cry. "Dorothy Johnson was—is my mother."

Mack kept her eyes on the jury through Jess' direct examination. They weren't taking notes, but they didn't need to. The point of Eleanor's testimony was the emotion behind it.

After establishing the patterns of Dorothy's life and the close relationship between mother and daughter, Jess moved in for the most important segment of Eleanor's testimony. Even if Jefferson did choose to testify, that was still almost two weeks off. In the meantime, Jess wanted to leave the jury with the State's theory of the case.

"After your dad passed, did you ever know your mom to date?"

Eleanor pulled another tissue from the box on the witness stand. She hadn't stopped crying in the forty minutes she'd been testifying, and her nose was red and raw. "Some," she said. She wiped her eyes. "She'd tell me about dates, here and there. No one serious."

"Would she have told you if she was engaged in a romantic relationship or a sexual relationship with a much younger man?"

Eleanor laughed through her tears. "She sure would, but she didn't."

Jess paused. Mack wondered if she was formulating her next question or if the pause was for dramatic effect. "Did your mom ever mention being in a sexual relationship with the defendant in this case?"

Eleanor shook her head decisively. "Absolutely not."

"No further questions," Jess said. "Thank you, Ms. Johnson." She took her seat next to Mack. "That was brutal," she whispered as Noah gathered his papers and approached the podium.

"You did great, though."

Jess half smiled. "*She* did great. I just feel so bad for her."

Noah cleared his throat and shuffled his papers. "Did your mom tell you every time she had sex?" he asked, sounding rushed and unsure of himself.

Mack was shocked that he would take such an aggressive approach so early in his cross. His point was a good one—many parents, maybe even most parents, didn't tell their children about their sex lives—but it seemed to be lost on the jury. Mack counted seven jurors who sat back, arms crossed, and looked disgusted by the question.

By the time they wrapped for the weekend, Mack was feeling pretty good about the state of the case. They were taking the entire next week off, because Judge Haberfeld was taking her daughter to

New England to visit colleges. That would give the jury a total of twelve days to sit with the case as they understood it so far.

Noah had scored some minor points by confusing the issues or distracting from important evidence, but none of them seemed fatal to the State's case. The jurors appeared to understand the story, at least as far as their questions for witnesses indicated. They hadn't yet heard from the most damning witnesses, who would talk about the DNA results and Jefferson's police interview.

Meanwhile, Campbell had issued his statement, fully supporting Mack's denial of the allegations Dan Petrou had leveled against her, and Chief Corrigan had posted on the department website affirming that Ron Simon was in custody for Morgan Packer's murder and was believed to have acted alone. The chief apologized for ever having considered Mack to be a person of interest.

She wondered if any news outlets would find these statements or care about them if they did.

"Come in!" Jess called in response to Mack's knock at her office door. She was at her desk, using a small hand mirror to apply eye shadow.

"Why so fancy?" Mack asked, bemused. In all the time she'd known Jess, she had only seen her wear makeup for an occasional evening out. Never at lunchtime, and never on a weekday. Her friend was naturally very pretty, and the lack of makeup, combined with her freckled face, made her look younger than she was. Mack had long since stopped being annoyed when bartenders carded Jess but not her, despite the fact that Jess was five years older. She was resigned to the fact that her own youth spent disregarding the need for sunscreen had come back to bite her.

"Adam is picking me up for lunch," Jess said. Luckily, her focus on the mirror meant she missed Mack's rolling her eyes. "We're going for Cambodian food!"

"Do you even like Cambodian food?"

Jess finished with the mirror and stashed it and the makeup in her desk drawer. "I've never had it, but I'm excited about trying something new."

Mack suppressed her urge to scowl. She didn't care if Jess adopted a Khmer-noodle-only diet, but she didn't like feeling as if her friend's life was moving forward without her. "How are things going with him these days? Did you ever figure out if he has a license?"

Jess smiled. "Really well. I asked him about it. Turns out, he got a couple parking tickets once upon a time. His brother was supposed to pay them, but he didn't, so his license got suspended. Adam went to get it reinstated, but the fines were so steep he just decided to forget it."

"That makes sense," Mack acknowledged. "I mean, how much could he possibly be making as a forty-year-old bartender at a lesbian bar?"

"I know. It's weird, actually. I never thought I'd date anyone who never went to college, let alone grad school. But here we are, and I really like this guy—love him, maybe, even—and it'd be super shitty to hold his job against him, right?"

"Sure."

"Sure! And he makes good money. Or at least, I think he makes okay money. His house is nice. But does he rent or own? I don't feel like I can ask. I don't want to be the woman who challenges her boyfriend about his job, which he claims to love. He says he's wanted to be a bartender since he watched *Cocktail* as a kid. I actually had a long talk about this with Judge McPhee the other day. Do you know her?"

Everyone knew Helen McPhee. She was the youngest judge in Pima Superior Court history, appointed by the governor at only thirty-two. She had spent thirty years on the bench earning a reputation as a thoughtful yet no-nonsense judicial officer. A hanging judge, with a severe personal style to match. She kept her shoulder-length gray hair in a slicked bun at all times and favored black pantsuits even under her robes. Despite her fearsome public persona, however, she was passionate about supporting women in the law and often initiated mentoring relationships with attorneys who appeared before her.

"I was in chambers talking to her about how I did in a trial before her recently—you know how she likes to do those informal postmortems—and somehow Adam came up. I told her about this socioeconomic hang-up I'm wrestling with, but she was great. She said that when she was young, she dated a guy in construction and she really liked him. Engagement was on the table. But her mentor at the law firm told her she needed to marry another lawyer and apparently pushed it really hard, told her she'd never make partner with this construction guy around her neck like an albatross. So she took the advice, dumped the guy, and married a tax attorney."

Mack blinked. "Um, hasn't she notoriously been divorced and single for like forty years?"

"That's correct. She hated the tax guy, and left him after, like, six months, but construction guy had already moved on."

"Good for him. What was he supposed to do, sit around and wait for her?" Mack thought of Anna. There was no indication that the psychologist would ever call again, but Mack would pick up the phone if she did. She was proud of Judge McPhee's construction guy for being less pathetic than she was. As someone who often thought that she would die alone—and hoped she wouldn't be surrounded by cats when the time came—she understood the judge's point.

On the other hand, the more time Jess spent with Adam—and, by extension, the more time Mack spent with Adam—the more she wondered about the guy. She'd never seen him be anything other than kind, polite, and helpful, but there was something about him that rubbed her the wrong way. Maybe it was just jealousy, possessiveness. Maybe she was worried that Adam might be mooching off her high-performing friend. She didn't like the idea of Jess mother-wifing the guy, doing all the emotional and household labor while he was free to languish in perpetual adolescence. Jess' free time was already more limited, not because Adam forced her to stay home or anything, but because she wanted to spend more time with her boyfriend. All very natural, and yet Mack was uncomfortable with the changes.

"What are you going to do?" Mack asked. She wondered if she should tell Jess about her concerns, but she knew better. Never trash a friend's significant other, and don't even trash a friend's ex unless you're *very* sure the breakup is permanent. She didn't want to be blamed for any discord in Jess' relationship. All she could do was support her friend.

Jess looked at her watch and stood, grabbing her purse, phone, and jacket. "Right now, I'm going to lunch. The rest...I'll figure out another time."

Mack stood, too, and followed her out of the office. "To quote a very wise philosopher, 'If you're good, I'm good.' I support you in whatever you choose. If you two wind up getting married, I'll dance a jig at your wedding. Which I assume he will bartend himself."

Jess laughed, and her eyes softened. Mack worried she was about to cry.

"And if you break up, I'll dance a jig in your living room, just because I know watching me dance makes you laugh. I'll even throw in Elaine's little kicks, from that *Seinfeld* episode. Just for you."

CHAPTER TWENTY-FIVE

Mack glanced around at her spotless living room. She'd done laundry and dishes, vacuumed, and put things away. She'd finished the work she'd brought home for the weekend, and had even gone for a brief hike that morning. Her plan was to fill the evening with reality TV and a take-out burrito. Not for the first time, she thought how nice it would be to have a dog, like Jess did. Someone to share the space with, to greet her at the end of a long day. Anna still hadn't returned her text. She wondered if she was seeing someone else already.

The phone rang. It was Jess, asking if Mack could join her and Adam for dinner. Mack agreed to meet them at Adam's house for grilled shrimp and vegetables. She picked up a salad on her way across town, and was pleasantly surprised when, outside a small stucco house southeast of downtown, her GPS told her she'd arrived.

Jess pulled up behind the Saab and pulled a bag of ice out of her trunk. "Hey!" she called. "Come this way." The two women hugged and Jess led Mack through the RV gate and around the house into the backyard, where Adam was manning the grill and a cooler full of beer was waiting.

"Who else is coming?" Mack asked, eyeing the assortment of snacks and drinks laid out on the patio table.

"It's just us," Adam responded. He handed Mack a Kilt Lifter. It was a warm day for late March, and the bottle was sweating and cold in Mack's hand. Heaven. "I guess we went a little overboard."

"This is our first time hosting anything as a couple," Jess said. "And we actually have some exciting news."

Mack looked at Jess' outstretched hand, confused. "What's the news?"

Jess wiggled her ring finger.

The ring was lovely, with a moderately sized center stone. Bigger than Mack would have expected, frankly. Her heart sank. Of course, she was happy for her friend, but if Jess got married, Mack's social life, such as it was, would disappear. The whole thing felt rushed, and her instinct was to question their motives. She faked a smile.

"Congratulations!" she said brightly, gathering Jess into a tight hug. "You chose a great ring, Adam. How'd you propose?"

As Adam and Jess competed to tell her the story, which appeared to involve a hike with Jess' dog Shirley, Mack zoned out. She'd always thought that proposal stories were kind of dumb, and Jess used to agree with her. They joked that bragging about how you got engaged was a sure sign of having nothing more interesting to say. And now here she was, gushing over a ring given to her by a man she thought was a liar. Mack wondered if there was a way to wrangle a look in the garage. She wanted to see if Adam had a car.

The couple beamed at her from across the table, and Mack took a long, long drink of her beer.

"So your engagement party is…me?" Mack asked.

Jess laughed. "No, we just felt like having you over for dinner. We'll do a big engagement shindig another time."

"Oh." Mack started picking at the label on the beer bottle.

"Actually…" Jess said, after the silence had stretched long enough to be awkward. "Adam has something he wants to ask you."

Mack turned to face him.

"Sabrina Fisher," he said. "I used to live around the corner from her. Back when she died. I told Jess about it when we started dating, and she said you were the prosecutor assigned to the investigation. Did they ever figure out who killed her?"

Mack sipped her beer. "It's still a cold case, but I was the on-call attorney, went to the scene, so it's mine. No suspects."

Adam shuddered. "How terrible. I knew her a little, just from walking around the neighborhood. I'd see her on her bike sometimes. Wave to her mom. You know, neighbor stuff. When she went missing, the police canvassed the block to see if anyone knew anything. It was super creepy. I stopped walking that way, and actually wound up moving soon after. Not because of what happened, but I just changed jobs. But I never stopped thinking about her."

"Your case got him into true crime, and that's what he and I bonded over when we first started dating! So really, you're kind of responsible for our relationship. Crazy!"

Adam was saying all the right words. His story was common—Mack had talked to dozens of people with similar experiences. A crime close to home had gotten them interested in crime more broadly.

"Yeah," Mack said. The last sip of beer was sour in her mouth. "Crazy."

A timer rang, letting Adam know to take the corn off the grill. He and Jess carried platters to the patio table.

"Hey, Adam," Mack said. "Did you ever connect with Dave Barton? Not that it really matters anymore, I'm just curious."

Adam, sitting next to Jess on the other side of the table, sipped his water. "I left a couple messages, but he never called back. Must not have been so important after all."

Jess shrugged. She was playing with the short curls in the back of Adam's hair and looking at him adoringly. "Once Simon was arrested and you were reinstated, I'm sure Dave got busy on other cases. I asked Adam if he remembered anything, anyway, and he said he didn't. Right, babe?"

Mack thought Adam looked uncomfortable, but she didn't like PDA either.

"You know Paradise," he said. "The nights all run together. It's always a treat to see you, Mack, but I don't remember any particular times. And Jess showed me a picture of the girl, but I didn't recognize her. Customers don't really stand out unless they're a regular or they give me some huge tip or something."

Mack finished her beer and reached for a fresh one. "Well, that ties up that loose end. Excellent. If I think of it, I'll tell Dave when I next talk to him, and he'll call you back if he wants to get it firsthand."

Dinner was nice. They found an easy rhythm of Jess and Mack trading work stories, each trying to top the other and make Adam laugh. He seemed happy to serve as their audience, and Mack shook off the funk she'd been in earlier.

Maybe if she put herself out there and started dating, she might meet someone, too. Once again, images of double dates flashed through her mind. Instead of Anna, though, the face beside hers was blurry.

What was she looking for? Someone smart, funny, attractive… The same things everyone looked for. She finished her beer and saw that Jess and Adam were looking at her expectantly.

"Hmm?" she asked.

"Adam just asked you about our honeymoon, Sparky. I'm pushing for Bora Bora, but he thinks Caribbean. What do you think?"

Mack didn't want to vote. It was time to go home.

CHAPTER TWENTY-SIX

Mack was surprised by the second story in Dan Petrou's series. He clearly had a source in the office; Mack was still inclined to think it was Michael Brown, but still couldn't prove it.

The good news was, Mack wasn't the focus this time. Petrou was attacking the office, including Campbell, for failing to protect Benjamin Allen. If a security detail had been assigned to Mack, Allen's attack on her couldn't have happened. If he hadn't attacked her, he wouldn't have been in jail. If he hadn't been in jail, he wouldn't have been stabbed through the eye with a pencil and killed by his cellmate. Now, the cellie was facing murder charges and Allen's family was without their loved one, all because the Tucson District Attorney's Office hadn't taken the threats against Mack seriously.

Mack focused on her breathing, biting the inside of her cheek as she read the article a second time. She wanted to be sure she fully understood its implications. She knew that Campbell's support was as thin as a razor's edge, and this attack on his leadership wouldn't help matters. In fact, a security detail had been offered, but Mack had refused it. She wondered if that was documented anywhere.

If it was, its release could help repair any damage done to her relationship with Campbell. He could retreat behind her refusal. Mack hesitated. Even if there was such documentation, she wasn't sure she could do anything about the jail side of the article. Allen's cellmate did not have a history of violence or mental illness. There probably wasn't anything anyone could have done to predict the dangerous consequence of letting him have a pencil.

She sent Charlie a quick email, asking if the office wanted to respond to the article and if she would be permitted to issue her own statement. She also pointed out she had declined a protective detail, and that she hoped there would be an email documenting that somewhere.

Her phone rang almost immediately, and she was surprised to see Charlie's name on the screen.

"What we're not doing, Mack," he said, "is sending emails about this."

She cringed. "Sorry."

"It's okay," Charlie said. "Just, you know, we can't be too careful about generating paper that could be subject to a records request. I've got half a dozen people still trying to comply with the first one. We don't need to add to that burden."

Mack rubbed the back of her neck. She couldn't even imagine how many documents had to be reviewed—emails, sure, but also the contents of paper files that sometimes took up multiple bankers' boxes for a single case, not to mention her annual evaluations, minutes of meetings she'd attended, and who knew what else. It seemed like anything that had ever included her name was subject to the original request. It had taken her almost eight years on the job to generate all those records, and the expectation was that they would be fully reviewed within six months. She cleared her throat. "So you got my email about Campbell's statement? Is there something I should be doing?"

"I did. You're staying in the Community Liaison slot, although I think we'll all breathe a sigh of relief when the year is up and you can shuffle off back to a caseload and out of the executive suite."

Mack laughed, grateful for Charlie's sense of humor in a difficult time.

"As far as you're concerned," Charlie continued, "you're basically three monkeys. You hear no evil, you see no evil, and you certainly say nothing at all. Just keep your head down. Do your meetings, lead your trainings, and win your trial. Eventually, this will all blow over. The last thing you want to do is bring attention to yourself. That was a good idea about documenting the thing with the security detail, but even that I'm going to leave alone. Has Petrou contacted you directly?"

"No," Mack said. "Not a word. Which I think is kind of weird, right? Shouldn't he be giving me a chance to respond?"

"Maybe in the old days. Now, though, if you want to clarify the record, you have to reach out yourself. Journalism is changing, Mack, just like everything else. Plus, Petrou has always had a strained relationship with law enforcement anyway."

"Yeah, but you know if his house got burglarized, he'd be on the phone to the cops in a heartbeat."

Charlie laughed. "But of course. Eyes on the prize, Mack. You'll get through this."

Mack hung up and slumped back in her chair. Petrou had promised three stories. All things considered, the first two hadn't been that bad. Her eyes were dry and she had a throbbing headache. She wondered what surprises waited for them in the third one.

CHAPTER TWENTY-SEVEN

Long breaks during trial were a mixed bag. On the one hand, when Mack was carrying a full trial caseload, going dark gave her the opportunity to catch up on other matters: call other victims, check with detectives and the crime lab, respond to emails and calls from defense attorneys convinced that their clients deserved all of Mack's attention. On the other hand, now that she *wasn't* carrying a caseload, an open week stretched before her like a boring desert road. She tried to pack the days with public-safety trainings and other Community Liaison tasks, but that still left her with almost six hours with nothing to do.

Mack didn't do well with downtime. She'd already drafted and deleted three separate emails to Anna. The first was angry, raging against the psychologist for abandoning her in her time of need. She deleted that one because it included way too many obscenities. The second was pathetic, questioning why she meant so little to Anna that the other woman could leave without looking back. She deleted that one, too, because…ew. The third was Mack's favorite, and she hesitated before deleting that one. It was the most rational of the three, simply explaining why Mack was so hurt by Anna's actions and expressing a desire—mostly sincere—to rekindle their friendship. In order for that to happen, she wrote, Anna would need to apologize and explain why she had disappeared.

But, as she was about to click send at last, she realized that she wasn't ready for an apology and she didn't care about Anna's explanation. She just wanted to erase the last two months, and the sending of an adult email wasn't going to erase anything.

Actually, if she was being honest, she wanted to erase the last fourteen months. She wanted to go back in time, back to when she'd offered to take the Benjamin Allen case, and slap the file right out of that-Mack's hands. If she hadn't taken that fucking case, she'd still be working in Sex Crimes instead of the executive suite. She'd be preparing for a marathon instead of struggling through a three-mile run. There'd be no KGUN exposé. She might even still be dating Anna.

Restless, Mack crossed her office to the stack of boxes she still hadn't unpacked. She lifted the lid of the one on top and found the pile of photographs of trial victims that had been hanging in her previous office. She closed the lid. She didn't want to hang them here, down the hall from Campbell's office. She had looked to these photos when she needed inspiration on her darkest days— they were proof that she was doing the right thing, that she could get justice for victims, even in the hardest cases. It felt disingenuous to hang them here, where her darkest day was one in which she stumbled over her words in a speech at an old folks' home. She shouldn't need help getting through those days.

Mack couldn't face digging past the photos to see what else was in the box. Her statute books could wait. It wasn't like she needed them in the community liaison job anyway. Knowledge of the law wasn't a requirement for this position, which could easily be done by a non-lawyer. No one who came to this office would be impressed by her awards or degrees, which were also somewhere in that stack of boxes. She hardly spent any time there herself. She wanted to keep the office as blank as possible. She would be out of it in six months. No need to get comfortable.

She walked back to the window and leaned her forehead against its cool glass. She wondered what was going on with the Morgan Packer case. Ron Simon hadn't been in the system long enough for anything of substance to have happened, but there might be progress with Jeffrey Mayer. It would be easy to log into the file-management system and check Nan's notes. Wouldn't even take five minutes, and she'd have an up-to-date status report. She could check both cases while she was in there.

She wondered how Fern and Robin were doing, hoped they were getting some counseling. The guilt they felt had been palpable during Mack's time in Fern's home, and maybe a professional could help them move forward. If they were seeing someone, they might have told their assigned victim advocate, and the advocate would have entered it into the system. So, really, she could just check if there was a note about counseling, and then anything else she happened to see would be a bonus.

She stopped, her hand hovering over her mouse, realizing that this wasn't really about Fern and Robin. It was about her own boredom. She couldn't put the cases against Mayer or Simon at risk—she'd already done enough by her involvement in the investigation. She'd spent her whole career trusting the system, and she had to trust it now. Fern and Robin would get justice, and hopefully that would be enough to bring them peace.

She left the office. A Diet Coke would be enough of a distraction for now.

CHAPTER TWENTY-EIGHT

Ideally, Mack and Jess prepped their witnesses before jury selection started. That way, if there was an issue, it could be dealt with before everyone had wasted time picking a jury and double jeopardy had attached. They'd never talked about that preference, just always did it that way.

Unfortunately, conditions were rarely ideal, and the Jefferson trial certainly wasn't. Wendy Orr, the DNA analyst, was out on maternity leave until they were already in trial—they hadn't yet talked to her. Jess could direct DNA-analyst testimony in her sleep, but she knew that Wendy had never testified before, and Jess regretted not prioritizing a pre-trial meeting with her despite her leave. The analyst seemed hesitant to testify, and Mack couldn't tell if it was from her lack of courtroom experience or some other reason.

They scheduled a meeting for Friday afternoon. Although the trial had gone smoothly so far, DNA would be the key to proving Jefferson had been present at the crime scene and committed the murder. Without solid testimony from Wendy, the jury would be left confused, and a confused jury was a jury that acquitted. Jess' anxiety was high, and that was making Mack nervous as well.

Wendy explained the evidence to Mack and Jess the way she would explain it to the jury. Despite Mack's best efforts to pay attention, the information was as tedious as it always was. DNA evidence was highly technical, and analysts were only willing to go so far. It was always up to the lawyers to really translate it into understandable terms in their closing arguments.

There were two important areas of Dorothy's body where DNA had been found. There was the vaginal swab, which contained one profile, a match to Frank Jefferson. They could definitely prove that Jefferson had engaged in sexual contact with Dorothy, which—despite Noah's opening—Jefferson had denied in his police interview. Given his denials and Dorothy's daughter's testimony that her mom had not been sexually active, they had a solid case for Jefferson raping Dorothy. If they could convince the jury that rape equaled murder, they were golden.

The second swab, however, was troubling. It was a breast swab with saliva. The sample contained a mix of two profiles, belonging to Jefferson and an unidentified male. When Jess first got the DNA results, she had assumed that the second profile had some innocent explanation. Perhaps it was secondary transfer from Jefferson, or maybe even contamination on scene from a cop or paramedic. Whatever the explanation was, she needed Wendy to be able to explain it to the jury in a way that wouldn't allow Noah to wiggle Jefferson off the hook. Jess was afraid Noah might be able to win a not guilty verdict based on the extraneous DNA.

Jess had discussed her theory with Wendy months before trial, and the analyst had seemed to agree with her. Now, however, Wendy was waffling.

"There's just no way to guarantee an innocent explanation," she said.

Jess played with her pen, frustrated.

Mack studied Wendy across the table, as the analyst pulled her long, frizzy brown hair back. They had been sitting together for almost an hour, and Mack wasn't sure she'd be able to pick the other woman out of a lineup. She looked like every new mom— exhausted, barely holding it together—from her hair to her outfit, a long-sleeved black jersey dress with a spit-up stain on the shoulder. Mack wondered how the jury would feel about her. They'd seated two young women, and she thought they were both moms. If Wendy testified that she'd just come back from FMLA, that might endear her to them. Hopefully, even the older jurors would remember what it was like when they were new parents and cut her some slack. Maybe they could even use her nerves in their favor—have her testify that she was worried about being out of phone reach in case something happened with the baby. Mack made a note to discuss that possibility with Jess later and tuned back in to what Wendy was saying.

"There is something interesting, though." She pointed at the chart in front of her, noting the DNA profiles from the saliva on Dorothy's breast. "Isn't it weird that the unidentified profile is really close to the victim's profile?"

Mack squinted. The crime lab made these charts every time a case went to trial, figuring they made the data easier for juries to understand—but that had never been Mack's experience with them. "What do you mean?"

"Look here," Wendy said She pointed at the first column of data. "This is the victim's DNA profile, right?"

Jess and Mack both nodded.

"And here's the exemplar we got from Jefferson via the search warrant, then the first profile from the swab, then the second profile from the swab."

So far, so good.

"Jefferson accounts for the first sample from the swab. See how it's a match at each data point? That's how we know he was one contributor." She covered the second and third columns, leaving only the victim's profile and the unidentified profile visible.

"See how the unidentified profile matches the victim profile at about half the locations? That's really unexpected if the contributor was, say, a paramedic or a cop sweating on the victim's body. It's not a match at every location, and we can see the unidentified contributor is a male, so we know it's not the victim's own DNA, but we'd only expect to see results like this if it was, like, a parent/child or sibling/sibling relationship."

"So maybe that's what happened," Mack said. "Eddie accidentally contaminated the crime scene when he was weeping over his poor dead naked mom."

"Eddie's her son?" Wendy asked. "That could definitely explain it."

Jess pulled a binder of police reports across the table and paged through them. "No, that doesn't make sense. Eddie wasn't there when police were on scene—he said he hadn't been to his mom's house in a week."

"Are you sure?" Wendy asked. "Because that really would be the only way to explain this so the jury would understand. It's the innocent explanation you want, I think."

Mack stared off into the middle space in front of her. Police had considered Eddie as a suspect when his mom was first found. Experience told them that murderers are usually connected to the victim, especially in cases where there's a possible financial motive. Eddie told police in his interview that he was cash-strapped when his mom had been killed, but two weeks later, he was driving a brand-new car. Had the insurance bailed him out of whatever difficulty he was in? Eddie claimed that he hadn't been at his mother's house in over a week, but what evidence did they have for that, really?

Eddie *was* there with Dorothy when she reported the burglary two weeks before her death. He told police she'd probably just misplaced her iPad, and there hadn't really been a burglary at all—which seemed like an odd thing for a man to say about his own mother. By all accounts, Dorothy was pretty with it. She lived alone, still drove, and had an active social life that included playing bingo. Eddie's girlfriend told police that he'd been with her all night before the discovery of his mother's body. Between that alibi and the rape, it had been a no-brainer for Kimberly to put Eddie on the back burner. The level of violence seemed too high for the victim's son to have committed the crime. Then the DNA results came in, hitting on Frank Jefferson, and the police never looked back.

Still, there were those cobwebs. Someone had let Jefferson into the house. It could be that he'd just knocked on the door, and Dorothy had let him in. But Eleanor had testified that her mom was very cautious. She didn't let people in unless she knew them, and there was no evidence to suggest that Dorothy and Jefferson had met before the murder.

Mack flipped through Jess' binder of reports to the fingerprint analysis from the burglary. The window had been wiped clean—no prints on the sill or glass. When police came back for the murder, Dorothy's children had both been fingerprinted, just to rule out their prints from consideration. They visited their mother often, so their prints would be expected to be there. And, in fact, both Eddie and Eleanor's prints were found.

But what if Eddie's alibi didn't hold water? What if he had been at his mother's house the night she was killed? He could have let Jefferson in, either through the Arcadia door or the front door, let Jefferson do the dirty work, and then spit on his mother's body before he let them both out and locked the door behind them.

But how to prove it?

"How long would it take," Mack asked, "if you had a known sample, to compare it to the unidentified? To know for sure if it was the son?"

Wendy chewed on the cuticle of her left thumb. "Is it an emergency? Related to the current case?" She looked worn out. They'd been talking for almost two hours without a break.

"That's exactly what it is," Jess said.

"Probably a couple days. I just need the sample."

They would need to get a DNA sample from Eddie, but they could cross that bridge later. Maybe Eleanor would be willing to help. The more pressing matter was Wendy's testimony. They agreed that, if Jess presented a variety of innocent explanations for the unidentified profile, Wendy would agree that they were possible. That would get them through direct testimony okay, but she couldn't control what the analyst got asked on cross. If Noah asked her whether the unidentified profile could belong to Eddie, she'd have to say yes.

"What if," Jess said later that night as she and Mack finished the salads they'd picked up for dinner on their way to Jess' house, "*this* is the additional investigation Noah was doing back in January?"

They had both changed into yoga pants and T-shirts, eager to leave the work week behind them. Mack was leaning against Jess' kitchen counter looking at her phone, and it took her a second to process the question. "What do you mean? You think he hired a DNA expert and figured out that Eddie might be that unidentified profile?"

"Well," Jess said. "What if he did?"

Mack thought it through. Noah was only required to disclose the name of an expert if it was someone he planned to call to testify. He hadn't disclosed anyone, so there would be no testimony. That meant, at worst, he had hired someone to tell him what questions to ask Wendy. That would have been a shot in the dark, but it might just pay off. Noah certainly wouldn't be the first defense attorney to take a big risk.

"Let's put our defense attorney hats on and play it all the way out," Mack said. "How would he do it? Have Jefferson testify that the sex was consensual, and then Eddie busted in on them?"

"Yes!" Jess said. "Eddie came in and was horrified to see his eighty-five-year-old mom with a thirty-something! He killed Dorothy in a rage. And then…"

"And then," Mack continued. "Jefferson didn't say anything to police because he didn't want to snitch. He has previous experience in the system. Snitching's the worst thing you can do, and he knows it."

They looked at each other with matching shocked expressions.

"Holy shit," Jess said. "I would bet you actual money that's where's Noah's heading. He didn't give notice that he's planning a third-party defense, but he knows no judge would actually keep it out if someone can testify to it."

It all hung together. She didn't believe the story, not for a second, but a jury might. It would take hours to prepare to counter. It was going to be a long weekend.

In the end, Wendy's testimony was anti-climactic, as DNA testimony always is. Jess showed Wendy's chart to the jury, who, if their facial expressions were any indication, couldn't make heads or tails of it. That was okay. Jess would clear it up in closing arguments. By the time Noah was going through the standard cross-examination questions on lab contamination, however, Mack was too bored to pretend to take notes.

She opened her laptop and looked at the to-do list she'd jotted down that morning during Wendy's direct. There wasn't much she could do from here about groceries and she couldn't call her mom, but there was one item she could check off the list.

She was happily browsing away on her favorite underwear website when she felt Jess nudge her in the side.

"What?" she whispered.

"I don't care if you shop online during trial," Jess said, "but *underwear?*"

Mack checked to see if anyone was sitting behind her. No one was. "I need underwear!" she whispered. "It's not, like, sexy panties or anything."

Jess rolled her eyes and pointedly lowered the lid of Mack's laptop without responding.

Wendy's cross didn't appear to have progressed very far. Noah was pushing hard against the results of the vaginal swab, which implicated his client alone. To Mack's surprise, though, he left the mixed profile on the breast swab alone. Maybe it confused him as much as it confused Jess and Mack. The jurors had a few questions, but none about the unidentified profile. Without bringing out that the profile could be Eddie's, Mack wasn't sure how Noah could develop the third-party defense she and Jess had cooked up.

"He'd have to call Jefferson," Jess said. She was thinking out loud during the morning break as they huddled in the attorney room at the back of the courtroom, reassessing after Wendy's unsurprisingly dull testimony. "And then recall Wendy. Maybe that's the plan? Dramatic effect?"

"I think we overthought it," Mack said. "We came up with a better defense than Noah did."

She hated it when she got all worked up about a potential issue which turned out to be nothing. All that wasted cortisol—not to mention the wasted weekend.

The most exciting part of the day happened without Noah or the jurors even noticing. Mack and Jess had discussed how to get Eddie's DNA without alerting him to their interest. They'd noticed that he brought a Starbucks coffee to court every morning. After Wendy's testimony, they had Kimberly impound the empty cup from the trash can where Eddie had dumped it on his way out of the courtroom and rush it to the lab for emergency testing. They hoped the results would be back quickly. Jess had overheard Eddie telling Eleanor that he was heading up to Park City as soon as the trial concluded. If Eddie was involved in his mother's murder, they didn't want the Jefferson trial to conclude without him, and they certainly didn't want him to leave their jurisdiction with questions left unanswered.

CHAPTER TWENTY-NINE

Adam was working that night, so Jess and Mack spent the day doing trial prep, had green curry shrimp from the local Thai place delivered for dinner, then sprawled on Mack's couch to watch an episode of the *The Bachelor*. The doorbell distracted them.

"You expecting anyone?" Jess asked.

None of Mack's friends were the pop-in sort. Even Jess always called first. The only person who had ever come over without calling was Anna, and Mack had finally written off the psychologist. It was time to move on. She'd briefly considered making a new Tinder profile, but thinking back to her experience—a woman whose profile photos had to have been taken at least ten years and forty pounds ago—quickly put the kibosh on that. Still, at least she'd had the thought. If Mack had been seeing a therapist, she was pretty sure that would count as progress.

Through the peephole, she saw Dave on the stoop, bouncing gently on his heels. He was obviously worked up about something as he came into the house.

"Good," he said, nodding at Jess. "I'm glad you're here. Saves me a phone call." The knees of his jeans and his tennis shoes were caked with dirt. Mack cringed as he sat on her couch. "I have bad news, ladies. Potentially very bad news. I came here straight from the crime scene. Northeast of town, in the desert, but not far off the 10. A body."

Mack looked at him, confused. Bodies were found every day. Why should this one be news bad enough to bring Dave to her house after nine on a Saturday night?

Jess cleared her throat. "You're going to need to spell that out for us a little."

Dave stood up and walked to the Arcadia door, peering into the backyard. "She was found in a Rubbermaid tub."

Mack dropped her beer, spilling Orange Blossom across her rug. "*What?*"

"Somebody tried to set her on fire but it didn't catch, so the guy tossed her in the desert in a Rubbermaid bin, same kind as Morgan Packer. Name's Jane Gould. Her purse was in the bin with her. She was a dancer at Bandaids, a strip club up in Phoenix, but was visiting her mom in Tucson. Mom last saw her yesterday evening. Jane was meeting up with some friends but she never came home. We're in the process of tracking the friends and getting her phone records. This is bad, Mack."

"Ron Simon's been in custody since you arrested him a month ago, right? There's no chance he got out?"

"That was my first call, but the jail confirmed he's being held nonbondable," Dave said. "I even had them physically check his cell. He was right where he was supposed to be. The M.O. is too similar to be someone else. So either—"

"Either Simon didn't do it alone, or Simon didn't do it at all," Mack finished. "You're not here to ask me where I was last night, are you?"

Dave rubbed his forehead. "I don't suppose you've got some great alibi?"

"Of course not. I worked late, came home, and went to bed. All of those things I did alone, until Jess got here about ten this morning."

Mack's toes itched, and she flexed them against the floor, feeling the seam of her sock rub uncomfortably. She desperately wanted to get up, grab her keys, and take off. She could be halfway across Texas before anyone noticed she was gone. They'd never catch her.

Mack knew she wouldn't do well in jail, let alone prison. She wasn't even sure she could handle the whispers that would follow this latest news.

So much for Campbell standing by her. She'd be unemployed in record time, and although she lived well within her means, she couldn't afford the house for long without a job. She'd have to move back to Ohio, back with her mother.

She took a long, shaky breath. Then another. After the third, her head was clear. She needed a plan.

"Okay," she said. "Okay. If it wasn't Simon, we need to figure out who killed Morgan and Jane, too. Dave, did you guys ever follow up with the girls down on the Track? Maybe they'll know something, like who Morgan was working with when she disappeared."

"We never got that far. Once we ID'd Morgan, things tumbled loose pretty fast. We knew who her trafficker was, and it seemed like she was advertising on Craigslist, not working the Track."

"Did you ever call Adam back?" Jess asked. "I don't think he has much to offer, but you never know, you know."

"Call Adam back?" Dave asked. "Is that your bartender? I never got a message from him. I've been waiting for him to reach out, but it didn't seem so important once we nailed Simon. Now that Mack might wind up back on the table, though, I definitely want to talk to him."

Jess and Mack exchanged a look. "He said he called and left messages," Mack said.

Dave shook his head.

"Weird," Jess said. "Well, he must have left them on the wrong voice mail or something. I'll remind him and give him your direct line."

"I think the Track is our next step," Mack said. "I can do it. It wouldn't be part of any official investigation anyway. Just because she was soliciting online doesn't mean she wasn't working the old-fashioned way, too. Who else has put it together that Jane and Morgan were killed by the same person? Does everyone know?" She was calculating how much longer she'd have her badge, issued when she was hired to ease her way into crime scenes. She'd never once had to use it, but it might come in handy for the undercover work she was about to undertake. The girls on the Track wouldn't look closely enough to see that she was an attorney, not a cop.

"I'm not sure," Dave said. "There was no overlap between the cops at Morgan's scene and the cops tonight, except for me. I don't think there were any of the same crime-scene techs, either. So, no, I don't think anyone has noticed yet. I didn't exactly call attention to it."

"Why are you doing all this, Dave?" Mack asked. "You and I have always gotten along, we've always worked well together, but we've never been, well, friends."

Dave shrugged, his face and scalp red. "I know you," he said. "I trust you. Call it cop instinct. If anyone asks me about similarities between the two cases, I'll just say I didn't notice. Might make me look like a dope, but it can't come back to bite me."

"I'll take any time I can get, frankly." Mack turned and went into her bedroom. Saturday night was prime time on the Track. She might as well get started.

Jess quickly threw a sweatshirt on over her jeans and pulled on the TOMS she'd worn that morning. Dave raised his eyebrows but didn't try to convince them not to go. He knew them too well for that.

"You want me to come along?" he asked. "My wife doesn't expect me home at any particular time. You probably ought to have some backup."

"It's a no from me," she said. "You'll just scare them off. We may not look like johns, but at least we don't look like cops. You, on the other hand…"

"You'll look like cops there," Dave said.

Jess pulled a baseball cap on and checked herself out in Mack's foyer mirror. "This is the best we can do," she said. "It's worth a shot."

They climbed into Mack's old Saab and headed west across town to the stretch of Oracle Road known as the Track. This rundown area was north of downtown and not a place a casual driver would stumble across. People who found themselves on the Track wanted to find themselves there, and it accounted for almost half of Tucson's prostitution cases.

Oracle was bustling at that time of night, with girls prowling the street alone and in twos and threes, and parked cars containing prostitutes and johns who hadn't bothered to find a motel room for an hour. As Mack slowly rolled down the street, an assortment of women approached her car and, seeing who was inside, walked away, clucking their tongues. Finally, Mack saw the face she was looking for and parked.

"Hi, Ruthie," she said, getting out of the car and greeting a young woman in a short red skirt and black tube top. Ruthie Miller had been raped on the job some years before, and Mack had been the prosecutor. The case had ended with a plea, and the rapist was still behind bars. Ever since, Mack and Ruthie had had an understanding. Mack treated Ruthie with respect, and Ruthie gave Mack information when she had it. Ruthie's phone number changed often, and her government-issued "Obamaphone" was almost always out of minutes, but she seemed if not happy, exactly, then at least not angry to see Mack in her place of business.

"Hey, Ms. Wilson," Ruthie responded. "How you been?" Her eyes were dull and her hair was in disarray. She was using again. Jess waved from the passenger seat, and Ruthie raised a hand in greeting. They had met during preparation for Ruthie's trial, when Jess' job would have been to try to keep Ruthie from turning back to heroin before her testimony.

"Got a question for you." Mack leaned back against the driver's door, trying to look natural. She didn't want to attract attention from the other girls if she could help it. It could hurt Ruthie's reputation and livelihood if she was seen hanging out with cops, and in this neighborhood, there was no real difference between a prosecutor and an officer. Even in her ratty jeans, sweatshirt, and a baseball cap, Mack knew she looked like a representative of The Man. "Can we take you over to the Waffle House? Get you something to eat?"

Ruthie studied her, arms crossed over her chest and a sour look on her face. Mack could tell she was calculating whether the goodwill she would earn by agreeing was worth the income she'd lose.

"I can give you some cash," Mack offered. "I'm not sure how much I have, but whatever I've got in my wallet. Doesn't matter if you can help or not. It's just for your time."

Ruthie wordlessly got into the back seat.

The Waffle House was close, less than five minutes away, and Mack was grateful. Ruthie smelled terrible, like sweat and stale cigarettes and Mack didn't know what else. She longed to discreetly roll down the Saab's windows, but she didn't want to offend her source. Luckily, the competing odors of grease, bleach, and coffee overpowered everything else as they walked into the diner.

Mack and Jess stuck to coffee, wary of the food, but Ruthie took full advantage, ordering an omelet, pancakes, coffee, and orange juice. When the waitress left their table, Mack slipped the photos of Morgan Packer out of her pocket.

"Do you recognize this girl?" She was inclined to think that Morgan had mostly gotten clients online, but if she'd worked the Track at all, Ruthie ought to know her.

Ruthie studied the photo and Mack saw something flash across her eyes. "She in trouble?"

Mack shook her head and waited until the waitress set down their coffees. "She's dead. Her and another girl, a dancer from up in Phoenix. We think it might be related to their work."

"I don't know no dancers from out of town," Ruthie said. She handed the photo back to Mack. "But I do know this girl. Morgana, they called her. Haven't seen her in a long time. She was just a baby. I'm sorry she passed."

"Did you know her pimp?" Mack asked. She cringed at the word, but knew that if she started talking about "traffickers," Ruthie would clam up. As a rule, the girls on the Track didn't like to be reminded that they didn't work for themselves—that sex work wasn't their choice in the first place.

"I saw him some, when he'd drop her off. But you know I don't go talking to other girls' men. Short white guy, too old for that girl."

That was consistent with Mayer.

"You know when she got that tattoo on her neck?"

Ruthie emptied an individual cream into her cup and played with the lid. "No, she just told me her man got it for her, but I didn't need her to tell me that. Ain't no girls getting that on they own."

"She have any regulars?"

The waitress delivered Ruthie's meal and she dug in, not answering until she'd downed half the omelet and all of the pancakes. Mack watched her, wondering what Ruthie's drug of choice might be these days. When they'd met, she was casually using meth and more seriously using heroin, but Mack didn't see any of the physical signs of meth use now. The sweet tooth and skinny limbs, however, screamed heroin. Mack sighed; heroin was the worst. She rarely saw cocaine or meth overdoses, but it was a short path from heroin to synthetic opioids, and not many people came back from those. Ruthie was smart, and she cared about people. She was only in her mid-twenties, but she was already an old-timer who looked out for new girls on the Track. She was funny, when she was sober. She hadn't deserved the violent mom, the abusive stepdad, the spiral into drugs and homelessness.

None of them did.

Ruthie pushed back her plate and signaled the waitress for more coffee. "There was one guy I saw a few times," she said. "Not long before I stopped seeing your girl. He never picked her up, but he'd sit and watch her some. We only noticed him cuz he had a big new truck. Stood out down here, you know?"

"Did you get a good look at him?" Jess asked.

Ruthie scowled. "Just another white guy. Good looking, but I couldn't tell you nothing specific. Whenever he saw us watching him, he drove off."

Jess leaned in close to Mack and whispered, "Simon mentioned a good-looking guy hanging around outside the motel the day he hired Morgan. Maybe that's the direction we should be looking in. Remember Beth's neighbor, Joe? Maybe Morgan got hooked up with a new pimp, and he kept a closer watch than Mayer did."

"Are there any other girls we should talk to, Ruthie?" Mack asked. "Anyone else who knew Morgan or could tell us about the guy watching her?"

"She kept to herself, mostly. You know I try to look out for people, so I butted in, but she didn't talk much to the other girls. Never seemed comfortable down here, you know? Always on edge. Like she didn't belong. The other girls thought she was stuck up, but I think she was just scared. She was just a kid."

"Anything else you can tell us?" Jess asked.

Ruthie took a last bite of her omelet and stood up, ready to get back to work. "She was sweet. Wanted to be a vet. For dogs and cats. Liked animals. She fed the strays that came around. It's a real shame she gone."

Mack drained her coffee. Ruthie was right. It was a real shame.

CHAPTER THIRTY

Wendy called from the crime lab Monday morning. Some equipment had gone down over the weekend, so Eddie's sample hadn't been run yet. It would be at least Thursday before they had any results. Jess pulled her hair loose from her carefully arranged updo.

"We don't have until Thursday," she said to Mack. "We're going to rest tomorrow, and the jury will have it Wednesday, unless Noah does end up calling Jefferson and then recalling Wendy. If Eddie leaves for Utah as soon as we get a verdict, we lose him. Extraditing him will be a nightmare. We're going to have to do something before the trial ends."

"Do what?" Mack asked. She was slumped in a chair across from Jess' desk and feeling punchy. Of *course* the crime lab had run into delays. She couldn't remember the last time things had gone smoothly. Why would this be any different? "We don't have a good reason to stop him."

"We have to make a decision about who's really to blame for Dorothy's death. Frank Jefferson killed her, but he was acting at Eddie's direction. I believe—and you believe it, too, regardless of your protests—that Eddie is really responsible for his mother's death. I say we scoop him in court. Keep him from getting away."

Jess was wearing a navy pinstripe skirt suit over a beige silk shell. She looked like every lawyer Mack had ever seen on television, and yet it was clear that she had lost her mind. She looked down at her own outfit—a beige pantsuit over a navy silk shell. People said that when trial partners started to dress alike, it meant that they were on the same page and more likely to win. Mack had always suspected there was some truth to that. When cases weren't going well, attorneys could feel it.

"Why not just grab him outside the courtroom as he's leaving tomorrow? That way, the jury doesn't see anything. If we have police arrest him in the courtroom, that's a mistrial."

Jess shrugged. "Maybe mistrying Jefferson wouldn't be the worst thing in the world—if it means we get Eddie. I'm worried that an officer stationed outside the door might miss him in the crowd."

"If we cause a mistrial, we don't get a second shot." Mack was growing frustrated with Jess' unwillingness to see reason.

Jess stood and crossed to the mirror behind her door. She started carefully gathering her hair into a ponytail. "So we try to get him at lunch," she said, patting a final strand into place. "If that doesn't work, though, I think we have to risk it. Our theory is that he hired someone to kill his *mom*. We can't just let him walk free."

"You're in too deep, Jess. You're not seeing things clearly. Yes, that's our working theory, but it's not something we can prove. Not yet. And we don't know if we'll ever be able to prove it, because we don't know what the DNA results will be. What if we blow up the Jefferson trial by arresting Eddie in front of the jury and then the DNA comes back that it wasn't him? What if it was just some weird coincidence? What if Dorothy put a kid up for adoption and he turns out to be an EMT who dripped sweat on her? There are literally a hundred explanations, with varying degrees of crazy, that mean we'd be wrecking this case for nothing. What'll Eleanor think if we let Jefferson skate trying to take down Eddie? For that matter, what will Eddie think if he's not guilty and we have him arrested? That's a lawsuit if I've ever seen one."

Mack could see the fire blazing in her eyes.

"Let's talk to Eleanor," Jess said. "Let's see what she thinks."

When they headed over to wrap up the State's case, they found Eleanor waiting outside the courtroom. They beckoned her into a small side room, hoping Eddie wouldn't notice. They explained the situation, from the interesting DNA chart to the delay getting her brother's results from the Starbucks cup. As they finished talking about the cobwebs—which had led them to suspect that the murderer had been admitted to the home and had not broken in—Eleanor started nodding.

"I've had doubts myself," she said. "Eddie and our mom were never close. Ever since he was a kid, he's complained about how I'm the favorite. When he pulled up in that new truck after the insurance cleared, I wondered. But he's my brother. How confident are you about this?"

Jess and Mack hesitated. "Ms. Lafayette is very confident," Mack said. "I am somewhat less so. I think that a bird in the hand is worth two in the bush, as it were. I'm worried that, if Eddie wasn't involved—or, frankly, even if he was—we might lose the actual killer. There's no question but that Frank Jefferson pulled the trigger. I'm concerned that, if we go off after Eddie half-cocked, Jefferson may not face consequences for that."

"I suggested that we talk to you," Jess said. "I think you know whether or not your brother was behind this. Not consciously, of course, but I think there's some part of you that knows if he would be capable of working with Jefferson to kill your mom. If you tell us now that you think he was involved, then I think we go forward. If you tell us you're not sure, or he wasn't involved, then we forget it. We convict Jefferson, and we wait to see what happens with the DNA. If the DNA comes back and implicates Eddie, we'll do our best. But by then, we'll be behind the curve."

"Can I have some time to think about it?" Eleanor asked.

"Of course," Mack said. "But not much."

They discussed the timeline for the remaining days of trial, and the importance of acting quickly if they were going to act. The two lawyers began to rise, ready to go into the courtroom.

"When we were kids," Eleanor said, "there was a time when I thought Eddie was going to kill me."

Jess and Mack sat back down.

Eleanor started playing with the long, beaded necklace she wore, running it through her fingers. "He had this plastic sword, and he got it against my neck. I was three years older, but he was strong, and he started choking me. I couldn't get away. I just got weaker and weaker, and eventually I stopped struggling. Thank God, our mom came in just in time. I remember she looked so scared, and he was just blank. Like nothing had even happened. He was just...cold."

She let the necklace fall back against her chest. "Let me think about it."

CHAPTER THIRTY-ONE

Noah called to report that Jefferson's girlfriend, Theresa Carter, was nine months pregnant. The doctors planned to induce her in twenty-four hours, which meant she would be unavailable to testify on Wednesday afternoon as scheduled. Instead, Noah proposed that she testify that afternoon, out of order. This was easy to agree to. They didn't expect Tessie to have much to say that would hurt the State's case. Jess had interviewed her months earlier, before the trial had been delayed until March, and Tessie had said her boyfriend stayed at her house the night of the murder. He couldn't have gone out, she said, because he didn't know the alarm code, so he couldn't leave her house after she'd set the alarm.

Mack had rolled her eyes when Jess related the story, and rolled them again when Tessie gave the same story—plus a whole bunch of impermissible character evidence that Judge Haberfeld refused to preclude—on direct examination. It was clear that Tessie loved her boyfriend, though she readily admitted that her unborn baby was not his child. They had broken up about a month before he was arrested, but then had gotten back together after his incarceration. Once Jefferson was out of custody, they planned to get married and have him raise the child as his own. Tessie Jefferson. It was too gross for words.

Tessie testified well for Noah on direct. She seemed calm and honest, a good demeanor for a defendant's significant other.

"How did you and Frank meet?" Noah asked after she introduced herself. His shirt collar was not frayed, and his suit looked new. Mack wondered again if his opening-statement outfit had been coincidental or calculated.

Tessie turned to the jury, and Mack tried to hide a smile. She could always tell when a witness had consumed too much court television.

"I was working as a nurse at an urgent care clinic, and Frank came in." Her hands were deep in the sleeves of her oversized brown cardigan, and she looked like the nurse she was. Cool under pressure.

"Was Frank injured, or—was he—he was—was he sick, or why was he seeking treatment that day?"

Tessie smiled. "He had a cut on his hand. It was love at first suture."

"And you started—did you start dating right away?" Noah seemed unused to conducting direct examination. Avoiding asking leading questions was tripping him up. That might give Jess and Mack the opportunity to object when he directed Jefferson. Even if the objections were overruled, they would further throw him off his game.

"Not exactly. He came back the next day to ask for my number, but I said no, you know, because he was my patient? It didn't seem appropriate."

"So, how did you start dating?"

Tessie blushed, and Mack understood the appeal. Tessie seemed like the perfect partner for a lying rapist and murderer: warm, compassionate, forgiving.

"When he came back to get the stitches out, he asked me out again. At that point, he wasn't my patient anymore, so I said yes, absolutely."

Of course, that was before he'd gone to prison, this most recent time, for that other home burglary.

"He had his troubles," she said. She had a kind face, but her forehead was creased with concern as she discussed Jefferson's past.

"But that's all behind him now. He's grown into the man I always knew he could be." She patted her very swollen stomach. "He's a hard worker, and dedicated to me and our family." The belly rub was a little too much for Mack.

She perked up when Jess began her cross and pressed gently on some of Tessie's testimony. Dealing with defendants' friends and family on cross was always tricky, and Mack was glad that Tessie was Jess' witness, especially given the added wrinkle of the pregnancy. Push too hard, and the jury might feel bad for the witness. Fail to push hard enough, and the witness could skate right past holes in their direct testimony. This was especially true when it was Mack or Jess handling the questioning, since they both looked much younger than their ages. Young female attorneys were held to higher standards by juries, even when the jurors themselves were young and female. It would all come down to whether or not Jess had built up enough credibility to justify going a little hard on the murderer's very pregnant girlfriend.

Although Tessie introduced Jefferson to her family and friends early on, he had not reciprocated. The only connection of his she'd met was his half-brother Donnie, who ran a pool-cleaning company. Jefferson worked for Donnie on and off, when he wasn't in custody. He didn't have any other family, he'd explained, and most of his friends had cut him off during his first incarceration. Now, though, he had been clean for over three years, and Tessie regretted that he didn't have more social connections to see what a wonderful man he'd blossomed into.

"So, you've been dating Frank for about five years, right?" That was a nice touch, calling him Frank. It showed that Jess, too, thought of Jefferson as a person with a family and a life outside of the crime he'd committed. Built credibility with the jury.

"Yes."

Tessie was older than Jefferson, Mack thought. She was probably on the wrong side of forty, while he wasn't even thirty-five yet. It was surprising that her doctors had been willing to let her testify at all—her pregnancy had to be high risk.

"And you love him?"

"We love each other."

Tessie was pushing back. Jess could use that.

"And you trust him?

"Of course we trust each other."

Technically, the other woman wasn't answering the questions Jess was asking, but she wasn't about to interrupt the rhythm she was building. Once she'd lulled Tessie into reflexive answering, she'd ask one that wasn't a softball.

"And you've lived in the same house the whole time, right?"

"Yes. It was my mom's house, before she passed."

"Okay. But in five years, you've never told Frank the alarm code?"

Tessie paused and looked at Jefferson before answering. "No, I—no."

"Okay." Jess checked something off on the pad of paper in front of her at the podium. Mack smiled. If the jurors didn't see how stupid that claim was, there was no helping them. Jess had done a great job leaving Tessie her dignity—hadn't gone too far and asked a "why" question, giving the witness a chance to explain away her nonsensical answer.

"In your years dating Frank, I assume you've had an active sex life?"

Mack looked up, surprised. They hadn't discussed this.

Tessie blushed and hadn't even opened her mouth when Noah jumped up. "Relevance! I mean, objection, Judge! My objection is relevance."

Judge Haberfeld looked unimpressed, glaring at Jess over her glasses. "Ms. Lafayette?"

Jess smiled. "I need a very short leash, Judge."

The judge pursed her lips. "Very short," she said. "Go ahead."

Jess turned back to Tessie, who looked confused. "Do you want me to repeat my question?"

Tessie shook her head. She didn't face the jury this time, simply stared at the table in front of her. "I don't need you to repeat it. We had an average sex life, I'd say."

"Frank ever get rough with you, sexually?"

Tessie's head jerked up. "What? Frank never raped me, if that's what you're implying."

"Not at all," Jess said, reaching for her cup and taking a sip of water as Tessie glared at her. "I'm asking if you and Frank engaged in consensual BDSM activities."

"I'm not comfortable talking about our sex life," Tessie said.

Jess looked at her intently. A long silence passed. Jess cleared her throat and turned to the judge. "I'd ask that the witness be directed to answer the question," she said quietly.

"You need to answer, ma'am," Judge Haberfeld said.

Tessie looked at Jefferson. Mack glanced at him, hoping she could see him without drawing the jury's attention to him. He was shaking his head slightly. That was interesting. There was something there, but he didn't want the jury to know about it.

"We never did anything that wasn't consensual," Tessie said. "I liked it just as much as he did."

"So, Frank enjoyed rough sex?"

Tessie nodded hesitantly.

"Is that a yes?" Jess asked.

"Yes," Tessie said, sounding defeated.

Jess made another check mark on her piece of paper and moved to her next topic, which was Tessie's motive for testifying.

Something about Tessie's earlier testimony tickled the back of Mack's brain. She shuffled through the papers in front of her until she found the report summarizing the police interview with Eleanor Johnson, Dorothy's daughter. The police had asked Eleanor what companies Dorothy contracted with for lawn care, house cleaning, and other services. They thought maybe the murderer had known Dorothy and had a money-related motive. Eleanor provided police with a list of all the companies she knew about, including companies her mother had moved away from over the years.

Dorothy had a pool in her backyard and contracted with Corcoran Pool Cleaning. Her previous company, however, had been DJPC LLC. DJ…Donnie Jefferson? Could Frank Jefferson have cleaned Dorothy's pool during his time working for his brother's company? If so, he might well have met Eddie during one of his trips to the house.

Mack leaned toward Kimberly. "Anyone follow up on DJPC?" she whispered.

"No. We didn't go back to any of the historical companies. We figured that if someone had a beef with Dorothy, it was probably rooted in a present-day conflict. I mean, who commits murder because of ancient history, you know? And then, when the DNA came back, we figured we didn't need to waste time on that follow-up."

Jess came back to the prosecution table to ask if Mack had any additional questions. Mack beckoned her closer and told her what she'd found in the reports. Jess pulled her long hair over her left shoulder and straightened the collar of her blouse, then returned to the podium.

"Frank used to work for his brother Donnie, right?"

Tessie nodded.

"Is that a yes?" Jess asked. She said it in a friendly way, and no one other than Mack would have noticed the slight edge to her voice.

The first rule of cross examination is that you never ask a question you don't already know the answer to. The second rule is that, if the answer doesn't matter, you can forget the first rule. Ultimately, it didn't matter to the case against Jefferson if Eddie was or wasn't involved. Whatever Tessie said would do no harm to the case they had, and might help the case they were hoping to build against Eddie.

"Yes."

"And Donnie's company is called DJPC, right?"

"Yes."

"Donnie Jefferson Pool Cleaning?"

"Yes."

"Do you know what Frank did for Donnie?"

"Objection," Noah said. "Relevance."

Jess turned to the judge, folding her hands on the podium to look just the right amount of bored.

"Overruled," Judge Haberfeld said. "But get to your point, Ms. Lafayette."

"Thank you, Judge." Jess turned back to the witness stand. "Do you need me to repeat my question?"

"No," Tessie said. "Frank cleaned pools for Donnie. He went to customers' houses, and he cleaned their pools once a week or however often the contract was for."

Jess bit her lip, and Mack recognized her hesitation. She wasn't quite sure how to play this. Mack didn't think Tessie knew anything about a possible connection between her boyfriend and the victim, so she hoped Jess continued teeing up easy questions.

"Did you know that Donnie's company was responsible for cleaning Dorothy Johnson's pool? The victim in this case?"

Tessie's jaw dropped, and Mack heard a juror gasp.

"Objection!" Noah shouted, standing. "Facts not in evidence!"

Jess smiled. "It's on Bates 97, Judge. So defense had notice of the fact. And I'm putting it in evidence as we speak."

Judge Haberfeld coughed and appeared to be hiding a smile of her own. "Go on," she said.

"I don't know what you're talking about," Tessie said.

Jess approached the stand and showed Tessie the report. "See?" she asked. "Did you know Donnie's company cleaned Dorothy's pool? Looks like he stopped about a year before she was murdered."

"No," Tessie said flatly. "I didn't know that."

"Frank never mentioned it?" Jess asked, still sweet. "After he was charged with Dorothy's murder? 'Gee, what a weird coincidence, I cleaned her pool when I worked for Donnie'?"

"Objection!" Noah called. "Argumentative!"

"Overruled. Answer the question."

"Never," Tessie said.

Jess glanced back at Mack, who shook her head subtly. The third rule of cross is never let the witness draw a conclusion. If Jess asked Tessie whether she thought that was weird, or unlikely, or meant something, that would give her the opportunity to defend Jefferson. If Jess left it hanging, either Noah would try to clean it up on redirect—which might or might not work—or he'd avoid it, since he didn't know what would happen any more than Jess did. Either way, Jess could argue it in her closing. *Was that the reaction of an innocent man, ladies and gentlemen? Of course not.*

Jess settled in at the prosecution table as Noah began his redirect, trying to salvage what he could from Tessie's testimony. "Do you see it now?" Jess whispered to Mack. "They met while Jefferson was cleaning Dorothy's pool and must have struck up a friendship. That's the connection."

"I see it," Mack said. "It's too bad we can't call Eddie to testify. He'd just plead the fifth."

Jess pursed her lips and tilted her head. "Would he, do you think? I'm not sure. He might be so confident he's getting away with it that he gets cocky. We could try. I'm sure I noticed him on the witness list. At this point, I'm not sure there's enough that we'd have to have counsel appointed for him. We could just put him up there and see what happens."

"I don't think so," Mack said. "I think we have to get him into custody, preferably without blowing up the case against Jefferson. I still think we can get them both."

Jess turned her full attention to Noah's redirect.

CHAPTER THIRTY-TWO

Through cell phone records and interviews with Jane Gould's friends, Dave was able to piece together a timeline of her final days. Only twenty-three, Jane had been performing at the Phoenix strip club for almost two years, earning enough to attend ASU full time during the day. She had been on track to graduate with a bachelor's in psychology in three and a half years. She planned to dance her way through grad school, too, and to make it through with no debt. Her mother didn't approve of her choice, but she acknowledged that it made financial sense. In addition to working and being a student, Jane had a large group of close friends from high school she still tried to see whenever she could. Every once in a while, she took a long weekend off from the club to come down and reconnect with people.

Jane had driven to Tucson from her apartment in Phoenix Friday morning. That day, she had lunch at a local Mexican restaurant with her mom and aunt, and the three of them went shopping. Dinner at home, and an early bedtime for Jane and her mom both. Her cell phone hadn't been used after about 9:30. The next day, they were up early and worked in her mom's garden until midafternoon.

Then Jane showered, changed, and took an Uber to meet up with some high-school friends. They went to the Tucson Renaissance Festival, which was much smaller than Phoenix's equivalent, but another friend was running the face-painting booth and the group wanted to say hello.

At the festival, Jane stuck close to her friends. They each had a few beers and shared a turkey leg. When her friends were ready to go early in the evening, Jane decided to stay. She'd catch a ride with Georgia, the face painter, when the festival ended, and they'd meet the group on Fourth Avenue, a popular neighborhood full of bars and restaurants.

Georgia told Dave she'd manned the booth until the festival closed at ten, so Jane had made herself scarce. When she was ready to go, Georgia called Jane but got no response. She waited around for a while, called a few more times, and then took off—texting Jane first to suggest she catch her own Uber. Jane was sweet, Georgia said, but kind of a flake. Georgia figured maybe she'd met someone or gone ahead without her. Jane's phone records confirmed the calls and texts, but GPS data showed she hadn't left the festival. Dave sent a detective, who found Jane's phone ringing at the bottom of a trash can.

No one saw her since she left Georgia at the face-painting booth, and no one came forward in response to signs posted around the festival grounds asking for information. Where she had been—and who she had met there—remained a mystery.

That evening, Jess and Adam went to Mack's house, so Adam could help Mack assemble some bookshelves. She and Anna had never finished unpacking Mack's home office, and the stack of boxes had finally driven her to action. Mack thought about hiring a handyman but instead decided she and Adam could handle it without professional help, and Jess had cheerfully offered Adam's services in exchange for dinner. Which, Mack thought, was a bargain.

They had been building together in easy silence for some time when Adam asked if Mack had heard from Anna recently.

The question caught Mack off guard and she dropped her screwdriver. "Um, no."

Adam looked around the room. Jess was in the kitchen fixing drinks. "Don't tell Jess I told you this, but we both think you could do better."

"Oh," Mack said, uncomfortable. "Thank you?"

"Jess told me some of what happened—not, like, the whole story or anything—but it seems pretty clear that she sucks."

Mack nodded, fighting the urge to defend her ex-girlfriend.

Jess delivered two Dogfish Heads and a bowl of crackers before excusing herself back to the couch. They continued working in silence, less comfortable this time.

"Are you working on anything else, other than your trial with Jess?" Adam asked.

"I've got a homicide investigation," Mack said, focused on the shelving instructions. "A girl disappeared this weekend at the Ren Faire. Turned up dead."

"Seriously?" Adam asked, surprised. "That's where I was working this weekend!"

Mack put down her Allen wrench. "You were working at the Tucson Renaissance Faire? Doing what?"

"Bartending. Rocky's there every year and offers me some extra cash to help. I've done it a few years in a row now. It's always a good time—I get to dress up a little, talk to the weirdos. Since Jess was in trial and working this weekend anyway, I figured it was good timing. With the wedding coming up, every little bit of income helps, you know?"

Mack pulled her phone from her pocket and scrolled until she found Jane's picture. "Do you remember seeing this girl?"

Adam glanced over. "Nope. Was she drinking? Even if she was, I probably wouldn't have noticed her unless she was in costume. Like, I've bartended at the Phoenix comic convention before, and unless they're dressed like the best Harley Quinn ever, I don't even see them."

Mack put her phone away, her adrenaline surge fading. It was just a coincidence. The chances that Adam had seen Jane were slim to none, and the chance that he saw anything relevant to her murder was even lower. She wondered whether she should ask him to give Dave a call. It seemed pretty clear that he had nothing of importance to contribute.

"I thought you weren't supposed to have a caseload right now."

"You're not wrong," Mack said. "But we think it's related to this other case that I'm interested in, so I've been working this one, too. Just, you know, kind of unofficially."

She felt Adam watching her and wondered if her tone had been a little too breezy. She didn't think Jess had told him the whole story of Morgan's murder and Mack's subsequent involvement in the investigation, but maybe she was wrong. If he already knew, he probably thought Mack was crazy for not talking about it. Of course, if he didn't know, she might sound like a lunatic anyway, involved in a murder investigation for fun. Weirdest of all, he might even think she did it.

The shelf in front of her was starting to come together, but she needed a break. She needed to calm down. She needed to go for a long walk. She needed a beer.

CHAPTER THIRTY-THREE

The last witness for the state in the Jefferson trial was the case agent, Kimberly Watson. Mack had invested several hours in preparing her to testify but was still nervous as they walked into the courtroom that morning. Kimberly didn't seem to understand the importance of the cobwebs in the guestroom window and kept mixing up which investigation each set of photographs came from. She hadn't been there when Jess and Mack had talked to Eleanor, and Mack thought maybe that was a mistake. If Kimberly had heard Eleanor's story, she might better understand the stakes.

Jess had decided that Mack should try to use Kimberly's testimony to shake Eddie. They wanted him to hear that they suspected someone had let Jefferson into the house and didn't think Jefferson had developed some independent motive to want Dorothy dead. If they could preempt Noah's "aha" moment on the photographs, Eddie might let go of the cool attitude he'd maintained throughout the trial. If he thought they were onto him, he might try to flee. They had an officer stationed outside the courtroom door, ready to scoop him if he tried.

As case agent for the murder investigation, it was Kimberly's job to tie together loose ends for the jury. They needed to understand how the case had unfolded, how Jefferson had been identified, and what he'd said in his interview. Jess and Mack's goal was always to put on a case in as close to chronological order as possible. That's how legal television shows did it, and that's what jurors were used to. Unfortunately, the actions of the case agent often influenced the actions of the crime-scene techs, whose results then influenced the case agent, and so on. The threads of an investigation could wind up a confusing knot, and it was up to Kimberly to untangle it for the jurors. Mack wasn't optimistic.

At least Kimberly had taken their wardrobe notes to heart. Her shoulder-length brown hair was down and curled. She wore light makeup—just enough for the female jurors to notice—and an emerald-green blouse under a beige suit. She had left her service weapon in her purse. She looked more like a bank teller than a police detective, which was exactly what Mack was going for. She looked credible, easygoing, not intimidating. If she could keep that up through several hours of testimony, they might win this thing yet.

Mack had Kimberly walk the jury through what a case agent was and what Kimberly's responsibility was with regard to the investigation. She had been the first detective called to the scene at Dorothy's house and had directed the collection of evidence. Although she hadn't been present at the burglary scene, the foundation for those photographs had been laid by a previous witness—one of the crime scene techs. Jess and Mack had spent hours staring at the pictures and had spotted something important just the previous day. It might cost them the burglary count, but it would cut Noah off at the knees, and Jess thought it would make the murder count against Jefferson a lock.

"You're familiar with this photo," Mack said, putting the picture of the broken window up on the screen, "which was taken when Dorothy's house was burglarized, two weeks before the murder."

"I am," Kimberly said. She was prepared for this line of questioning—Mack had called her that morning to review their plan.

"You're a homicide detective now, but have you ever investigated burglary cases?"

"I have. Early in my career, as a patrol officer, I investigated at least thirty burglaries of homes and businesses."

"Have you seen cases where windows were broken to get into homes?"

"Yes."

"Window screens slashed to get into homes?"

"Yes."

"When a window is broken to get into a home, would you expect to find shards of broken glass?"

"I would," Kimberly said. "Inside the home."

Mack zoomed in on the window ledge, where there were shards of glass visible *outside* the home. "So not like this?"

"Objection!" Noah called.

Judge Haberfeld summoned the lawyers to the bench. "What's your objection, Mr. Gardener?"

"My understanding from pre-trial interviews is that the State's intention was to say that this window was the point of entrance for my client when he allegedly committed the murder. Now they're talking about someone breaking the window from inside the house two weeks earlier. They've changed their theory without notice to the defense."

"So your objection is…?"

"Relevance," Noah said. "My objection is relevance."

Judge Haberfeld turned to Mack.

"Defense counsel already knows that this window was not the point of entry for his client when he murdered Dorothy, as will become clear from the photographs depicting cobwebs on this window at the time of her death. The point I'm building to is that the 'burglary' was staged in order to make it look like the homicide was related to the theft of Dorothy's iPad."

Noah spluttered. "But—but—but—no one has indicated anything of the sort at any point up 'til now."

Mack shrugged. "You have all the same photographs and testimony that we have. If you think the burglary was related to the murder, argue that. The State gets to put on whatever case we want so long as we comply with the rules—which we're doing. There's no requirement that we tell you, in advance, how each fact fits."

Both lawyers faced Judge Haberfeld, waiting for her decision. She looked angrier than usual. "In the future," she said, "there is absolutely no reason for you to address each other during bench conferences. Please address all comments to me. If, and only if, I want someone to respond to something the other side has said, I will ask. Understood?"

The lawyers agreed, and she waved them back to their respective positions.

"Objection overruled," the judge said. "You can answer."

Kimberly studied the image. "No," she said. "That glass is on the outside of the window ledge."

"So based on your training and experience, what would you think happened here?"

"Someone broke the window from inside the room."

Mack looked at the jury. Five of them were taking notes. Perfect. They were on board. Noah would have to fight to recover his momentum. She risked a glance at the defense table. Jefferson was sitting impassively, as he had throughout trial. It was as if he wasn't even listening. Noah, on the other hand, was frantically scribbling on a pad of paper. Mack assumed he was revising his cross-examination.

If Mack looked toward the courtroom clock, she could see Eddie's face. Instead of his usual bland expression, he looked pale and serious. Better and better.

Mack moved on, guiding Kimberly through an explanation of what she did when she received the DNA results implicating Frank Jefferson. She'd researched him, figured out where to find him, and made contact. He was brought in and interviewed. Kimberly knew he wasn't new to the system, but she read him his rights and recorded the interview per department protocol. Mack played the tape for the jury, so they got to watch Jefferson deny knowing Dorothy in real time.

As the video played, Mack glanced back at the jurors. Two were watching the interview intently. Two were taking notes. Three were watching Jefferson at the defense table. Mack wondered if his lack of reaction was as off-putting to the jurors as it was to her. She always wanted defendants to show remorse when confronted with their lies and was almost always disappointed. She could count on one hand the number of defendants she'd seen react to their recorded interviews. The remaining jurors stared off into the middle distance, apparently disengaged.

Typical.

She wondered again whether or not Jefferson would choose to testify. His prior felony convictions would normally mean that he would exercise his right to refuse, since that would open him up to cross examination about his priors, which would reveal to the jury that he was a felon. Under the circumstances, though, it might be worth it. Noah had to find some way to explain the DNA, and so far it didn't seem like the jury was buying the implication that the lab had gotten it wrong. If Jefferson testified and admitted to a consensual sexual relationship with Dorothy, at least he'd be giving them an alternative explanation for the DNA. Mack wasn't sure it would be enough to sway their opinions, but it was probably worth a try.

The taped interview was short. Once the biographical details and introductions were over, it took less than ten minutes. Jefferson was clearly visible on the overhead camera, slumped back in his chair with his arms crossed over his chest. Mack knew he'd been kept in the interview room for almost three hours before Kimberly came in to start the interview. In all that time, no one had told him why he was being held. Despite that, he seemed calm and disinterested in what was happening. Even when Kimberly started asking pointed questions about Dorothy's murder, Jefferson maintained his flat affect. He showed none of the panic or stress that Mack would have expected from an innocent man.

Perhaps most notably, he didn't react at all to the crime scene photographs Kimberly showed him. Innocent people react to crime scene photos. Mack thought back to her own interview with Dave and how strongly she'd reacted just to his words, let alone to the photos. If the audio was muted on Jefferson's interview, though, no one would be able to tell what he and Kimberly were talking about.

After Kimberly's testimony concluded, Mack ducked into the hallway to confirm that Officer Morales was still standing guard. If Eddie was going to make a run for it, this would be the time, once it was clear that the State's theory was that there had been an inside accomplice.

"The State rests, Judge," Jess said. Mack heard a sharp intake of breath from a juror and the scribble of a pen. Clearly, someone was expecting more. She wondered if they were waiting for the accomplice to be identified. There wasn't time to dwell on that, however, since Eddie was standing up, gathering his laptop bag and jacket, and quietly saying goodbye to his sister.

Mack watched him walk out of the courtroom. She counted to thirty in her mind, then followed after him. As the courtroom door closed behind her, she saw Eddie in handcuffs, Officer Morales reading him his rights. Eddie's face was red, and his jaw was clenched. Mack didn't envy the detective who would be tasked with interviewing him. That would be an uphill battle. Eddie was too smart to be tricked into a confession and too angry to invoke.

Mack returned to the courtroom to find that the jury had been dismissed, and all eyes were on her. She sat next to Jess and whispered, "What's going on?"

"Eleanor started crying when you followed Eddie out. I guess she figured out what was happening. Judge is waiting for your report. I'm also thinking about dismissing the burglary count. I don't think we have enough to argue it both ways at this point, and I want the murder conviction."

Mack disagreed with dismissing the burglary count and wanted to make sure they discussed it before Jess went rogue. She got to her feet. "Judge, Eddie Johnson has been arrested. He was taken into custody in the hallway and will be transported to the police station from here."

"Thank you," Judge Haberfeld said. "Mr. Gardener?"

Noah rose. "Judge, at this time, I'd ask for a mistrial. This case was predicated on the State's belief that my client acted alone. Now that they've arrested the victim's own son, right outside the courtroom. I think my client has been unfairly prejudiced, and the only remedy is a mistrial."

Judge Haberfeld stared at Noah, a blank look on her face. "Where's the prejudice, Mr. Gardener? The jury has no way of knowing that anything untoward has happened, and that's the point of a mistrial—to remedy the situation if the process gets tainted for the jury. How could the arrest have any bearing on their verdict if they don't even know about it?"

"My client might have done things differently if he'd known Eddie was going to be charged with—or even just suspected of—the same crime."

Jess cleared her throat. "Your Honor, if I may?"

"Go on."

"Counsel appears to be presupposing that Eddie was arrested for involvement in his mother's death. I just want to put on the record that I haven't said anything to lead defense to that conclusion. Eddie could just as easily have been arrested for unpaid parking tickets or tax evasion."

Noah laughed. "Don't be ridiculous. Of course he was arrested for suspected involvement in the murder. You've been building to that all week. If he was being arrested for tax evasion, it wouldn't have happened here and now, and his sister wouldn't have started crying about it in court."

Judge Haberfeld raised a hand. "You both raise interesting points. As we've previously discussed, however, you are to direct those points to *me*, not to each other. Am I understood, Mr. Gardener?"

Noah didn't look contrite so much as furious.

Judge Haberfeld turned to Jess. "Ms. Lafayette, what charge was Eddie arrested on?"

"He wasn't arrested on a specific charge, Judge. But he is suspected of working with Mr. Jefferson to coordinate the murder of Dorothy Johnson. Certain facts have come to light during the course of the trial that led police to the decision to arrest him today, but to be clear, no indictment currently exists against him. And, again, I'd like to reiterate that he was arrested outside the knowledge of the jury. If any of them notice that he isn't in the courtroom when the verdict is read, it can't be prejudicial—they will have already reached their verdict."

"Thank you," the judge said. "Mr. Gardener, what would your client have done differently if he'd known Eddie was going to be arrested?"

"I can't know that, Judge, because that's not what happened. Maybe he would have pleaded. He's indicated to me that he does not intend to testify, so I intended to rest before we got sidetracked. Given this change, though, maybe he would have testified and said Eddie made him do it. That's my whole point—we can't know what he would have done if things had developed differently, and that's the prejudice."

"Is there the possibility for a plea, Ms. Lafayette?"

Jess glanced at Mack. They had discussed that issue before Kimberly made the decision to arrest Eddie. They probably should have talked about it with James Harris, or possibly even Michael Brown, but they had decided to ask for forgiveness rather than permission. Eleanor was on board, hoping that Jefferson would turn on her brother, and her approval was what mattered to Jess most.

"Yes, Judge. If Mr. Jefferson is interested in pleading guilty to first degree murder, the State will offer life with the possibility of release after twenty-five years. As a term of that plea, Mr. Jefferson will have to be reinterviewed and agree to testify against Eddie."

"Mr. Gardener, do you want a minute to talk to your client?"

The defense attorney bent over Jefferson, and the two men whispered to each other for a moment. Noah eventually straightened up, a defeated look on his face. "Judge, Mr. Jefferson has indicated that he would not be interested in accepting such an offer."

"What about testifying? Would he like to reassess that decision?"

"No, Judge."

"Counsel, may I address your client directly?"

Noah looked sick. Mack understood his dilemma. He couldn't prevent the judge from talking to his client, but he also couldn't prevent his client from saying something stupid. This was a no-win situation. He looked resigned and sat beside Jefferson.

"Sir," Judge Haberfeld said. "Have you been following the conversation?"

Noah nudged Jefferson, who stood. "I think so. They've arrested Eddie, saying he's involved in this murder that I've been falsely accused of."

Judge Haberfeld pursed her lips, a look known and feared around the courthouse. "Your lawyer is saying that you might have made some different decisions if you had known before trial that Eddie was going to be arrested. He says you might have pleaded guilty or chosen to testify."

"No, ma'am," Jefferson said. "I wouldn't have pleaded guilty to anything, and I wouldn't testify against Eddie. I don't have anything to say about Eddie. I wasn't involved in this crime, regardless of whether he was or not."

"Okay, then," the judge said. "No prejudice appearing, I am denying the defense motion for mistrial. Jury instructions?"

The judge, Jess, and Noah moved on to talk about jury instructions and the schedule for closing arguments, and Mack sat back, stunned. She had thought Jefferson really had to testify and had invested over fifteen hours in her preparation. Instead, he was rolling over and playing dead. She wondered if Noah had a trick up his sleeve for closings. So far, it seemed like an open-and-shut conviction, and Noah had a reputation for being better than that.

Mack felt Kimberly nudge her shoulder and tuned back in to the discussion.

"In opening statements," Jess said, "defense indicated the jury would hear that the defendant had a consensual sexual relationship with the victim. During the trial, however, no evidence has been introduced to support that defense. Because there's no evidence, Mr. Gardener should be precluded from making that argument."

"That seems to make sense. Counsel?"

Noah stood and tapped his pen on the table several times before answering. "I do intend to make that argument, Judge. The State indicates there's no evidence to support it, but there's also no evidence against it. There's been no evidence one way or another about how that DNA got there, so it's a reasonable inference for me to argue it was consensual."

"There absolutely *was* evidence against that inference," Judge Haberfeld said. "The victim's daughter testified that her mother was not in a sexual relationship. There was a chance to get your evidence in—your client could have testified to it. If he had, you could argue it. It's possible that his girlfriend could have testified to it, even. I'm not punishing your client for exercising his right not to testify, but I'm also not going to let him use that right as a sword and a shield."

"Judge," Noah said, and Mack was surprised he had more to say. "I'm going to ask you for leave to brief the issue for reconsideration. I really think this could be an appellate issue, and I want to make the best record I can."

Mack cringed. Any time a defense attorney started talking about the appellate record, her hackles went up. Although she agreed that Noah shouldn't be able to make his argument, she worried about the judge's statements regarding Jefferson's failure to testify. The jury would be explicitly instructed not to consider it, but it was clear that the judge *had* considered it.

"Briefing is not necessary, Mr. Gardener," Judge Haberfeld said. Her voice left no room for argument. "I'm confident that the record, as you've made it, will preserve any relevant issues for appeal. I will not change my mind. If the jury convicts, and if I'm wrong, the appellate courts will tell me."

If the jury did convict, would an appellate court find the judge's decision to preclude the defense argument grounds to reverse? The last thing Mack wanted was to have to try this case a second time.

"What do we do about the burglary charge?" Mack asked once they were back in Jess' office. Jess seemed lost in thought, preparing for her closing arguments.

"Hmm?" she said absently. "Oh, I think I need to dismiss it. It's not charged with accomplice liability, and we spent today showing that the window was broken from the inside out. How can I go in there and argue that Jefferson did it?"

Mack chose her words carefully. "We've had a couple things come up in this trial where, if we make the wrong decision, we know we're going to have to try it again, right?"

"Yes."

"I think this is another one. Noah is looking for a reason to mistry this. We've spent a lot of time talking about his strategy, and what his plan is, and I'm now at the point where I think his plan is just 'mistrial.' So if we drop the burg', he gets to ask for a mistrial again, because if Jefferson isn't charged with it, then why did the jury get to hear about it? I think we *have* to leave the burg' in place. You can argue it or not argue it, whatever seems right. But I don't think you can dismiss it."

Jess looked at her steadily. "I appreciate your position," she said. "But I think I need to dismiss it. Let me sleep on it. I'll decide in the morning."

CHAPTER THIRTY-FOUR

Mack knew that Jess didn't like splitting the State's two closing arguments between two lawyers. She trusted Mack and liked her argument style, but she'd made it clear this was *her* case, and she wanted to be the one the jury heard from on its last day.

Mack respected her choice and did her best to play the role of calm, supportive second chair. She made sure Jess' slide presentation was working, filled a cup with water and left it for Jess at the podium, and generally tried to make the process as smooth as possible. This didn't come naturally to her—*she* wanted to be the one making the arguments, convincing the jury, performing—but she knew her place and didn't complain.

"What did you decide about the burglary?" she whispered as they stood waiting for Judge Haberfeld to take the bench.

"You were right," she said. "I'm leaving it in."

Mack was relieved. She would take careful notes of how the jurors responded to Jess' first argument. Combined with similar notes on the defense close, they would help guide Jess through her rebuttal. What points were resonating? Who needed a little more persuasion?

"...for all these reasons, I ask you to make the only choice supported by the evidence and find the defendant guilty on all counts. Thank you."

"Thank you, State," Judge Haberfeld said. "Defense close?"

"Thank you, ladies and gentlemen," Noah said. Thanking the jury was a waste of time, and starting by thanking them was a waste of an opportunity for a great opening line. "You are here because jury service is one of the most important civic duties that Americans have. You are contributing to a sacred tenet of the law here in the United States: trial by a jury of your peers.

"In this case, my client, Frank Jefferson, had no motive to commit the heinous crimes he's been accused of." Noah paused to take a drink of his water and straighten his tie. "The only reason he's been accused of those crimes, in fact, is that the cops were lazy. They didn't want to do the work, the investigation, necessary to solve this vicious murder. They didn't want to look under rocks, and look into records, and really figure out who knew the victim and wanted her dead. So they framed my client. And even with the full force of the *government* brought to bear against my client, they couldn't give you a reason why he would have done it! They couldn't give you a reason, ladies and gentlemen, because there was no reason."

It wasn't a bad argument, Mack thought, but it wasn't one that was likely to go anywhere. The jury had already been instructed, and Jess would reiterate in her second close that motive was not required. Sometimes people killed for no reason—or at least no reason anyone ever learned.

"How do we know the police framed Frank, ladies and gentlemen? Two ways. First, there's the DNA. The government offered you no explanation for the second DNA profile on the victim's breast swabs. I would submit to you that their failure to offer you *any* concrete explanation of that other profile constitutes reasonable doubt right there!"

Mack nudged Jess to object. Jess had been taking notes on points she wanted to be sure to address in her rebuttal close, and she jotted down *second DNA profile* but didn't say anything. It would be bad form to object, and it wouldn't get her anywhere. She could deal with it later.

"My client's DNA was already in the system," Noah said, "so it could have been planted in the crime lab. It would be easier to plant evidence than to investigate the case—that's what the officers in this investigation thought.

"But even if you're not convinced by the DNA, ladies and gentlemen, let's talk about those mysterious cobwebs. When we started this trial, the government wanted you to believe that Frank broke into the victim's house through the guestroom window on two separate occasions—first to steal her iPad and then to kill her. But then, we all saw the cobwebs on the windowsill. We all sat here and looked at the photos with glass outside on the ledge from that first so-called 'burglary.' Someone broke the window from inside the house. And Frank certainly didn't come in through that window to commit a murder. You've seen my client during this trial. He's no offensive tackle, but he's no running back, either."

Mack didn't know what that meant, but two of the older men on the jury smiled and nodded appreciatively. She nudged Jess again.

"So if my client didn't come in through the window, what was the point of talking about the burglary? The government wasn't able to prove that Frank committed that crime, any more than they were able to prove that he killed anyone! The point, I submit to you, ladies and gentlemen, was to poison you against my client. To show you what a bad, scary dude he is and trick you into convicting him of crimes they couldn't prove and he didn't commit.

"And how else do we know he didn't commit those crimes? He was at Tessie's house! He didn't have the code to her alarm! He couldn't have left without her knowing, and she sat up there on the witness stand and told you that he was home that night."

Mack felt a headache starting to form behind her left eye. One of the few places where she and Jess disagreed about trial strategy was objections during closing arguments, and she itched to object to every improper statement Noah was making. Facts not in evidence! *Ad hominem* attacks! Nuh-uh!

Instead, she forced herself to maintain a neutral facial expression and tried to focus on Noah's uninspiring, circular argument.

After close to an hour, he thanked the jury a second time, asked them to acquit his client, and sat.

Jess got up, crossed to the front of the jury box, and made eye contact with each of the fourteen jurors in turn. Her navy-blue skirt suit was well tailored to her slim frame. Her pearls were carefully chosen—understated, professional, trustworthy. Mack put her pen down and pushed her notepad away. There was nothing left to write. The entire case depended on what Jess would say next. That's how it always felt, anyway. Mack knew the electricity that must be surging through Jess. Her toes curled in her black pumps, a habit she'd developed in elementary school to ground herself during presentations.

"Defense counsel," Jess said, her voice clear and loud, "needs you to believe that because we don't know what was going through his client's head when he raped, tortured, and murdered Dorothy Johnson, he must not have done it."

She clicked the remote, and the same portrait of Dorothy Mack had shown in opening statements appeared on the screen.

"You know, however, that that's not an accurate statement of the law. You have all the law that applies to this case—it's in your jury instructions, which Judge Haberfeld read to you this morning. And you know from those instructions, that the State does not have to prove motive. Sometimes people do things for reasons we can never understand. It's terrible, but it's true. The question for you, is whether you are firmly convinced, beyond a reasonable doubt, that Frank Jefferson killed Dorothy."

Another photo appeared on the screen. This one was a crime-scene photo, showing the devastation that had been wrought on Dorothy's lovely face.

"Here's what's been proven. The defendant worked for his brother Donnie's pool-cleaning company. That company used to clean Dorothy's pool. The defendant's DNA was found on Dorothy's vaginal swab and on her breast. Her daughter came before you and told you that Dorothy wasn't having a consensual sexual relationship with the defendant, or with anyone else. And that makes sense, because the defendant denied ever knowing Dorothy. Even when confronted with the DNA results. Even when given a chance to explain to Detective Watson.

"Ladies and gentlemen, when you go back into the jury room and begin your deliberations, you're going to talk about what defense counsel and I have said in our closing arguments. Remember, what the lawyers say is not evidence. Our arguments are provided to help explain and interpret the evidence. But you're going to talk about them, and one of you might want to talk about the defense's assertion that the police officers in this case were so lazy they framed this totally random guy, instead of taking the time to investigate this case fully.

"So let's talk about that. You heard *no* evidence that any of the police officers involved in this case knew the defendant. You heard *no* evidence that any of the crime scene techs or lab scientists involved in this case knew the defendant. You heard *no* evidence that anyone involved in this case had any reason to want the defendant to be guilty of these crimes.

"Now remember, you are not asked to leave your common sense at the door when you walk into that jury room. So I ask you, does it make sense that Tucson Police and the crime lab conspired together to frame this random 'dude' who never met Dorothy? I would suggest that that makes zero sense. It makes whatever is *less* than zero sense. What makes sense, ladies and gentlemen, is that the defendant horrifically raped, tortured, and killed Dorothy. So when you go into the back, and when you begin to deliberate, I ask you to come to the only verdict that makes common sense. I ask you to find the defendant guilty on all counts. Thank you."

Jess sat next to Mack, who gave her a fist bump under the table. She had done a phenomenal job. She'd skated right over the burglary and focused on what mattered—the murder and rape counts that would keep Jefferson in prison for the rest of his life. She'd said everything Mack had itched to say, said it well, and said it concisely. Mack herself was ready to file into the back with the jurors and vote to convict.

The courtroom stood as the jurors were dismissed to begin deliberating. When they were gone, Mack started packing up the computer and equipment.

"Anything before we break?" Judge Haberfeld asked.

Noah loosened his tie. "Yes, Judge," he said. "I'd like to request a mistrial for prosecutorial misconduct during rebuttal close."

Mack dropped the laptop, which luckily was only six inches above the surface of the table. All eyes in the courtroom shifted from Noah to Mack, and she blushed under the scrutiny.

Judge Haberfeld turned back to Noah and gestured for him to continue.

"In her rebuttal close, Ms. Lafayette referred several times to what I—as Mr. Jefferson's lawyer—'wanted the jury to believe.' This was done in a manner that suggested that Ms. Lafayette believes I was trying to mislead the jury or otherwise impugned my professionalism. As a result, she irreparably tainted the jury against me and against my client. It's impossible for him to receive a fair determination of guilt under these circumstances."

Jess stood very still. Her face was white. "I don't think I did, Judge. I am meticulous about what I say about defendants and defense attorneys during closing arguments, precisely so that we don't run into these very issues. I am certainly aware of the rule against making *ad hominem* attacks against the defendant. Perhaps my co-counsel has notes of my exact words" —she turned to Mack, who frowned, apologetic— "or perhaps our court reporter would be so good as to read them back to us?"

"No need," Judge Haberfeld said. "I took my own notes, and I have access to the live video record in my chambers. I'm going to take this under advisement for now and review the video. Please stay in the courtroom."

Mack finished packing up the audio-video equipment, resisting the urge to talk to Jess. That would only wind them both up. Jess was sitting on the edge of the prosecution table, her head buried in her phone. Mack knew she was reviewing her argument, trying to decide what the likelihood of a mistrial was. Mack wasn't sure herself. The line between permissible responses to defense arguments and impermissible attacks on the character of the defense attorney—including suggesting that they were lying—was thin. She thought Jess was on the right side of it, but ultimately Judge Haberfeld was the one whose opinion would matter.

After twenty minutes, the judge swept back into the courtroom, robes open and fluttering around her as she sat.

"I've reviewed my notes, as well as the video. It's very close. I am inclined to agree with Mr. Gardener that you went too far, Ms. Lafayette, in saying that the defendant wanted or needed the jury to believe things in order to find him not guilty. That amounts to a personal attack, and to burden shifting, frankly."

Jess paled even further. Mack could see the muscles in her jaw clench.

"That being said, I'm not sure you went far enough to warrant a mistrial. I want to review some appellate cases and figure out where the line is. Further, my bailiff informs me that the jury has selected a foreperson and adjourned for the day. They'll be back tomorrow at eight thirty."

She paused, and it felt like everyone in the room was collectively holding their breath. Mack snuck a glance at Jess. She was rigid, her arms crossed over her chest. Her left foot pressed hard into the industrial carpet.

The judge took off her glasses and rubbed her eyes. "Much as I hate to have them come back if I do decide to grant the mistrial, I don't see another option. I'm going to ask you all to be back here at eight fifteen. I will make my ruling, and we'll proceed from there."

Jess was silent all the way back to the office. Mack followed her, wheeling their trial cart.

Jess pulled off her suit jacket and collapsed into her chair, her hair in disarray. "I've been doing this job almost fifteen years," she said.

Mack picked a piece of lint off her sleeve.

"That's too fucking long to make mistakes like this. And I didn't. I'm sure I didn't. Did I?"

Mack swallowed hard. Jess was always honest with her, even when the truth hurt, and she owed her friend the same.

"I'm not sure," she said. "I think it was close. Hopefully the case law is in our favor and Haberfeld does the right thing."

Jess didn't respond. Mack waited until it was clear that no answer was coming. She left her friend's office and went to her own to grab her purse. Neither of them would be sleeping well.

CHAPTER THIRTY-FIVE

Mack finally dozed off on the couch with an old episode of *Sister Wives* playing quietly on the television. She dreamed of Anna chasing her through an open-air market. Her phone buzzed on the coffee table and she woke with a start. Jess. She cleared her throat.

"Did I wake you?"

Mack sat up fully. "S'okay," she said. "I'm up. What time is it?"

"Just after three. Can you let me in?"

The line went dead. Mack stood and stretched. It took her a minute to understand the question. When she did, she shuffled to her front door, where she found Jess in black yoga pants and an Elizabeth Warren tank top, shivering slightly in the cool desert night. She had a large Circle K coffee in each hand. She handed one to Mack.

"I was a jerk earlier."

Mack took a long sip of coffee. Light and sweet, just the way she liked it. "I was, too," she said. "I should have been more supportive. There's nothing to apologize for. It wasn't keeping me up, or anything."

Jess cracked a small smile. She looked Mack up and down and found her ratty llama-print pajamas unacceptable. "Get in the car—but change first. Hiking clothes, please."

Jess waited in the foyer while Mack threw on her own black yoga pants and a St. Kitts T-shirt from a long-ago vacation. Her hiking boots and a Yankees hat rounded out the ensemble.

Mack slid into the passenger seat of Jess' Infiniti and accepted the protein bar she was handed. "Where are we going?"

"Tanque Verde trailhead," Jess said. "I want to take a look at where Morgan's body was found. I know we've reviewed the photos, but I want to see it closer to how it would have looked when Beth found the body."

Mack relaxed. The trailhead was only fifteen minutes from her house, given the empty streets. Jess had quiet music playing that Mack didn't recognize, so she sipped her coffee and enjoyed the drive. Jess' car was luxurious by any measure, but compared to Mack's ancient Saab, it was a dream. It had been a long time since she'd had an adventure and, though this wouldn't have been her first choice, it felt good to be *doing* something again.

Theirs was the only car in the trailhead's parking area. Jess handed Mack a bottle of water and got out. They stopped by a large rock, recognizing it from the crime-scene photos.

"So, the bin was here," Jess said, her voice making Mack jump in the silence. They looked around. "Clearly visible from the parking area."

"Agreed," Mack said. "So how could Joe be sure Beth was the one to find the body?"

Jess pursed her lips. "Maybe he didn't care who found it. Maybe Beth was a fail-safe."

"What do you mean?"

"Maybe he just needed someone to find it. He set Beth up so if no one found it Friday night, she'd find it Saturday morning."

"Why would he care about the timing?"

Jess shrugged. "I don't know. Maybe he had an alibi for Friday night? Someone who could vouch for his whereabouts if he was ever a suspect?"

That made as much sense as anything else—which wasn't much.

"I wish we could ask Anna," Mack said.

"Hmm," Jess said. "I'm not sure she'd have much to offer on this one, frankly."

Ruthie had promised to call if she saw the man in the pickup again, but Mack suspected that was a dead end. He wasn't targeting girls on the Track—Jane Gould proved that. Mack wasn't sure where Jess' theory got them. They couldn't start asking every man in Tucson if he had an alibi for that Friday night.

Jess looked around, her hands on her hips. Finally satisfied, she turned back to Mack. "Since we're here," she said, pulling a flashlight from the small backpack she carried, "let's hike."

Mack tried to decide whether she was kidding. Jess tossed her a second flashlight and walked down the well-marked trail and into the scrub. Mack trudged after her. It wasn't like she could get back to sleep at this point anyway.

After they'd both showered and changed at Mack's house, they were in court by 8:10, waiting for Judge Haberfeld to take the bench. The hike had done Jess some good, and she seemed resigned to her fate. "Whatever happens, happens," she said as they walked into the building. "Maybe, if it mistries, we try him *with* Eddie next time. That wouldn't be so bad."

Mack thought—but didn't say—if it mistried, Judge Haberfeld was unlikely to let them try Jefferson again. She would only declare a mistrial if she found that Jess had engaged in prosecutorial misconduct. There would be no second bite at the apple.

Noah looked like he hadn't slept much, either. Mack studied him as he sat at the defense table, stifling yawns. Jefferson, stiff and silent, sat beside him. She wondered what their relationship was. Had Noah encouraged Jefferson to take a plea given the strength of the case against him, or had he fought for trial, confident he could overcome anything Jess threw in his path? There was no way to tell.

Judge Haberfeld appeared at 8:16 and waved everyone back into their seats. Kimberly wasn't there—she would wait for the verdict at police headquarters, where she could catch up on cases that had been left on hold during the trial. Eleanor, however, was there in the first row of the gallery, chewing a thumbnail as she waited for the judge's ruling.

"I will issue a written minute entry," Judge Haberfeld said without preamble, "summarizing the reasons for my ruling, but the short version is that I'm denying the motion for mistrial. The jury will continue deliberating."

Jess let out a shaky breath. Despite the earlier bravado, Mack knew how much a mistrial would sting her. Especially a mistrial Jess herself had caused. She was relieved that all their work hadn't been wasted. Yet. The verdict would ultimately determine that.

They gave their contact information to Judge Haberfeld's bailiff and retreated to their offices to wait for the jury. Jefferson would be kept in a holding cell just off the courtroom until a verdict. When he left the jail that morning, they'd given him a bologna sandwich and an orange as a bagged lunch. Mack hoped it would be the last meal he ever ate with a viable chance at freedom.

The bailiff called just after noon. The jury was ready and would return at 1:30. Jess pushed her salad away, and Mack set down the crackers she was eating. They both felt sick. A quick jury on an easy case was a good sign—it almost always meant a guilty verdict. This hadn't been an easy case, though, and a fast verdict on a circumstantial case often meant trouble.

Jess called Kimberly and Eleanor, and they sat, unable to focus on anything else, until it was time to return to the courtroom.

The clerk cleared her throat before she read the first verdict form. Mack could feel her heartbeat in her molars. Nothing was as painful as the moments between the foreperson handing the folder of verdict forms to the bailiff, the judge reviewing them, and the clerk starting to read.

"As to Count One: First Degree Murder, we the jury, duly impaneled, do find the defendant guilty."

Mack felt her muscles relax. The other counts didn't matter, not really. First degree meant Jefferson would spend his life behind bars. She gave Eleanor a tight smile. The anxiety of waiting for the wheels of justice to turn was over.

After the remaining verdicts had been read—guilty on all counts related to the rape and murder, not guilty on the counts related to the first burglary—Judge Haberfeld thanked the jury for their service and released them. None of them wanted to stay and talk to the lawyers.

Mack was pleased with the way the jury had split the baby. That would make it much more difficult for Jefferson to win an appeal, since the jury had demonstrated its willingness and ability to consider the evidence fairly and acquit Jefferson when warranted.

Eleanor stood awkwardly, arms wrapped tightly around herself, as Jefferson was led out of the room by the deputy. She didn't look at him as he passed. She hugged Jess when the prosecutors approached.

"Thank you," she said. She looked sad and worried. Mack looked at her outfit. Eleanor had always been well dressed during trial, usually opting for muted colors and natural fibers, but today her face was washed out against her black cardigan.

"You're welcome," Jess said. "This doesn't bring your mom back, but we did what we could for her and to protect the community."

Eleanor chewed her lower lip. "Shouldn't I feel better? Getting the guilty verdict, being done with the trial?"

Mack shrugged. "The system worked, but that's not the same thing as 'closure' or even 'justice.' You don't have to worry about Jefferson. He'll pay for his crimes, and he won't ever hurt anyone again. Unfortunately, that's really all the system can do. There's no way to fix the harm that's already been done."

"And what happens to Eddie?" Eleanor asked. Jess and Mack made eye contact but didn't respond. "That's anyone's guess, I suppose?"

"We'll do what we can," Jess said. "You'll be kept informed, of course. If there comes a time when we're able to indict, your victim advocate will reach out to you."

Eleanor's smile didn't reach her eyes. "Thanks for taking the time to chat."

"Thank you for coming to trial," Jess said. "I know Dorothy appreciates your standing up for her."

Eleanor's shoulders dropped, and she looked ten years older. "My mother doesn't appreciate anything. She's dead. She would have wanted me to celebrate her life—me and Eddie. She didn't— wouldn't, doesn't—want any part of this." She turned abruptly and pushed through the courtroom doors.

Who could argue with that? They had said the things they were trained to say, but Mack knew such platitudes were little comfort to victims.

Noah was slowly packing his messenger bag. He had surely overheard the conversation with Eleanor. He crossed the room and held out a hand to Jess. She did not take it.

"Always a pleasure working with you," he said, putting the hand in his pocket.

Jess nodded tersely, clearly not ready to forgive him for the mistrial motions. Her jaw was clenched again. Mack wondered if she'd ever seen an orthodontist. Surely that was taking a toll on her teeth.

Noah left the courtroom. They waited until they were reasonably confident that he'd caught an elevator before following.

In the hallway, Juror Eight was looking at her phone. A younger Hispanic woman, Mack had never gotten a good read on her. She had seemed disengaged, took minimal notes, asked no questions of the witnesses. Mack assumed that she, like many jurors, was only there because she hadn't come up with a good enough reason to get released during *voir dire*.

Mack smiled at her as they started to pass but was surprised when she spoke.

"Can I talk to you guys?" she asked, putting her phone in her pocket. "Just for a minute, please?"

Jess and Mack stopped. They waved goodbye to Kimberly, but the detective didn't appear to notice. Mack wondered if she would think about this case again, or if she would have forgotten Frank Jefferson by the time the elevator doors opened.

"How can we help you?" Jess asked.

"He's going to get the death penalty, right?" Juror Eight asked.

Jess and Mack looked at each other, matching expressions of confusion on their faces.

"No," Jess said. "This wasn't a death-penalty case. If it had been, that would have been up to you jurors, but since the State wasn't asking for the death penalty, it's not an issue."

The juror scowled. "Why not?"

Jess raised her eyebrows, surprised. "Well," she said, and Mack could tell she was stalling for time. "Well, there are certain legal standards that have to be met for a case to be eligible for the death penalty, and this one wasn't deemed to be an appropriate candidate."

Juror Eight rolled her eyes. "I see guys from my neighborhood get death when their buddies are killed in home invasions," she said. "And this white guy gets nothing?"

Mack caught herself on the verge of arguing. Felony murder was death-penalty eligible, sure, but Mack had never seen anyone actually *get* the death penalty in a situation where a civilian killed a co-conspirator. But that wasn't the point, and neither was the complex analysis of aggravating factors and mitigation that went on in decisions to seek the death penalty. It seemed like the only things Mack saw on the news lately were stories about the system failing—it was too harsh on black and brown men, too lenient on white men. Female victims were ignored, while female defendants were treated more harshly than men who committed similar crimes.

Times when the system got it right didn't make for compelling television. That's why all the true-crime shows and podcasts and books featured unsolved murders and wrongful convictions. Juror Eight was angry because she perceived that Jefferson was benefiting from racial stereotypes. That would be enough to upset anyone.

"I want to write a letter about this," the juror continued. "Who should I write it to?"

Jess looked confused, so Mack took half a step forward. "Probably District Attorney Peter Campbell," she said. "He's the elected official in charge of the office that Ms. Lafayette and I work for. He is personally involved in every case where the State considers the death penalty, regardless of whether or not we actually wind up asking for it. So, he's up to speed on this case, and he was involved in the decision. He'd be the best person to write to."

Juror Eight pulled out her phone and typed that into a note, confirming with Mack that she'd spelled Campbell's name right. She walked away, shaking her head.

"Another satisfied participant in the justice system," Mack said when the juror was out of sight. "Do you think she'll really write to Campbell?"

Jess shrugged and rubbed her forehead. "I'm not sure. I couldn't tell if she wanted to write to Campbell or the media or, like, the ACLU. I hope she doesn't. None of us needs any additional scrutiny right now, and you need it even less than I do. Come on, let's get out of here."

Mack felt unsettled. Her after-verdict ritual—win, lose, or draw—was to get a drink with Anna. This was the first time in years that she found herself needing a different way to mark the occasion, and she wasn't sure how much celebrating she really felt like doing. What good was a guilty verdict on Jefferson, she thought, if Eddie Johnson walked free?

"Drinks?" she asked as they finally made their way onto an elevator.

"Sorry, no can do. Adam and I have plans. I haven't seen much of him lately, and we have lots to catch up on. Next week?"

"Sure," Mack said. "Of course. My schedule is…open."

CHAPTER THIRTY-SIX

Monday morning, Mack got to her office to find an email from Wendy at the crime lab. The results were in: the swabs from the Starbucks cup confirmed that it was Eddie's saliva on his mother's breast. Mack took a moment to quietly celebrate as she drank her coffee and checked her calendar and messages. Jess responded, saying that Kimberly was going to interview Eddie that afternoon and confront him with the new results. Hopefully, he'd come clean.

Since she had handled the Jefferson case, Jess would be the prosecutor, and Mack knew she would schedule a grand jury presentation in short order, regardless of the results of the interview. Jefferson's sentencing had been scheduled for three weeks down the road. Mack wondered if he might be willing to give an interview in the interim, implicate Eddie in exchange for a recommendation that the judge show leniency. She sent Jess an email suggesting it and was disappointed at the immediate response: according to Noah, Jefferson wasn't interested in talking about anything.

Mack's calendar was light that afternoon, so she agreed to go down to police headquarters and watch Kimberly's interview with Eddie, so Jess could catch up on other cases. A child molestation trial was set the following week, and Jess needed the afternoon to respond to accumulated emails and voice mails.

It was the first time she'd been to 270 South Stone since Dave interrogated her on the day Morgan was found. As she approached the imposing gray and brown stone building, she shivered despite the afternoon sun. She wondered how long it would take before her first association with police headquarters stopped being the time she was a murder suspect and went back to being the job she had always loved and fought so hard to get.

She blinked hard and walked into the building, signed into law-enforcement book, and was permitted without commentary to wander the hallways unescorted. She found Kimberly in her cubicle, chatting with some colleagues. When the detective saw Mack, she stood and led her back to the monitoring room.

"Have you decided how to play it?" Mack asked. This was the kind of situation where, in days gone by, she would have reached out to Anna for advice. The psychologist was a master at predicting which methods would work for any specific kind of criminal. Mack had never seen a detective who used Anna's ideas fail to get a confession. Over the years, she'd caught on to some of Anna's theories, but she wasn't sure what to do with Eddie. Was he a narcissist, a sociopath, or something else entirely? She didn't want to be responsible for the interview going south because she'd read him wrong.

"I don't play games," Kimberly said. "I'm a straight shooter. I'll tell him what we've got and what our theory of the case is, and see what he has to say. I never went for that Reid Technique, unscrew-the-lightbulb, hard-sell stuff."

Mack suppressed a smile. The Reid Technique was a law-enforcement interview approach that most of the macho cops she knew swore by, designed to give a systematic progression from denial to confession using manipulative and deceptive techniques. They bragged about attending Reid trainings and using Reid materials, then got shredded by defense attorneys who knew enough to challenge them. The research was clear: Reid was an outdated and deeply flawed system. Even cops Mack respected—like Dave—sometimes fell into the Reid trap.

Once Mack was ensconced in the monitoring room, Kimberly headed into the interview room where Eddie Johnson sat, looking bored and pulling at a hangnail. This was the first time Mack had seen him not wearing a suit. He favored skinny ties and pants that seemed a hair too short. He was a good-looking guy, average height and build, with a stylish haircut and expensive prescription glasses. In the orange jumpsuit, his tan skin looked washed out. He had three days of stubble and a bruise on his forearm. Mack wondered if he'd gotten into it with a fellow inmate.

Kimberly read him his rights, even though he'd already been advised by Officer Morales when he was arrested. Mack appreciated her thoroughness. Now they would have the advisement on the same video as the interview.

To Mack's surprise, Eddie didn't ask for a lawyer. Instead, he agreed to talk to Kimberly. He answered her introductory questions politely and showed no fear or nervousness about the process. Mack wondered if he had a criminal history. He seemed far too cool for someone who had just spent several days in county lockup. Hopefully, Kimberly's questions would unsettle him and lead to some answers.

After building rapport, Kimberly asked about Eddie's relationship with his mother. Mack expected a breezy answer, in line with Eddie's other answers thus far.

"Dorothy and I never really saw eye to eye," he said. Mack was surprised. This seemed almost too easy. "She always preferred my elder sister, Eleanor. Excellent Elder Ellie, that's what I called her as a kid. But that's a long ways from murder, Detective."

Kimberly agreed, and asked how he knew that his mother had preferred his sister.

Eddie laughed. "It wasn't hard to tell," he said. "It showed in everything that Ellie got handed to her while I had to earn it. College tuition, help buying a house, on and on. My parents both thought she was God's gift. But after my father passed, things got worse. Ellie would do things like come watch a movie with our mother, just for the fun of it. They'd cook dinner together. Go grocery shopping. Even go to bingo. Dorothy *loved* her bingo. Of course, I never got invited. I was expected at Christmas and on Mother's Day, but otherwise, I never heard much from either of them."

"That must have been hard," Kimberly said.

"It wasn't so bad. I found other things to occupy my time."

Kimberly asked about the insurance policy, but Eddie avoided the question. It was clear that he was willing to talk—but there were limits.

For an hour, Kimberly painstakingly pushed at the edges of what Eddie was interested in discussing. His disdain for his mother was palpable as he catalogued a lifetime of perceived injustice. Mack was confident that motive wouldn't be a problem in *this* trial. There'd be other problems if Kimberly couldn't work her way to some admissions.

As Eddie began to wind down, they took a break.

"What do you think?" Kimberly said, taking a seat in the monitoring room and drinking deeply from a bottle of water. "He's a hard nut to crack."

"I think you've done a great job letting him set the pace," Mack said. She really was impressed with how well Kimberly was handling him. After their experience in the Jefferson trial, she hadn't had much faith in the detective, but this interview had changed her opinion. "But I'd like to see you mix it up a little. He's a narcissist, right?"

"Absolutely," Kimberly said. "Hero of every story. Every slight he's ever imagined weighs on him. He's the smartest and best man who's ever lived."

"So, why not try a narcissistic injury? Worst-case scenario is he shuts down, but I don't see that happening. He's a talker. He might not fall for it—in which case, you'll have to shift gears pretty quickly. But I think it's worth a shot."

Kimberly watched Eddie through the one-way mirror. He was leaning back in his chair, hands behind his head. Mack wouldn't have been surprised if he'd started whistling. Looking closer, though, she saw his jaw clenching and unclenching. Maybe he wasn't as calm as he appeared.

"So Eddie," Kimberly said, reentering the interview room. "You've gone on and on about why you hated your mom, how terrible she was when you were a kid, blah blah blah. But you're a grown man now. Surely you've gotten past all that stuff?"

Eddie's face flushed an angry red, but he didn't respond.

"No? Still thinking about how mommy was mean to you? What that did to your life?" Kimberly leaned back in her chair, its front two legs leaving the ground. "Let's see. Most men who can't stop thinking about their mothers have…performance issues." She held up her index finger and curled it with an exaggerated frown.

"Fuck you," Eddie said. His voice had lost all hint of the friendly banter he had kept up for the previous hour. "I've never had an issue in that department. Want me to prove it to you?"

Kimberly laughed. "Okay, big man. So then why did you need Frank to fire the fatal shot? I mean, you should have been able to take care of her yourself, but you had to outsource it to the help?"

Eddie dropped his hands to the table and sat up straight in his chair. "I didn't *outsource* anything," he said.

"I mean, I know you were *there*, Eddie. You spit on her naked corpse. That's *grim*."

Eddie didn't respond. His hands clenched into fists.

"Spit," Kimberly said again. "Just spit, huh? Couldn't do what you really wanted to do? Had to outsource that to your pal, too?"

Eddie didn't respond.

"You couldn't pull the trigger? That's just pathetic. She was just a little old lady, but she still had so much power over you, you had to hand the gun off to a stranger? You couldn't do it yourself?"

Mack could only see Eddie in profile. Even so, she saw his reaction to Kimberly's words.

"He didn't pull the trigger," Eddie snarled. "*I* pulled the trigger. I let Frankie have his fun with the old bitch, but I'm the one who finished the job. *I'm* the one who finished her bingo card."

Kimberly smiled and sat back in her chair. "Why don't you tell me all about it?" she said. "Don't leave anything out."

It took Eddie almost another hour to explain the plot. He had actually been the one to refer Donnie Jefferson to his mother—they'd met when Donnie was cleaning Eddie's pool. But Donnie had apparently rubbed Dorothy the wrong way, and she'd fired him after a couple of months. When Donnie complained to Eddie, Eddie saw an opportunity to make his mother pay—and to come ahead financially on the deal.

"Donnie wasn't interested," Eddie said. "He didn't have the stones to get his hands dirty, but he put me in touch with his brother, who jumped at the chance. I didn't know the guy was some kind of sexual sadist who couldn't finish the job."

Eddie paid Frank $5,000 upfront, and another five grand after the deed was done. Eddie set up the burglary and stole the iPad to deflect attention. He knew that he'd be a prime suspect if his mother's murder wasn't associated with an earlier break-in. The presence of Frank's DNA in the system, however, was a complication neither of them had seen coming.

Eddie's admission, both to setting up the burglary and to pulling the trigger, threw Mack for a loop. Jefferson's murder conviction could wind up thrown out on appeal, since the jury had been told about the burglary.

This was a big fucking deal.

Jess and Mack had asked the jury to convict Frank Jefferson for committing the burglary, and now, Eddie was saying that the jury got it right and Jefferson had nothing to do with it. If Eddie and Jefferson had worked together to set up the burglary, to cover their tracks on the murder, and then been tried together, there wouldn't be an issue. The jury would still have heard about the burglary, because Eddie had set it up to further the murder conspiracy. But Judge Haberfeld would have instructed the jury not to consider the burglary in their deliberations about Jefferson, and life would have gone on.

It all came down to accomplice liability. Even though Jefferson hadn't pulled the trigger, he was legally equally guilty of the murder. It was charged first-degree, premeditated, but also as felony murder, because Dorothy had died in the course of the second burglary. Even without specifying that Jefferson was an accomplice, the felony murder conviction was righteous. She had died in the course of Jefferson committing a qualifying felony. It didn't matter that he wasn't the one who'd pulled the trigger.

As it stood, however, the police—and the Tucson District Attorney's Office—now had actual knowledge that Jefferson wasn't involved in a crime that a jury had heard the State accuse him of. If the murder conviction was good, what need was there to inform Judge Haberfeld and delay Jefferson's sentencing or agree to a new trial?

Trying Jefferson and Eddie together on the basis of the new evidence would be a cleaner solution. Maybe. The problem was that Eddie's implication of Jefferson couldn't come in at a joint trial, because co-defendants can't testify against each other.

Mack's head ached from thinking through the complicated permutations of what to do next. Jess would have a difficult decision ahead of her, and Mack didn't envy her the slightest bit. By the time Eddie's interview was over, Mack had already drawn up preliminary charging paperwork for Jess' review. She wondered if, unlike Frank's case, Eddie's was one where the office might seek the death penalty. Mack was ambivalent about capital punishment, but this was a case where she would support it. It was clear that Eddie would kill anyone who stood in his way. That kind of callous killer wouldn't be safe in any community, including a community behind bars.

CHAPTER THIRTY-SEVEN

Four months after Eddie Johnson confessed to his mother's murder, Mack had completed her ninth month as the Tucson District Attorney's Community Liaison. That left her with only three more months of purgatory to endure. Now that the Jefferson trial was over, she'd fallen into an easy rhythm of community speaking engagements and police agency trainings. She left work at work, her evenings were free for concerts, movies, or simply reading on the couch, her house was clean, and her refrigerator always had food in it. This was a pleasant change from her time in Sex Crimes, when she constantly felt like she was fighting to catch up.

Campbell hadn't said anything to her about where she'd be reassigned come October. Mack hoped that she would be allowed to go where she wanted. Although her first love would always be sex crimes, she was ready for something new. The Jefferson case had proven that she had what it took to try homicide cases, and Mack had enjoyed the challenge. Giving Eleanor Johnson a measure of justice for her mother had left Mack feeling righteous in a way she now missed. The story wasn't over yet, as Eddie's case worked its way through the system, but at a minimum she'd been able to keep the community safe from any future threat from Frank Jefferson. Community Liaison didn't give her the same sense of moral superiority.

Jess suggested that Mack should consider pursuing a supervisor job, but that wasn't for her. She had spent far too much time sparring with Michael Brown to ever be appointed to a management position, and that was fine with her. She had seen too many good trial lawyers promoted out of trial caseloads and into roles they were neither qualified nor suited for. Mack wanted to stay in the trenches where she belonged.

Jess was focused on the Jane Gould investigation. The link between the homicide and the case against Ron Simon had not, apparently, been made by anyone other than Dave. No one had batted an eye when Jess offered to take on what looked like a dead-end case with no suspects and no leads. Jess and Mack, however, didn't see it that way. Jane's autopsy results had included some interesting DNA results, and Jess thought it might be a case that could benefit from the help of a genetic genealogist.

Typically, unknown DNA profiles from crime scenes were entered into CODIS, the national database, where they were run against all other samples. CODIS, however, only worked on exact matches. If Jane Gould's killer already had his profile in the system—for any reason, whether as a convicted felon or from an unsolved crime—it would hit. But if he'd managed to avoid law enforcement contact, a CODIS search would come up empty.

Genetic genealogists, however, wouldn't look for exact matches. They'd use the millions of profiles voluntarily submitted to family-tree genealogy websites and look for profiles that were close to the suspect profile. Identifying a possible last name or even a close family member could help law enforcement figure out who the suspect was.

Mack glanced at her calendar and noticed that November 11 was circled. Jess and Adam's wedding day, only four months off. Because they were both a little old for a first marriage, they had decided to go a non-traditional route. They'd be getting married at the courthouse, followed by a party in Adam's backyard. Jess had asked Mack to be her maid of honor, and Mack had hesitantly accepted. She wasn't sure she was the right choice to organize a bachelorette party or a bridal shower and whatever other duties she'd be asked to perform, but she was the only local bridesmaid and she wanted to help her friend in any way she could. They'd gone dress shopping, an experience Mack found thoroughly unsettling. "That one's nice," she'd said, shifting uneasily from foot to foot. "They're all nice."

She was distracted by her phone buzzing. A text from Jess. *Are you ok?*

Why wouldn't she be?

More texts popped up: her mom, two detectives, and three other prosecutors. She barely had time to look at them before her email alerted: Dan Petrou's third article was out.

Mack clicked to the reporter's story. This was the one she had been dreading since the public records request had come through. The new article made it clear that he hadn't just gone to the DA's office, either. He had also requested records from Tucson Police.

The article was impressively accurate. She *had* dated an expert witness from the Andersen trial, which *did* put the expert's credibility in doubt. She *had* been a suspect in the Morgan Packer homicide. She *had* gone rogue to investigate that case. Her investigation *had* resulted in an arrest that couldn't have been righteous, because then Jane Gould was killed.

Did Mack kill both girls? The office clearly thought she might have killed Morgan, since she was put on admin leave. Why was she allowed back into her job?

It was an excoriating piece—not just about Mack, but also the office and the justice system as a whole. Campbell was blamed for keeping her on board and making a possible killer the public face of the office. Tucson PD was blamed for not arresting her. The Pima County Superior Court was blamed for allowing her to try the Jefferson case. The State Bar was blamed for not disbarring her.

The integrity of every conviction she'd ever obtained was questioned. How could a possible murderer try a murder case? Petrou mused.

The reporter seemed not to understand that, regardless of whether or not Ron Simon had killed Morgan, he had undeniably raped her and participated in sex trafficking her. It wasn't as if an innocent man had been charged. Ron Simon was a piece of trash, and Mack had gotten him off the street. How many other girls were safe, now that Simon couldn't target them? And what about the 1999 victim—did Petrou care about getting justice for her? Apparently not.

It was clear that Petrou hadn't been firing in the dark with his public records requests. He knew exactly what he was looking for, and Mack couldn't begin to guess who his source had been. It couldn't just be Michael Brown or his brother the cop. Michael and his brother couldn't have known the details of Mack's role in the Ron Simon investigation. Either Dave must have leaked the story himself, or he'd told someone else who leaked.

Still reeling, Mack called Dave. His voice was tense as he swore he wasn't the leak. The article made him look bad, too, he argued. Clearly, he wasn't the source of Petrou's information.

"I think I know who it might be," he whispered. Mack wondered if he didn't want his co-workers to know he was talking to her. "But I don't want to say anything until I'm sure. I'll call you back after I do my own investigation."

Mack hung up, and her phone immediately lit up again, this time with a text from Rocky. Mack was flooded by a rush of guilt. The longer she went without responding to Rocky's texts, the more difficult it became to even think of talking to her. Mack was resigned to finding a new favorite bar.

Two things, the text read. *I know you're stressed, Pumpkin, but if you want someone to talk to about the latest news piece you know where to find me. Also, can you send me Jess' number? Something is going on with Adam, and I want to talk to her about it. I'm actually worried about him. He's missed a couple shifts lately, seems stressed. Maybe she knows what's up.*

Mack considered her response. The best option, she decided, was to give Rocky's number to Jess and let her decide how to proceed. As Mack started to type, her phone interrupted her. She was shocked to see Anna's name and picture on the screen. So shocked, she fumbled the phone and nearly dropped it.

"Anna?" she asked, incredulous. She'd given up ever hearing from her ex-girlfriend well before the third Petrou exposé. If Anna hadn't had the bandwidth to deal with her when no one really knew about Mack's issues, she certainly wouldn't be interested now that the media was carefully watching.

"Hi, Mack," Anna said. She sounded just the way Mack remembered—warm but professional. Mack felt her cheeks flush at the sound of her name. Despite everything that had happened, she still really liked Anna and wanted her in her life.

"Long time no talk," she said.

Anna laughed. "I see your name in the news here and there. Looks like you've been busy. I want to talk to you about a case one of your colleagues in Pinal County contacted me about."

Mack blinked. "You're calling to talk about a case?"

"Listen, I—I'm sorry. I shouldn't have bailed on you back in January. I just—I panicked, but we've always had such a good working relationship, and I thought maybe enough time had passed, so I—"

Mack couldn't believe it. "Respectfully, Dr. Lapin, get fucked. These have been the worst six months of my life. This has been the worst *year* of my life, and you were nowhere to be found. I don't care about your case. Ask someone else."

"I understand you're hurt."

Mack laughed. The back of her throat ached and she fought back tears. "Hurt? I stopped being 'hurt' round about Valentine's Day. Then I got mad. Now, I don't think about you at all." That wasn't true, but Mack hoped she sounded sincere enough Anna wouldn't question it.

The line was silent, and Mack wondered if Anna had hung up. "That's fair," the psychologist said finally. "Can you just"—she sighed, frustrated— "can you meet me? At my office? I really miss you, and I know you don't owe me anything, but I just want to talk to you, one more time. And then I promise you'll never hear from me again, if that's what you want."

Mack got up, suddenly restless in her confined office. She wanted to drop her phone and run, and keep running until she got far, far away from Tucson. Somewhere she could start a new life and never think about Anna Lapin again.

"Okay," she said. She wanted to get off the phone, and agreeing seemed like the fastest path. "Where and when?"

They agreed to meet at Anna's office in an hour. When they got off the phone, Mack threw herself back into her chair, trying to decide whether or not to tell Jess about the call. She knew that her friend had her best interests at heart, but Jess' tendencies to distrust Anna made her hesitate. Anna's office was fifteen minutes from Mack's, and she sat, watching the clock, until fifty minutes had passed. Her phone was still in her hand, but she hadn't reached out to Jess. She hadn't yet decided whether she was actually going to meet the psychologist. Impulsively, she grabbed her purse and headed for the door. She couldn't resist seeing what Anna had to say for herself.

CHAPTER THIRTY-EIGHT

Anna's office was on the second floor of an anonymous building in the northwest part of town. It was a quiet neighborhood, and Mack was sure that the businesses on either side of Anna's didn't know what kind of clients were coming to Saguaro Wren Counseling PLLC. Anna and two other practitioners shared a conference room, which they used for group therapy sessions, and each had an individual office for one-on-one meetings with patients.

The suite was empty when Mack arrived—she walked into the unlocked lobby to find Anna's door ajar and the desk light on. Anna's purse was hanging on the hook behind the door, so Mack assumed she'd just stepped out to use the restroom. She sat on the midcentury modern gray cloth couch that took up the entirety of one of the small office's walls and pulled out her phone. After five minutes passed, with no sign of anyone else coming or going, Mack noticed Anna's phone on her desk.

Odd, she thought. *She usually grabs her phone even when she's just going to the bathroom.* She tapped the screen and saw notifications spanning the last half hour. That was odd, too. Anna was meticulous about clearing her notifications promptly.

Concerned, Mack checked the communal restroom, three doors down. Its stalls were empty.

Mack looked at her own phone. There were four missed calls, all from Jess.

Jess picked up on the first ring. "Hey, thanks for calling me back." She sounded stressed. "This is going to sound crazy— it *is* crazy—I think I've lost my mind, but—well—I—I think it's possible that Adam is a murderer."

"Excuse me?" Mack asked. She went back into Anna's office— still empty. She scanned the carpet to see if Anna had left a note that might have fallen to the floor. Nothing.

"You know how I sent the DNA stuff to that genetic genealogist?"

"Mm-hmm," Mack said. She put her phone on speaker and set it on the desk, the better to search the drawers. If Anna came in now, she'd be pissed, but Mack knew there was no point hurrying Jess, and she needed both hands free.

"Well, I got the report back this afternoon. And I'm reading through it, and it came back suggesting that the DNA on Jane Gould belongs to a close male relative of someone named Mark Bennett."

"And?"

"And Adam's brother's name is Mark."

"Yikes. Well, Mark Bennett's got to be a pretty common name." She pulled Anna's purse from its hook and dug through it. "Even here in Arizona. Who's to say it's the same family?"

"There's a photo. It could be Adam's twin. And I just, I don't know, it feels right, somehow. Like, when you told me you were a suspect, my immediate reaction was 'Fuck no!' But when I read this report, my stomach dropped and I thought 'Fuck, no wonder he's been lying to me.' We really haven't been together very long. He came on so strong, and I never really noticed that I don't know him all that well."

"And?"

"And think about what we know about Joe. Adam could totally be Joe."

Mack rubbed the back of her neck. "Well, it sounds like we're both having pretty bizarre afternoons. Not to add to your stress, but I'm in a bit of a pickle. I am at Anna's office—we were supposed to meet—but she's not here. She left her purse and phone. Should I call the police?"

"Mack, saying this out loud makes me feel like a psycho, and if I'm wrong I'll appreciate it if we never mention it again, but I think it's possible that Adam might have taken Anna."

"*Taken* her? What does that mean?"

"He's been talking about her a lot recently, but I wrote it off as him trying to take an interest in my good friend Mack's life. I mean, I've told him about all the bullshit you went through with her. So I just wonder if, maybe, he has her? I know it's crazy, but it's just, like, this feeling I have."

"Okay," Mack said. "Okay, just—I mean—give me a second." She dropped Anna's purse and braced herself against the wall. This was insane. Jess had lost whatever tenuous grip she had on reality, and her pre-wedding jitters had taken over her brain. Some brides-to-be worried their fiancés might be cheating on them, but Jess was all about go big or go home. Someday they'd laugh about this—but not until Jess had received some pretty serious therapy.

And yet...hadn't Mack always had her doubts about Adam? Hadn't he always seemed just a little bit...off? Was it possible?

"Where would he take her, Jess? Maybe I should have a look? If you're wrong, it's no harm, no foul. I'll just say I was looking for you. But if he actually killed those girls and now he has Anna... Well, we don't have any time to waste."

"They'd be at his house." Jess' voice was strained and tight. "I'll meet you there."

"You don't have to do that. I can go."

Jess laughed. "There's no way I'm letting to go there by yourself. I'd never forgive myself if something happened to you. But, Mack?"

"Yeah?"

"Why don't you call Dave, too? Just in case."

Dave didn't answer his phone. He was probably trying to track down the source for the Petrou article. She shot him a text with Adam's address and a second one: *Need your help. Wear a vest. ASAP.*

Given the nature of her clientele, Anna had long ago decided that she was safer with firearm close at hand, and she had one in almost every room of her home. For additional protection, she also always kept a gun in her office. They'd fought about it—Mack was afraid a rogue patient might grab it and Anna would wind up shot, while Anna trusted her ability to beat a bad guy to the trigger. Now, though, Mack was grateful for Anna's caution. She grabbed the handgun out of the bottom drawer of the desk and slipped it—and Anna's phone—into the psychologist's purse. She wasn't sure she remembered how to use the gun—that one-day class she'd taken had been more theory than practice—but she knew how to hold it. Hopefully, that would be enough.

CHAPTER THIRTY-NINE

Rocky answered on the first ring. "This isn't a great time, Pumpkin. You could have just texted me Jess' number."

"Sorry," Mack said, remembering for the first time since Anna had called that Rocky was trying to reach Jess because she was concerned about Adam. "I'm just—are you at the bar, by any chance?"

"Just walking in," Rocky said. "Adam was supposed to open, but I got a call about half an hour ago from the barback saying he never showed and she was locked out. So I drove down to open up. You need something?"

Mack's mind raced. "So he's not there?"

"No. What's going on?"

"Call me back if he shows up," Mack said. "I'll explain later." She ended the call as she pulled onto Adam's street. She parked the Saab half a block from his house, in front of a vacant lot. The block backed onto the desert, and she had a clear view of the mountains in the distance. She had no idea what, if any, cameras Adam might have set up. She checked her watch. Jess should be there any minute, and she wasn't sure whether she should wait. She knew that Anna kept the gun loaded, but she didn't know if its safety was on or off. She wasn't even sure the gun had a safety.

A sleek Infiniti pulled up behind her. Jess had changed out of her work clothes into the black yoga pants and tank top she kept under her desk. Mack glanced down at her own outfit—a navy blue suit over a pink Oxford shirt and beige pumps. Of the two of them, Jess looked more ready for action.

"Should we go in?" Mack asked. She shrugged off her jacket and tossed it into the car, then grabbed the gun from the passenger seat, careful not to point it anywhere near Jess.

"Do you know how to use that thing?" Jess asked.

"Definitely no. I thought you might."

"Never learned," Jess said.

Adam's garage door was closed, and no lights were visible behind the living room curtains.

"Should we wait for Dave?" Mack asked. She was feeling less brave than she had in Anna's office.

Jess grimaced. "If he's got her, we can't afford to wait."

"You don't even like Anna. You've been telling me how shitty she is for months."

"Yeah, well, I like you, and I know you're going to do this, with or without me." Jess pulled her hair into a tight bun. "He sometimes leaves the back door unlocked. You knock on the front door, and I'll take that" —she pointed at the gun— "and try the back." She bit her lip. "This is so messed up, Mack."

Mack handed over the gun.

"I wish we had walkie-talkies," Jess said.

"We have the next best thing," Mack said. She pulled out her phone and dialed Jess' number. "Just keep it in your pocket. If he's home, try not to disconnect the call. If things seem fine, I'll hang up, and you can make like you just decided to surprise him. Okay?"

The women took a final deep breath. They exchanged a quick hug and Jess circled around the house low, moving like she hoped to avoid any surveillance cameras.

Mack squared her shoulders, went up to Adam's front door, and rang the bell.

She counted to thirty before ringing again. Still no response. As she turned away, the door opened. It was Jess.

"No sign of him," Jess said, "but we should check every room."

"That's standard," Mack said, thinking back to the countless SWAT officers she'd put on the stand. "Clear the house. Of course."

Jess led the way, the gun at waist level, her finger on the trigger. Mack had no idea what would happen if Jess tried to actually use the gun, but she looked like she knew what she was doing.

The house had an open floor plan, the foyer flowing into the living room and kitchen. They moved room to room, confirming that no one was there.

There was a black leather jacket draped over one of the kitchen chairs. Mack checked the tag. "Anna's."

"She was here," Jess said.

The lights were off. The setting sun provided the only illumination. There were no signs of life.

The hallway on the south side of the house led to two bedrooms and a guest bath, if Mack recalled correctly from the engagement dinner. All three doors were closed.

There was a sudden sound, and Mack jumped.

The ice maker.

Mack squeezed Jess' shoulder reassuringly.

They were running out of places to look, and Mack feared that they were wasting time.

The guest room and closet were empty. There was a blinking light in the guest bathroom, and Mack's heart thumped wildly.

"Air freshener," Jess whispered.

They crept into the primary bedroom's en suite bath. Jess moved toward the closet, but Mack grabbed her arm. There was something in the tub. They inched closer, their breath shallow and rapid. In the light of Mack's phone's flash, she saw a dark heap, not moving.

A body.

Anna.

Mack groped for the psychologist's wrist and almost collapsed with relief to find a pulse. Anna was unconscious, not dead. Mack examined her for signs of injury. There was no blood, no visible bruising—though much of Anna's body was hidden from view by her long pants and turtleneck sweater. No sign of a head wound. Mack thought back to her lifeguard training, courtesy of her stints at the JCC's Camp Wise every summer. Anna didn't have a history of fainting or low blood sugar.

Again, a noise startled Mack.

This time, it was Jess throwing up on the tile floor.

"This is different," Jess said, wiping her mouth and tossing a towel over the puddle of vomit. "It's not just me being crazy."

"I'm sorry you were going to marry a killer," Mack whispered.

Jess heaved again, and Mack rubbed her back.

"Is Anna okay?" Jess asked when she was able.

"I think she will be. We know he used GHB on the other victims, so I think it's safe to say she'll have a killer headache when she wakes up."

Jess glared at her use of the word "killer."

"Sorry," Mack said.

Her phone rang. She frantically rejected the call. Her heart was pounding. "Dave," she whispered.

"We better check the garage," Jess whispered back. "And you should text Dave. Silently."

Mack moved her thumb over her phone's screen. *Think we found killer. Come in. Dr. Lapin here, passed out but seems okay.*

They heard the front door open and close.

"Mack?" Dave called.

Jess bolted from the room and came back with Dave, both of them whispering furiously.

"You up to speed?" Mack asked.

"Yes," he said, moving to Anna's body and performing the same exam Mack had just gone through. "GHB?"

"We assume so," Jess said.

"If so, she'll be fine with some fluids and time to rest. I need to call for backup."

"Not yet," Mack said. "We don't have time. We haven't finished clearing the house. You two check the garage. I'm staying with Anna. Fine or not, she's vulnerable. We can't leave her alone."

"No," Jess said. "You go. I'll stay."

Mack started to argue, but Jess raised a hand.

"Seriously," Jess said. "I can't hunt for my fiancé, and you shouldn't be guarding your ex-girlfriend." She handed Mack the gun. Mack was surprised to find it slick with sweat. Dave looked at it and seemed to want to say something, but bit his tongue and led the way out of the room.

"You got my six?" Dave asked as they approached the door to the garage.

Mack swallowed hard. "Yes."

Dave took a deep breath. "Here we go." He burst into the garage. Mack tightened her grip on the gun, ready to shoot at the slightest sign of trouble.

"Clear!" Dave called. He came back into the house and touched Mack on the shoulder. She relaxed and let him take the gun. He fiddled with it and handed it back to her. She tucked it into her waistband.

"You know how to use that thing?" he asked.

"Big no," Mack said.

Dave grimaced. "That's what I thought. You had the hammer back—totally unsafe. At least now, with it decocked, you won't accidentally shoot yourself. To fire it, you'll have to pull *really* hard."

They found Jess sitting beside the tub, arms folded around her knees. "Can we call for backup now?" She sounded young and scared.

"Okay," Mack said, but she needed a moment to think. "You're right, Jess, we should call this in. But once the cops get here, none of us will be allowed anywhere near this case. We'll be walled off. We'll be more than walled off. Walled off will look like an invitation. We'll be *Garrity*-ed and interviewed, and that won't be the end of it. By the time they're done with us, admin leave will be the best-case scenario."

"But we didn't do anything wrong."

Dave shook his head. "She's right," he said. "At this point we've burglarized a house, and for all anybody knows we're the ones who brought Anna here."

Jess pulled her knees tighter against her chest. "So, what then?"

Mack sat on the side of the tub. "So don't you want to know what was going on here? I mean, you were going to marry Adam, Jess, and now we think he killed two women and almost killed a third. He's got my ex-girlfriend unconscious in his bathroom! And now God knows where he is. We need some answers before police get here."

Jess looked at her blankly. "I don't understand."

"Maybe we should" —Mack raised her eyebrows— "have a look around before we make the call. See if we can figure out where he might have gone."

"You can't be serious," Jess said. "Dave, tell her she can't be serious."

"I don't know," Dave said, crossing his arms over his chest. "I mean, in for a penny, right? I have gloves in my car. We could have a look around. I think it's up to you, Jess. Do you want to know, or would you rather keep out of it?"

Jess leaned against the bathroom counter, staring down at Anna. She bit her lower lip. Her face was gray, almost green, and Mack worried she was about to throw up again.

"I want to know," Jess said.

"Well," Dave said, "we should probably start with what I found in the garage." He stepped out of the room, returning quickly with three sets of latex gloves and a large flashlight.

Jess fumbled with her engagement ring, took it off, and moved to drop it onto the counter.

"Wait," Mack said. "Hang on to it, for now at least."

Jess thrust the ring into her pocket. "Hey, I can probably get a few grand for it."

"Sure," Mack said. "That, too. Fuck that guy. Get yours, girl. We can take the money and go to Vegas. Meet you someone new."

Jess laughed shakily, and Dave led them through the house, turning on the lights as they went.

They filed into the two-and-a-half-car garage. One bay was filled with an extended-cab Ford pickup. Just like Joe the friendly neighbor had. So they'd been right about that all along. And Adam did drive, after all, license or not. A chest freezer hummed against the back wall, beside a stack of Rubbermaid bins.

"Dave?" Mack said.

Dave rolled his eyes but opened the freezer. All three of them held their breath.

"Empty," he said. "Staining on the bottom, though. I bet that'll be good evidence on Morgan's case."

Mack shuddered. Morgan had spent her final moments in that innocuous-looking freezer as her heart slowed and stopped.

Mack was grateful that the medical examiner thought she'd been unconscious.

"Should we look in the bins?" Dave asked.

Jess shook her head. "If we had more time, I would say yes. But we need to get moving. I want to go back to the guest room— Adam never let me in there. He said it was a 'work in progress' and he didn't want me to see it until it was done. I always thought that was weird, but I put it aside. Just like everything else. God, I feel like such an idiot."

At first glance, it looked like a normal guest bedroom. Queen-sized bed, carefully made, matching nightstands, dresser. The closet door was ajar, and Mack flipped on the lights. The closet was bare except for a small green-and-white-striped cardboard box, like Mack's mom kept old family photographs in.

"Anything in the dresser?" she called.

"Nope," Dave said.

"Nothing in the nightstand," Jess said.

"This has to be it, then." Mack pulled the box off the shelf and took it into the bedroom. She set it on the bed. "You want to do the honors, Jessica?"

CHAPTER FORTY

Jess' hands were shaking as she pulled up the lid. There was a small steno pad in the box. Underneath it was a stack of photographs, all clearly postmortem. Jane Gould. Morgan Packer. Sabrina Fisher. Plus, four other girls none of them recognized.

"Shit," Mack said. "I didn't even connect Sabrina's case to the other two. I should have seen it when he tried to burn Jane's body. Morgan was frozen, so of course he couldn't burn her. And—and—these must mean—"

"There are more victims," Jess whispered. She looked back into the box. "What's this?" she asked, pulling out another photograph, this one creased and battered.

She handed it to Mack, who peered at it. A skinny white guy with spiky brown hair and wearing a white tank top, laughing in front of an ATV.

"That's Adam, right?" Mack asked.

Jess looked again. "Yeah. Younger, but it's him."

Mack shook her head. There was something familiar about the photo, but she couldn't place it.

"Jewelry," Jess said, digging deeper into the box. "Souvenirs?"

"We can check with the families," Dave said.

"God, I hope he didn't take this off a body," Jess said, tossing her engagement ring into the box. She shuddered and ran out of the room. Seconds later, they could hear her retching.

"Heavy shit," Dave said.

"Makes me feel a little better about being single, though," Mack said.

Dave laughed. "Don't tell my wife."

Mack reached for the steno pad.

"You sure you want to read that? It could be...well, you know what it could be."

Mack considered it. She assumed that the other items in the box were trophies from Adam's kills. That made the notebook too important to ignore. She opened it.

It was a journal. There must have been earlier volumes somewhere, because this one covered only the previous year. He didn't write in it every day, but most days there were at least a few sentences about the pretty girls he'd encountered. He followed women at the grocery store, stalked patrons from the bar. *Is that why he took the job at Paradise in the first place?* Mack wondered. He certainly seemed obsessed with lesbians. His entries often expressed a desire to show them what sex could be with "a real man." He reveled in fantasies of drugging and raping women.

She flipped back and forth through the pages.

The night Morgan and Mack met, Morgan had used her sister's ID, but Adam hadn't realized that and had memorized the address. He later scoped out the house—maybe more than once—and must have seen Morgan and followed her to Mayer's apartment. From there, it was easy to stalk her and eventually scoop her and kill her. Mack could picture him rereading the entries related to Morgan, reveling in the violence he'd perpetrated.

When she came across a description of a woman who must have been herself, Mack felt sick. It had been written before Adam knew who she was, but he'd apparently been watching her for some time, and to say that he was attracted to her would be an understatement. Mack had never had any idea the Paradise bartender might be interested in her as anything more than a reliably good tipper.

When he saw Mack and Anna kiss the same night she'd met Morgan, though, he was enraged. He'd assumed Mack must be gay, but the confirmation was more than he could bear. He wasn't sure what to do about it, until that night in October when he first saw Jess. If he couldn't have Mack, he'd settle for her best friend.

He seemed to enjoy the poetic irony of a serial killer dating a prosecutor. He described at some length how easy it had been to manipulate Jess into falling for him, relished the feelings of superiority he derived from their relationship. He was *much* smarter than the two prosecutors, who were completely taken in by his act.

Mack wanted to put the notebook down, close the box, go straight to any bar but Paradise. Jess and Dave could call police if they wanted to, but Mack had other priorities. There wasn't enough beer in the world to erase the horrific things she'd read, but she could try.

No, sack up, girl. This needs to be read.

A trickle of fear ran down her spine at Adam's account of the night Mack and Anna had met Jess for drinks. The flattering way he'd carded Anna? He was getting her address from her license. He didn't have a plan, not yet, but he already knew he wanted to be able to find her.

He'd dumped Morgan's body because Jess was going to stay the night at his house for the first time. He regretted giving up his trophy, but he couldn't take the risk of Jess finding it in his freezer.

I'm going to be sick, Mack thought.

During his next shift, he deleted Paradise's surveillance footage. He didn't want Morgan traced back to the bar.

As his relationship with Jess became more serious, the frequency of his journal entries decreased. She was, apparently, keeping him busy enough that he didn't need to follow other women. Then Dorothy's trial started, and Jess was working longer hours. Left to his own devices, Adam got bored—and Jane Gould paid the price. Jess hadn't told him about Ron Simon's arrest for Morgan's murder, so he didn't realize that killing again would actually make her busier.

The night he told Mack about knowing Sabrina, he wrote a long entry—longer than those describing the murders of Morgan and Jane. The pleasure he took from discussing a murder he himself had committed with two homicide prosecutors was repulsive.

Mack closed the notebook and dropped it back in the box. She wished there was more about Sabrina's murder. How had he found her? Why had he done it? She supposed those were questions that would remain unanswered.

Though Mack wasn't a psychologist, she'd spent enough time with Anna—and read enough evaluations of sex criminals—to make some educated guesses about Adam. He was intelligent, but he was also a narcissist, a sociopath, a sadist.

She wondered if it was just a coincidence that he'd taken Anna the same day she was going to meet Mack for the first time in months. He had written that Jess seemed to be pulling away, and he wanted to reel her back in. He knew from Jess that Anna had treated Mack badly, and figured she'd turn to him if Mack's ex was killed. Plus, once Anna was out of the way, perhaps there might be room for him in Mack's world.

CHAPTER FORTY-ONE

"What do we tell police when they get here?" Mack asked. They had reconvened in the living room, sipping water bottles and trying to regulate their nervous systems. It had taken Mack the better part of an hour to read Adam's journal. Jess still looked gray, and Mack worried that she wasn't done throwing up.

"We're going to tell them the whole truth and nothing but the truth, right up until we went exploring," Dave said. "And then we're just going to leave out the rest of it. None of us did anything wrong. We need to remember that, okay?"

Mack and Jess nodded.

"Okay," Mack said. "I'm going to go back to Anna. Dave, I think Jess needs to get out of here."

"You sure you're okay to stay with Dr. Lapin?" Dave asked.

"We'll be fine," Mack said. She found Anna in exactly the same position they'd left her in, twisted at the bottom of the tub with her left arm hanging over the side. Mack confirmed she was still breathing, then leaned back against the side of the tub. She was still trying to process Adam's murder book.

A noise—halfway between a screech and a slam—came from somewhere. Mack jumped, then realized it was just Dave and Jess leaving the house. She let her head drop against her chest. She was exhausted.

There was a rustling noise in the bedroom. She got up, relieved that Dave had come back so quickly. Hopefully, he'd have backup with him.

The bathroom light flicked on. The figure standing there in silhouette was taller than Dave, lean and muscular, his tight and dirt-streaked T-shirt emphasizing his strength.

Adam.

As her eyes adjusted to the light, Mack was shocked by the cruel look on his face and the revolver in his hand. He looked comfortable, holding the gun in a loose one-handed grip.

"Fuck," Mack swore. She was so focused on the gun, it took her a minute to notice the long-handled shovel he held in his other hand. In a flash, she realized where he'd been—in the desert behind his house, digging a grave for Anna.

Adam gestured with the gun, and Mack put her hands in the air.

"I didn't expect to see you today, Mack. I kind of thought we'd see you tomorrow, after your friend was reported missing."

"I—I came over looking for Jess and came in because—because the door was unlocked. I thought maybe she was in the bedroom—resting. Let me just take Anna and leave. We can forget this ever happened."

Adam laughed. "No, I don't think so. I think you'll both stay right here."

Mack let out a shaky breath and swallowed hard against the rising lump in her throat.

"It's a shame," Adam said. The gun was pointing right at Mack's face, and she couldn't see anything else. "I had it all played out in my mind, how it would go tomorrow. Anna'd be reported missing, maybe by a colleague when she didn't show up for work, and you'd call Jess, and I'd be there, and I'd tell her to invite you over. You shouldn't be alone at a time like that, right? I'd go out to get some dinner, and you'd be here when I got back. I'd pick up some comfort food. Pasta, or soup. I'd come in, and you'd look up from the couch, your face tear-stained and red but still beautiful. I'd set down the food and give you a big hug, and you'd be grateful that I was providing for you, taking care of you in your time of need."

Sweat poured down Mack's back. This was the end. Adam would kill her and Anna before Dave and his backup ever came. Where was Jess? Had she gotten out of the house, or had Adam found her first? She couldn't let herself believe that. Jess was safe. She had to be with Dave, in his car. She *had* to be.

Adam could shoot Anna from where he stood, if he changed the angle of the gun just a little bit.

His gun.

Gun.

Slowly, she moved her right hand toward her waistband.

Maybe there was still a chance.

There was a sudden noise from somewhere in the house. Adam started, set the gun on the bathroom counter, and gripped the shovel with both hands.

When he returned his attention to Mack, she had Anna's gun pointed at him. She was surprised to note that she wasn't shaking. She'd had trouble holding the gun still that time on the range, for Christ's sake, and here she was pointing one at an actual human being without a tremble.

"Put the shovel down, Adam," she said. "It's over."

He took a step toward her.

"Stop right there," she said. "I swear, you take one more step and I'll—"

The winning smile Jess had fallen for spread across his face. "You're not going to shoot me, Mack. I know you."

He raised the shovel over his head and took another step.

And Mack squeezed the trigger, just the way they'd taught her.

CHAPTER FORTY-TWO

Maybe it was just an echo amplified by the bathroom tile, but it sounded as if there were two gunshots. Mack threw herself into the tub, covering Anna's body with her own. Her ears rang, and the smell of propellant overwhelmed her. She couldn't tell if she'd been hit or if the pain in her arms and legs was just adrenaline. She focused on staying very still, didn't want to accelerate blood loss by panicking. Plus, if Adam thought she was dead, maybe he'd back off.

A hand on Mack's shoulder brought her back into the moment. It was Jess, sobbing. When she saw that Mack hadn't been shot, she gathered her into a tight hug.

"Adam's here!" Mack said frantically. "We're not safe. We have to get out of here."

"It's okay," another voice said. Dave. "It's okay, Mack."

"We really need to learn how to use these things," Jess said, nodding at the gun Mack had dropped on the floor. "You missed, Annie Oakley."

Mack laughed in spite of herself. They were both crying now, the cortisol of the previous hours starting to ebb.

"Luckily," Dave said, offering Mack a hand up. "I didn't miss. One and done, center mass."

Adam's body lay sprawled on the bathroom floor, a pool of blood spreading beneath it. She shuddered. "Is he dead?"

Dave felt his neck, careful to keep his shoes out of the gore. "Yep."

"We heard a noise," Jess said. "He came in the back door. I've been telling him he needs to grease it for months, but I guess we're lucky he didn't."

"How's Dr. Lapin?" Dave asked.

Anna was still unconscious in the bathtub. Mack had almost forgotten about her in the panic of the last few moments.

"No change. Did you call it in?"

"I did. EMTs are on their way."

"Thanks."

"Look," Dave said. "Any second now this place will be crawling with cops. You know, police-involved shootings are a hot-button issue, and two prosecutors on scene will raise questions. But here's what happened: Jess came to see her fiancé at his home. She brought a friend. The friend was worried and called me. When I got here, Adam was armed and threatening to kill Mack and Dr. Lapin. They'll go through the motions and then quietly close the case, along with three local murders, and hopefully some out-of-jurisdiction ones, too. Adam was a serial killer. No one is going to want to look too closely at any of this."

"Nan Chin will have to know," Mack mused, "so she can dismiss the murder charge against Ron Simon."

"That can wait a little," Jess said. "He's in custody on the sex-trafficking count anyway. We know Adam killed Morgan because of the genetic genealogy results. Nan'll find that out in the course of the investigation, when TPD tells her what they found in the box. The lab will do a confirmation test with Adam's DNA, and she'll dismiss the murder charge against Simon, no prejudice."

Mack cleared her throat. "I need to thank you both," she said. "You put yourselves at risk—again—for me. I am lucky to have you. Jess, I'm sorry I got you into this."

Jess' laugh rang out harsh and brittle. She picked up a framed photo of her and Adam and smashed the glass against the counter.

"Adam got us into this," she said. "You don't have anything to apologize for."

They heard sirens, faint at first, then closer. It was over.

CHAPTER FORTY-THREE

After the two rookie patrol officers gave her permission and she agreed to an interview whenever was convenient for the assigned detective, Mack rode with the still-unconscious Anna to the hospital. As Dave had predicted, the rookies didn't seem overly eager to investigate the dead guy once they saw the drugged psychologist in his bathtub and the witnesses' assortment of badges.

At the ER, nurses quickly hooked Anna to an IV and took blood in order to figure out what had been used to drug her.

"He used GHB on someone else," Mack told the nurse, whose name tag read *Lorraine* and indicated that she'd worked at the hospital for twelve years. "I'm not sure if that helps."

"It might. Do you know when it might have been administered? Or how much?"

Mack shrugged. "Is she going to be okay?"

Lorraine squeezed Mack's arm. "There's nothing we can really do for GHB overdose other than supportive treatment. We'll keep her breathing, keep pushing fluids. Her pulse is strong, and she's in good shape. That helps. I can't promise you anything, but it looks pretty good."

"Would…would it have made any difference if she'd gotten to the hospital sooner?"

Lorraine shook her head, her sympathetic look almost more than Mack could bear. "Not really," she said. "Do you want to stay with her? Sometimes it helps."

Mack bit her lip. Anna's family was in California. Mack didn't know anything about Anna's life over the last six months. She might have a girlfriend. Even if she was still single, there might be a friend she'd rather have by her side, rather than her ex-girlfriend the murder suspect. Mack was exhausted, desperately in need of a shower, and wanted to go back to Adam's house. She didn't want to leave Jess alone, under the circumstances.

Lorraine looked at her expectantly.

Mack nodded.

"Hey," Anna said, faintly.

Mack looked up from her phone, where Jess was filling her in by text on the investigation, and broke into a smile. "Hey there. That was some nap, there, Doc. We've been in this room almost ten hours."

Anna tried to sit up and grunted. "What happened? Were we in a car accident? I feel like hell."

Mack explained what she knew, which wasn't much. The doctors were relatively confident that Anna hadn't been raped. They'd found no injection site for the GHB. Anna couldn't remember seeing Adam at her office, so she had no explanation for how the drug had been administered. The last thing she recalled was looking at a patient file, waiting for Mack to arrive. Then blackness until the beeping of hospital machinery woke her.

"I owe you an apology," Anna said. Her eyes were starting to close already. "It feels like I'm constantly apologizing to you in hospital rooms. This whole last year. Just hospital apologies."

Mack laughed and squeezed Anna's hand. "Twice isn't always. Apologies can wait. Why don't you rest?"

Anna's hand went slack in Mack's as she fell asleep.

While Anna slept, Mack drove to her house and returned with a tote bag full of pajamas, toiletries, and the book she found on Anna's bedside table. She'd resisted the urge to snoop around the house, unsure whether she wanted to know if Anna had moved on. It was easier to focus on doing the next thing that needed to be done, rather than her feelings.

The gun had been impounded by the responding officers—they hadn't had a problem with Mack's smooth explanation that she'd pulled it from Anna's purse, which she claimed to have found in Adam's house along with its owner. She called Jess from her car to check in. She seemed okay, acknowledging the trauma they'd been through but not dwelling on it.

Anna was grateful for her belongings, and even more grateful for the large coffee Mack had picked up. Mack watched her out of the corner of her eye, wondering if she'd get right on her phone to summon someone else to her side. But Anna left her phone on the bedside table and drank her coffee, trashy daytime TV playing in the background.

After two nights in the hospital, Anna was released, still fighting a bad headache but otherwise fine. The doctor advised her to take it easy for a few days, but there was no need for a follow-up appointment and there were no long-term consequences anticipated.

Mack drove her home. They hadn't revisited whatever Anna had started to say when she first awoke, and Mack was hoping she could drop Anna off and leave before she remembered. Anna hated unresolved conflict.

"Come in for a minute?" she asked as Mack pulled into her driveway.

Mack saw no indication of an ulterior motive. "I can't stay for long," she said. "I need to go see Jess. She's not doing so well, you know, with everything that happened."

Anna gave a half smile. "Oh, of course," she said. "Jess needs you."

Anna got settled on the couch, comfortable in the baggy pajamas Mack had gotten her for Christmas. "You want something to drink, or something?"

Mack shook her head. "You okay?" she asked. "Because I should—"

"I never finished apologizing to you."

Mack sank into a plush armchair. So much for an easy escape.

"Mack, I'm really sorry for how I behaved when you called me about…the body…and you being the subject of that investigation."

"It's fine," Mack said. If she moved a fraction of an inch to her left, she could see the front door. It wasn't more than twenty feet away. If she ran for it, there was no way Anna could catch her.

"It's not fine," Anna said. "I behaved badly. I regretted it as soon as we got off the phone, and I've regretted it ever since."

"Okay," Mack said.

"And it's not even the first time I've behaved badly toward you. I mean, last year, with Allen…It was my fault he was able to get to you—if I'd just listened to you and not freaked the fuck out, you wouldn't have been alone in your apartment. But that's what I do. I panic and I run and then you wind up getting hurt for it."

"I don't want to—"

"I just—this isn't an excuse, it's just that—well—my patients' wives and girlfriends *never* believe that the men they love have done something terrible. I mean, how many moms have we seen who choose their men over their daughters when the girl discloses abuse? And, you know, my parents' relationship was all my dad lying and my mom forgiving him. So I told myself years ago that I would never get taken in by anyone's lies. So when you told me… all that…I just panicked. I was afraid you had turned out to be just another liar. So I ran."

"I mean, cool," Mack said. She stood up and paced the small living room. "Still shitty, though."

Anna rubbed the back of her neck. "There's more to it than just that. Mack, can you sit down and listen to me?"

Mack leaned against the fireplace mantel. "What else could there be?"

"Detective Caldwell called me. The day you were put on admin leave."

"Craig?" Mack asked.

"Yeah."

"What did he want?"

"He told me he was doing me a favor. Calling as a courtesy, to warn me that I was about to find myself under investigation for being your accomplice. Said to stay away from you if I wanted to have any shot at not blowing up my life."

"And you listened to him?" Mack pushed off the mantel and resumed pacing. She felt herself beginning to panic.

"He said both of us could get charged. They had enough to charge you already, he said, and I had to save myself. I didn't see anything I could do to protect you—anything I could do to help the situation. I figured you'd be able to focus better on getting yourself out of trouble if I wasn't around."

"That's a bullshit excuse. You've known me for almost eight years, Anna. You know I wouldn't *murder a teenager* and dump her body in the desert." The sudden anger that flooded Mack's body ebbed, replaced by hot tears. "You should have known, anyway. Dave Barton knew. Jess knew."

Anna sighed and leaned back against the couch cushion.

"Of course Jess knew," Anna said. "I could never live up to the incredible Jess."

Mack had to get out of that house. Immediately.

"I have to go," she said. "Maybe we can have a drink sometime. Maybe we can be friends again, some day."

"I'd like that," Anna said. "You've always been a great friend, Mack, and I'm sorry I wasn't a better one."

Mack laughed, the sound harsh and loud.

"You weren't supposed to be my friend. That's the problem. You were supposed to be my girlfriend! You were supposed to be on my side, to help me through the worst shit I've ever had to deal with. You weren't supposed to ditch me at the first sign of trouble. I could have died, Anna! I came to find you, and I could have been killed. But I did it anyway, and I dragged Jess and Dave into danger with me, because that's what you're supposed to do."

Anna hung her head.

"So fuck you," Mack continued. "I was hoping I could get out of here without this nonsense cathartic bullshit. But apparently not. So, fine. Now you get to hear how I feel. I am so angry, Anna. I swear to God, I wish I'd left you there with Adam. But now I'm angry for even thinking that, because that's not who I want to be in the world. I don't want to be the guy who leaves a friend for dead. I want to be a helper. I've spent my whole life being a helper, but you weren't there the *one time* I needed you. Oh, actually, I'm sorry. As you so helpfully pointed out, I've needed you two times, and both times you've cut me loose. Perfect."

She was crying in earnest now, fighting the urge to wipe her face and seek comfort from Anna, who wasn't even looking at her. Her eyes were focused on her thumb, where she was carefully picking a hangnail.

"So I'm angry at you for abandoning me," Mack went on. "And I'm angry at myself for wishing I'd left you with Adam, and I'm really mad at Adam for hurting my friend and killing a bunch of women and getting me into this mess. And I don't understand why he didn't target me, and I'm angry at myself for caring about that. I mean, he was a serial killer, and he was in my home, and he never wanted to kill me, and I'm sitting here going, 'Why didn't he choose me?' which has got to be the most fucked-up thing that's ever happened in the history of the world. But I wouldn't know he was a serial killer if it wasn't for you—and I'm mad at you for that, too."

Overwhelmed by that last admission, Mack collapsed on the couch, covered her face with her hands, and gave in to the sobs wracking her body. Anna sat beside her and put an arm around her shoulder.

"Shhh," Anna said. "It's okay to cry it out. That's a whole lot of anger you've been carrying, and it's hard to face that. You've probably been angry with me, in some way that maybe you haven't even admitted to yourself, since Allen." She had her psychologist voice on, and Mack was struck by a flare of hatred that faded as soon as she recognized it. "Have you considered talking to someone about it? Not me, obviously, but I could refer you to someone."

Mack played with a hole in the knee of her jeans. "I'm okay, but thanks. I don't need anyone's help, and I don't want any referral you could give me anyway. I just need to start running more, I think."

Anna didn't say anything.

Long minutes passed. Finally able to take deep breaths without shuddering, Mack shrugged off Anna's hand and stood, rubbing her palms, wet with tears, on the legs of her jeans.

"I'm going to go now," she said.

"Okay," Anna said. "Let me know when you get home safe?"

"I don't think so," Mack said. "But I'm fine. Thank you."

Anna followed her to the front door. "I really am sorry."

Mack shrugged. "I'm sure we'll see each other around." She went to her car and didn't look back. She wasn't sure if she wanted to see Anna waiting at the door or not. The truth—which she had not told Anna despite an overwhelming urge—was that she still harbored romantic feelings for the psychologist. Those feelings were complicated, of course, by her anger and hurt, but they weren't gone. Mack wasn't sure they'd ever go away completely.

CHAPTER FORTY-FOUR

That Thursday evening, at Jess' encouragement, Mack returned to Paradise.

"It isn't the bar's fault, or your friend's fault, that I can't tell when someone is a murderer," Jess had said. "You've known Rocky a long time. You owe it to her to go back, at least once."

Mack hesitated in the doorway, fought the urge to turn right around and drive home. There were a few women, heads bent over their phones, seated at the bar. The place smelled like stale beer and old popcorn.

It's okay, Mack thought, forcing herself to walk to the bar and take a stool. She made sure to pick one with a view of the front door.

She'd never seen the bartender before, a cute young woman who greeted Mack with a smile, which Mack half-heartedly returned. She ordered an Angry Orchard. Adam had known her drink—she'd never had to ask.

Mack was almost done with her drink and thinking of heading back home when Rocky came out of the back office looking wary. She smiled hesitantly when she spotted Mack.

"I haven't responded to your texts," Mack said. "I'm sorry, Rocks. It's been a crazy time."

Rocky took a seat beside her and signaled the bartender for two more ciders. "It's been crazy for all of us." She looked tired. Her hair was slightly too long for the fauxhawk she usually wore, and her blue polo had a hole in the seam. "I kind of thought you might call after…well, *after*, but I know I shouldn't have been surprised not to hear from you."

They drank in silence for a long while. "I assume you know what happened?" Mack finally said.

"Some. A cop came by to clean out Adam's locker. Told me a little. I saw a little more on the news, but it seems like they're still keeping it all pretty quiet. I assume even more will come out later, once everything is all wrapped up, right?"

"I think so," Mack said. "You know, I was there when he…when he was shot." She didn't mourn Adam's passing, but it was difficult to think about that night without getting choked up. This had been the second time in just over a year that she had come so close to evil, and she—all of them—had been lucky to get out with their lives.

"Shit."

"Yeah."

Rocky signaled the bartender for two tequila shots.

"Shots, Rocks?"

Rocky shrugged and downed the shot, foregoing the salt and lime. "Seems like maybe we both could use them."

Mack couldn't disagree.

"Were there…" Rocky looked like she couldn't figure out what she wanted to say. "Were there many of them? Victims, I mean."

"Some," Mack said.

"Shit. Do you want to talk about it?"

She didn't—certainly not with Rocky. Even she and Jess had mostly avoided the topic. But there was a question on her mind. "You didn't have any idea?" She knew the answer was no—what else could it be?—but still, she had to ask, had to confirm that Rocky hadn't somehow, for some reason, set Jess or Anna up.

"Of course not," Rocky said, "but I didn't know him that well. He came in one day, great résumé, told me about his gay sister. I needed a bartender. Then five years later—never a complaint, never an issue—I find out he's stalking women from my bar. Killing them." Her eyes went wide. "Oh God, *he* must have been the one to delete the surveillance footage!"

"You thought it was me," Mack said softly.

"I was shitty about that, Mack, and I'm sorry. Listen, I need you to know, I never wanted anything like this to happen, especially not to you or your friends. I thought Adam was keeping us safe—keeping the homophobes away, walking women to their Ubers, you know. I trusted him as much as I've ever trusted any bartender. More than I've trusted any man since my dad died."

Mack understood. Adam had won Jess over, despite her misgivings. He was good at charming women, especially smart, suspicious ones who didn't trust men. Even she hadn't seen what he really was. Her worst-case scenario was that he had a DUI in his past, not a corpse in his freezer.

She looked at her watch. It was almost eight. Pretty soon, the karaoke singers would start their warmups and the bar would get busy. With two Angry Orchards and a shot inside her, she knew she wasn't fit to drive, but there was a good taco place a few doors down.

"Want to get some dinner?" she asked, sliding off her barstool and pulling her wallet out of her purse.

Rocky waved off her credit card. "Tonight's on me. I'll pass on dinner, though."

Mack turned to leave.

"Hey, Mack," Rocky said, and she came back. The other woman seemed to be struggling with what to say. "Is Anna okay?"

Mack shrugged. "I don't really know. Physically, she's fine. But she's been through a lot. We haven't talked much over the last six months."

Rocky studied her, and Mack suddenly felt self-conscious. She hadn't mentioned the breakup to Rocky because it had never seemed relevant, but maybe Mack had been hiding behind the safety of having a girlfriend to keep Rocky at arm's length.

"You know," Rocky said. "If you'd asked me to dinner any time over the last ten years, I would have been the happiest woman in Tucson. I've wanted to be more than just your bartender since I first met you, Mack. But I've always been just a sympathetic ear, huh?"

Mack blushed. She knew that Rocky was attracted to her, but butches weren't her type. "I've always valued your friendship, Rocks."

Rocky scowled. "Don't do that. You're better than that, and I'm sure as hell better than that. We've never been friends, I just didn't realize it until tonight. You came in here to, what, make sure I knew I hired a serial killer?"

"I—I thought you'd...I thought you'd want...Actually, Rocky, I'm not sure what I thought."

Rocky pushed away her unfinished cider and got to her feet. "Actually, Mack, I don't care what you thought."

CHAPTER FORTY-FIVE

It was clear that Adam had killed Sabrina, Morgan, and Jane, but there were still loose ends Dave needed to tie up. There was no real reason for Mack to come with him, but she had been so much a part of the investigation so far that he invited her along when he went to meet with Beth Shankar, the hiker who had discovered Morgan's body. Mack agreed to go.

"What if he had an accomplice?" he asked as they drove.

Mack had read Adam's journal, and there was no room in his twisted fantasies for an accomplice. He prided himself on working alone. She didn't argue the point, though. A day out of the office was nothing to turn up her nose at. She was happy to spend the day with Dave and, hopefully, get some firsthand answers to the questions Adam had left behind him.

Mack was surprised by the pretty woman who greeted them at the door to a nondescript apartment on the east side of town. She had assumed that Adam had chosen Beth because she was plain or even ugly—an easy target. Stupid, she thought. *He targeted Jess, and she's lovely. Even Anna swooned over him.*

Beth, a petite brunette in a Mets cap, was dressed in workout clothes and a hydration backpack. Clearly, finding Morgan's body had not deterred her from hiking. Mack liked her already. As Dave showed her the photo lineup he had prepared—including Adam's photo in the group of six, each carefully selected for their similar looks—Mack noticed a photo of Beth kissing the cheek of an attractive blonde and wondered if she was just another pretty lesbian Adam had taken in. Dave had said she was attracted to Joe, but maybe he'd misinterpreted. Maybe she was simply interested in making a new friend, a hiking buddy. Maybe she was just bisexual.

She leaned in and took a closer look. There were Christmas lights in the background and she wondered... Was it possible?

Beth studied the six-pack. "I don't want to get this wrong," she said. She bit her lip, and Mack blushed. The hiker was *very* pretty.

"There's no wrong answer," Dave said. "Joe might not be there. But if he is, let me know."

Beth continued studying the photos. Finally, she tapped the third picture. "This is him."

"Okay," Dave said. "Now, I don't want you to use a percentage or anything, but how confident are you?"

"Oh, I'm a hundred percent sure. No doubt whatsoever."

Dave had her write that under photo three and sign her name. She had identified Adam, and so they'd been right all along—he'd posed as Joe to make sure Morgan's body was discovered on his schedule.

"Can I ask you a question," Mack said, "about this other picture?"

"Oh," Beth said. "That's just an old friend."

"Where was this taken?"

Beth picked up the photo and looked closely at it. "You know," she said. "I actually know the answer to that. It was at Paradise—it's a lesbian bar near here?"

Mack and Dave exchanged looks.

Son of a bitch, that's how he found her in the first place. He set up a customer to find Morgan's body. I bet he got her address the same way he got Morgan's and Anna's—from their ID. He must have changed his hair and dressed differently enough as Joe that she didn't recognize him.

Beth walked them to the door and put her hand on Mack's arm as they said goodbye. "Here's my card," she said, squeezing gently. "In case you need anything else from me."

"Oh," Mack said, "I won't—I mean—I don't—I mean—"

Dave took the card Beth was offering and slid it into the pocket of Mack's Oxford. "She means thank you," he said, smiling.

"I don't want to tell you what to do," Dave said as they put on their seat belts and pulled away from Beth's apartment. "And it's really none of my business. But you should call her."

Mack leaned back against the leather seat and looked at Beth's card, a cell number written on the back. She was an engineer at Raytheon. Mack couldn't picture herself having anything in common with an engineer at a defense contractor.

"Would that be appropriate?" Mack asked. "Isn't she a witness?"

Dave glanced at her. "A witness to what? The case against Adam Bennett resolved pretty conclusively when I shot him." He cleared his throat. "I didn't bring this up before, but there's some gossip going around about you and Dr. Lapin. I didn't hear much, but from what I've heard…Anyway, I think you should call Beth."

They did both like hiking. That was something. She'd done more with less. Mack slipped the card back into her pocket.

Their next stop was the Pima County Jail, where they'd set up a visit with Ron Simon. To avoid stepping on Nan's toes, since she was the prosecutor handling the Simon case, Mack would watch from a monitoring room as Dave conducted the meeting.

As they waited for Simon, she focused on breathing through her mouth. The stench of unwashed bodies, bad food, and dirty clothes permeated the jail.

"This is the main reason I could never be a defense attorney," she said to Dave, only half joking. "They're in here three times a week! I might be here once a year, and even then it might take me days to wash the stink out of my hair."

Dave rubbed his shaved head. "Weirdly, I don't have that problem."

Jail hadn't done anything positive for Simon's appearance. He'd gained weight since his booking picture was taken, and his skin looked waxy and dull against his orange jumpsuit. His gray hair was uncombed and badly in need of a cut.

"Where's my lawyer?" Simon asked when he was led, handcuffed and with a waist chain, into the concrete block interview room. A sheriff's deputy stood near the door, ready to intervene if Simon tried to attack Dave, who had turned in his firearm when they checked in. "You can't talk to me without my lawyer."

"This is just a friendly chat," Dave said. "Nothing to do with the charges you're facing. You're not getting charged with anything else, so no lawyer needed."

Simon sat heavily and waited, hands clasped on the table in front of him.

Dave took another copy of the lineup he'd showed Beth out of a folder and placed it in front of Simon, just out of reach. "Last time we talked, you told me you saw Morgan's pimp outside the motel room. Are any of these men the guy you saw?"

Simon studied the photos. His bored look morphed into something calculating. Predatory. Mack shivered. It was easy to see Simon as a violent man. "What do I get if I tell you?"

"Nah," Dave said. "That's not what we're doing." He slid the six-pack back into the folder and stood.

"He's there, Detective. I can tell you who he is."

Dave sat back down. "What do you want?"

Simon smiled. He was missing his right incisor, and it lent his face a malicious look. "I want you to put in a good word with Ms. Chin. I've got a prison plea, and I want probation."

Dave stood again and left the room.

Mack met him in the hallway. "Do you at least want to talk with Nan?" she asked. "See if she's open to giving him something?"

"No need," Dave said. "He told me what I need to know. He said the guy he saw was in the lineup. The other five guys are all cops. If any of these guys was hanging around outside Morgan's hotel room, it was Adam."

Mack was troubled by a question she'd been unable to answer in the days since finding Adam's box of souvenirs.

"You remember we found the picture of Sabrina Fisher in with the other victims?"

Dave kept his eyes on the road. "Yeah. I was on scene when they found her, I don't know if you knew that."

"You were? I don't remember that! I was the prosecutor that got called out."

Dave smiled. "Oh, I remember. I went home and told my wife all about the new prosecutor who looked like she was about to throw up on my murder scene."

Mack laughed.

"I wasn't a sergeant, then. Had just barely promoted up to detective, actually. I wasn't the case agent, but I was there to assist because I'd just gone to an arson training up in Nevada."

"Do you remember the couple that found her? The young guy and his girlfriend on their ATVs?"

Dave considered the question. "You think that might have been Adam?"

"Yeah."

"Interesting," Dave said. "Especially since we know he set Beth up. How would it have worked, though? He killed her, dumped her out there, set the fire, then drove home to get his girlfriend and went back to the scene?"

"I guess," Mack said. "It reminds me of that old joke—well, it's not a joke, I guess, it's like a riddle—about the sociopath at the funeral. Do you know that one?"

Dave shook his head.

"A sociopath goes to a funeral and sees a girl he thinks is cute. Three weeks later, he kills the dead guy's brother. How come?"

"I have no idea, Mackenzie."

"Because he thought she'd come to the brother's funeral, too."

Dave laughed. "Good one, Mack, but I don't see the connection."

Mack debated how to explain her point. "He wanted the credit. He wanted to see attention get paid. He didn't want Sabrina's body to just decompose and disappear. He wanted to see police trying to figure it out, to see their panic and disgust. The cops were the girl he wanted to see, I guess is what I'm saying. But he didn't want to get caught, of course, so that's why he bullied his girlfriend into giving fake info."

They drove in silence for a while. "This is kind of gross," Dave said finally. "But have you thought about what he was doing at Paradise in the first place?"

"What do you mean?"

"Well, you came to the scene when Sabrina was found. He could have found out your name pretty easily, right? And back then, you probably weren't as careful about your online security as you are now. Maybe he, well, you know."

"What are you saying, Dave? Maybe I led him to Paradise? Maybe this whole thing is my fault?"

"Of course not! Never mind. Forget I said anything."

But Mack couldn't forget. What if Adam had tracked her down, figured out that Paradise was one of her hangouts, and followed her there? He was obsessed with her—his journal made that clear. What if the obsession went back much further than they suspected? There was no way to know for sure. Once again, she regretted that Adam had died before they'd had the chance to interview him.

As the sun set, casting a golden light that softened even the Track, the working girls started to come out. Mack was shocked at how young most of them looked.

Eventually, Ruthie appeared. She wore denim short-shorts and a cropped blue tee. Even in the heat of a July night, she looked cold.

"You'll stay here?" Mack asked Dave.

He handed her a single photo of Adam. "I'm not trying to spook anyone."

She took the picture and got out of the car. Ruthie rolled her eyes as she saw Mack approaching, and Mack knew she stood out in her jeans and Oxford shirt.

"Ms. Wilson, what you want?" Ruthie asked. "I gotta work."

Mack handed her Adam's picture. "Is this the guy you saw watching Morgan?"

Ruthie squinted at the photo. "I'm not sure. White guys all look the same. Mighta been."

Mack looked at her. She had goose bumps on her arms, but her face and eyes were clear. She didn't look like she was using.

"Would dinner help you know for sure?"

"Honest, Ms. Wilson," Ruthie said. "No cap. It could be him, but I don't remember. I see guys who look like this every night and twice on Fridays. Did he kill that girl?"

"Yeah," Mack said. She pulled five twenty-dollar bills out of her pocket. "Thanks for looking. How about you get yourself something to eat and a room for the night?"

Ruthie stuffed the bills into her purse. "Thank you. You stay safe out there. Ms. Wilson?"

"Yeah, Ruthie?"

"Can you, um, can you not come round here no more? I mean, I'm happy to help you and you've always been cool to me, but these other girls, they starting to ask questions about why I'm in tight with the lady cop."

Mack laughed and returned to Dave's unmarked car. She turned back and saw that Ruthie had already found a customer. Her hundred dollars would almost certainly go to Ruthie's pimp or into her veins, but it seemed like the least Mack could do. If Ruthie wanted to get out of the lifestyle, to finally get clean, Mack would do anything she could to help, but she couldn't force the girl to live the life she wanted for her. Ruthie's whole life had been filled with other people making her choices for her. Mack couldn't promise never to show up on the Track again looking for answers, but she would try to respect Ruthie's request.

"Was it him?" Dave asked.

Mack shrugged. "No idea. It was a long time ago, and Ruthie's seen a lot of men since then. She couldn't rule him out."

That would have to be enough.

CHAPTER FORTY-SIX

Mack was stretched out in her hammock, a cold bottle of Magic Hat #9 in her hand, the sunset painting her backyard a brilliant red. The Sabrina Fisher file was sitting on the cooler where she had put it after confirming that Adam was the guy on the ATV who'd "found" her burning body.

Son of a bitch, she thought, the beer suddenly bitter. *He set the whole thing up, even way back then.*

Jess was due in an hour or so. They'd agreed to help each other make online dating profiles—Jess would write Mack's, and vice versa. Jess was ready to start dating again. She wasn't going to let memories of her mistake with Adam stand in her way.

The phone rang.

"I know who the leak was," Dave said, by way of a greeting.

Mack's muscles tensed, the bottle slipping as she sat up. She watched it crash to the concrete patio and shatter. A dark puddle spread around the shards of glass, and Mack was reminded of Adam's bloody body on the tile floor of his bathroom.

"You know Craig Caldwell, right?"

"Of course. He—" Mack stopped herself from mentioning what Anna had told her about Detective Caldwell. Craig had been Dave's longtime partner in the Sex Crimes unit. He'd been there that day, when Mack presented to the homicide detectives and it blew up so spectacularly. He hadn't been willing to look at her.

"We've worked together since the Academy," Dave said, sadly. "He's the godfather of my oldest son. We don't see eye to eye on everything, but he's always been a good friend. He was on vacation the day Morgan's body was found, so he wasn't around for your..."

"My *interview*?" Mack asked.

"Yeah. But I filled him in when he got back. I didn't know he'd hooked up with that group of officers that was out to get you, so I've been updating him this whole time. Just, you know, as friends. Frankly, I thought he was on our team—he offered to help me with the case, and now I know why. He's been passing information to Petrou. He didn't care if he brought me down in the process. I'll never trust the sonofabitch again."

Mack knew how closely Dave guarded his family. If he had trusted Craig enough to name him godfather to Ricky, they were basically brothers. That made the betrayal tremendous. She wouldn't add to it by mentioning Craig's call to Anna. Not yet, anyway.

"One more thing," Dave said, "and I'll let you get back to your evening. The DNA came back on Sabrina Fisher."

"Oh?" Mack asked. She suspected she knew what the results would be.

"It was Adam," Dave said. "Just like we thought."

After they hung up, Dave sent Mack an email with several attachments. As she clicked through them, she found that he'd provided everything she'd need to get Craig fired for breaching department policy. He'd admitted to talking to the media about an ongoing investigation, without regard for the truth. Admitted having called Anna, having warned her away from Mack. Laughed about it—bragged about it—because he knew he was cutting Mack off from her support network. Tightening the noose. Even admitted that he'd targeted Mack for reasons unrelated to her job performance.

She sank back into the hammock, considering what to do. With Adam's death she had been officially cleared—again. She and Dave and Jess had solved at least three murders and prevented a fourth, and justice had been served.

Petrou would never issue a retraction or even an apology, and it would be a waste of time to ask for one. What would getting Craig fired accomplish? Would it make her feel any better? He and Michael Brown had worked hard to ruin her life, but in the final analysis, what actual impact had either of them had?

Maybe it would be better to keep what she knew in her back pocket. Her year as Community Liaison would be up in two months, and Campbell had already notified her, through Michael Brown, that her next assignment would be homicide. She would return to trying cases, to getting justice where she could. She and Jess would work together, or they'd finally start following the rules and recruit junior attorneys to second-chair them.

Mack grabbed another #9 from the cooler. She had more important things than Michael Brown and Craig Caldwell to think about, like Jess' dating profile and Beth Shankar's business card, which she had moved to her wallet. Maybe Jess would find the man of her dreams, get married, and become a stay-at-home mom. Maybe they'd both still be single at eighty, tottering around the nursing home together and raising hell.

Maybe Beth had a favorite bar, someplace other than Paradise. Maybe she'd agree to meet Mack there—but they'd have a boring first date and never speak again. Or maybe they'd fall in love and live happily ever after. The world was full of possibilities.

The beer was cold and Mack enjoyed the feeling of the glass against her hand. Her phone buzzed with a text. She looked at the screen. Anna. Mack thought about reading it but decided to wait. There'd be time for that later. If there was any hope for a friendship with Anna, it would have to happen on Mack's terms. There was no need to rush it.

She took a long drink of her beer and fell back in the hammock. She watched the first few stars appear overhead and wondered what would happen next.

Acknowledgments

Somehow, bringing a second book into the world seems like a much bigger accomplishment than the first one. "I did it once, I should be able to do it again" was not the productivity mantra I thought it would be. It is my great privilege to have the chance to express my how appreciative I am for the many, *many* people who contributed to this process, either directly or indirectly.

I'm exceedingly grateful to the team at Bella Books, especially Cath Walker and Heather Flournoy, for taking a chance on Mack and on me, and for all the support. Thank you for seeing Mack as the series character she yearned to be. You make this process feel so easy.

To everyone who read the first Mack book and asked for another, I wouldn't have done this without you. I'll forever be amazed at how many people were kind and generous with their time, attention, and words.

This book has benefited from the training and experience of innumerable police officers, attorneys, and judges I have known over my career, not to mention victim advocates, psychologists, and other criminal justice professionals. There are too many of you to name, but I am much obliged to you all.

I want to recognize everyone who helped me get the science, law, and process right in this book. Any mistakes I've made are my own, and you probably tried to warn me. I am especially grateful to Stefanie Walesch, Kyra and Vince Goddard, Erin Pedicone, Jenny Carper, Rebecca Kennelly, Katie Staab, Jim Seeger, and Drs. Tina Garby, Holly Salisbury, and Nicole Pondell. If the government ever reads our texts, show them this book. You (hopefully) won't get charged with conspiracy.

AR, my incredible and inspirational cousin, shares great resources and lets me talk to a normal human once a month, and for those things I am forever in her debt. Please don't read this book.

My parents, yet again, are major contributors to my ability to get words from my brain onto a page and have them be (mostly) intelligible English. Thank you to Victoria Jones for your unwavering confidence that I can do anything I set my mind to. Thank you to Josh Pachter for your editing skills and willingness to spend so very many hours on the phone. You've made me very aware of how much I sigh, nod, and pace. One space after a period. I'll get there someday.

Lela Mae Winer, my great-aunt, passed as I was writing the first draft of this book. A voracious reader, I know she would have loved this.

Many thanks to my real-life pal in crime-fighting, Elizabeth Reamer. I would try hard cases with you any day and will ride into battle by your side as a fierce and unyielding ally. I appreciate your willingness to entertain insane phone calls about homicide investigations and to hold me accountable on my green boxes. This book, like the world, is better because you are in it.

Finally, endless gratitude to Eli Ditlevson who is the most fun and my favorite across all categories. Your support and patience are limitless. It's not always easy to live with a writer, and you manage it with the same grace and style you bring to the rest of your life. Thank you.

Bella Books, Inc.

Women. Books. Even Better Together.

P.O. Box 10543

Tallahassee, FL 32302

Phone: (800) 729-4992

www.BellaBooks.com

More Titles from Bella Books

Mabel and Everything After – Hannah Safren
978-1-64247-390-2 | 274 pgs | paperback: $17.95 | eBook: $9.99
A law student and a wannabe brewery owner find that the path to a fairy tale happily-ever-after is often the long and scenic route.

To Be With You – TJ O'Shea
978-1-64247-419-0 | 348 pgs | paperback: $19.95 | eBook: $9.99
Sometimes the choice is between loving safely or loving bravely.

I Dare You to Love Me – Lori G. Matthews
978-1-64247-389-6 | 292 pgs | paperback: $18.95 | eBook: $9.99
An enemy-to-lovers romance about daring to follow your heart, even when it's the hardest thing to do.

The Lady Adventurers Club - Karen Frost
978-1-64247-414-5 | 300 pgs | paperback: $18.95 | eBook: $9.99
Four women. One undiscovered Egyptian tomb. One (maybe) angry Egyptian goddess. What could possibly go wrong?

Golden Hour - Kat Jackson
978-1-64247-397-1 | 250 pgs | paperback: $17.95 | eBook: $9.99
Life would be so much easier if Lina were afraid of something basic—like spiders—instead of something significant. Something like real, true, healthy love.

Schuss – E. J. Noyes
978-1-64247-430-5 | 276 pgs | paperback: $17.95 | eBook: $9.99
They're best friends who both want something more, but what if admitting it ruins the best friendship either of them have had?

Printed in the USA
CPSIA information can be obtained
at www.ICGtesting.com
JSHW022126111023
49953JS00001B/2